GREEN DRAGON

Sarah Jestin

GREEN DRAGON

DOUBLE DRAGON

CHAPTER ONE

Chest heaving, legs burning, Meeryle had to stop running. She was feeling her weight acutely. The race back to the village against Leena was a rather stupid challenge on Meeryle's part, given her lack of condition.

Leena ran past her. When she realized her friend was no longer moving, the tall girl stopped and backtracked.

"C'mon! Pick up your feet!"

Meeryle shook her head, panting. "I... can't... run... any... farther." She leaned forward, her hands on her knees, and tried to catch her breath. Her eyes closed, she took in deep breaths, willing her heart not to burst out of her chest. Her thick dark hair was in her face and would stay there, at least for the time being. Nothing ever seemed to hold it and today was no exception.

"By the way, you were going the wrong way. The village is over there."

Meeryle shook her head. When would she get a sense of direction?

Still trying to catch her breath, she leaned against a tree, thinking that as much as she hated it, doing more tromping around was necessary. And putting a stop to sweetcakes. At least the ones in the morning.

Suddenly, the trunk moved against Meeryle's back. It didn't sway like a normal tree would, a slow movement back and forth, but expanded and deflated as if it had taken in a deep breath. Startled, she stood straighter and took a step forward, wanting to tell Leena about the strange feeling. But her friend wasn't paying her any attention; she was a few steps away, staring at the tree, gaping. When Meeryle turned to look at the tree, her eyes couldn't focus properly. For some reason, the tree seemed fuzzy. Meeryle blinked twice. The tree moved again, but not like before. It rippled, from the bottom up, and suddenly became bigger and taller. The top swung toward her, the branches shifting and changing shape. They fused together to become a bird-like head, while the trunk and the bottom branches melded and transformed into a lithe body.

Meeryle froze in place. Time had stopped. A strange detachment allowed her to examine the creature with interest. Covered with green scales, it reminded her of a lizard and a cat at the same time, possessing an alien grace and beauty. The head was shorter and wider than she would have expected given the length of the neck. But when Meeryle looked into its eyes, she unfroze. The eyes were a deep ruby red.

She was looking into the eyes of a dragon.

Meeryle surrendered to terror. Without any thought of what she was doing or where she was going, the girl ran for her life-faster than she ever had, faster than she thought possible. Her fear blocked every sound except for her heartbeat. The forest was reduced to the ground beneath her feet and the tree closest to her. Once she passed it, only the next one mattered. She didn't know how she managed to avoid running into them, but her feet had a life of their own. As long as she didn't think, her body was in control and it was moving along as fast as it could.

At one point, Leena had passed her, but Meeryle didn't know when. She blinked, and her friend was in front of her. Absurdly, she observed that Leena's tunic had a grass stain on the bottom left and that her usually shiny and neat light brown hair was now loose and decorated with twigs and leaves. She noticed with shock that Leena's precious green scarf-the one marking her status as an apprentice-Healer-was gone.

Meeryle's brain took control over her body. She was suddenly conscious that her breath had long ago run out, that she had already exerted herself with the race, and that the ground was uneven. She tripped and slid on her stomach for what felt like furlongs. The ground was not only uneven, but also riddled with rocks and roots.

She didn't remember yelling, but must have said something since Leena stopped in her tracks, turned, ran back to her, and dropped on her knees by her side. "Meeryle, are you badly hurt?" Her words came out as fast as her breath allowed her. Her face was blotchy red, sweat ran down her forehead, and a branch must have been responsible for the tear in her right sleeve. She was in no better shape than Meeryle.

"I don't know yet, but you look like you're at the end of your roll too."

"Tell me about it. I never thought I could run so fast. And I have no clue how I managed to avoid all these darn roots! It looks like one got the better of you. Your foot's still stuck in it."

"Really?" Meeryle was surprised. Only then did she notice that she couldn't feel her foot, or any part of her body, accurately. Everything was suddenly blurred in pain. Her chest was burning, her hands felt raw from her slide, and the only thing she could really hear was the thumping of her heart.

"Here, it's out. Does it hurt when I do this?" Leena was doing something with her leg and foot. Meeryle looked back and saw Leena holding her foot, twisting it gently left and right.

"Ouch! And my hands hurt too."

Meeryle gathered herself up on all fours and winced when her hands touched the ground. She sat back on her heels to look at her hands. They were brown, just like her forearms. Below the remnants of earth, her skin was red in some places and deeply scraped in others. Never before had she found herself in such a state.

"They're going to feel worse tomorrow, you know." Leena was shaking her head at the condition of Meeryle's arms. "We need to clean these as quickly as possible. You don't want them to get infected." Leena grabbed her friend by the elbow to help her up. Meeryle stood, feeling a bit shaky. Breathing wasn't so hard anymore, but her legs felt stiff.

"Leena, I don't know if I can walk. My legs feel strange and my ankle hurts."

"Don't stop moving. Otherwise your muscles are going to cramp. Come on, let's go home."

"But... what about the dragon?"

"What?"

"The dragon. We saw a dragon." Now that the fear had run its course, the reality of the encounter hit Meeryle like a blow and took her back years, to when she had so firmly believed in dragons. Everyone had told her over and over again that these creatures didn't exist, that they were nothing more than stories for children.

Everyone was wrong. The dragon Meeryle had seen today certainly had not been a figment of her imagination and she had the most down-to-earth witness with her.

"I don't know what that was," said Leena, staring at her while chewing her bottom lip.

Meeryle blinked. "It was a dragon. What else could it be?" The elation of the moment was such that Meeryle heard her heartbeat better than the birds singing. "Why didn't you ever tell me there were dragons in the forest?" she asked dreamily.

"I didn't know. I'm not even sure it was a dragon!"

Meeryle shook herself, concentrating on her friend's words. Leena doubted her. The old feelings of frustration and shame at being mocked surged with such intensity, she gasped. "But it *was* a dragon." She tried to cross her arms to emphasize her point, but her scraped skin betrayed her. Instead, she put her knuckles on her hips, careful not to close her hands in a fist. "What else could it be, anyway? And how come no one ever told me there were dragons here?"

"Meeryle, no one's ever seen one before. Don't get mad at me because we were attacked by a stupid dragon. I've never been in this part of the forest before, and it's been a while since the Healer came here too. Calm down. It's gone, anyway. We should be safe."

Anger surfaced. "You don't get it, do you? A dragon! We're the first ones in the village to ever see a dragon! If I'd known there were dragons in our

9

area, I would have gone looking for them a long time ago."

"You what?" Leena gaped, eyes wide in surprise.

"You heard me! Dragons are... they're all I ever wanted to learn about. But I... I had to give up on them."

"Meaning you stopped believing in them, right?"

"I've always believed they existed. But everyone laughed so hard when I decided to make it my life's work that I decided never to mention it again." She looked at her friend earnestly. "Don't you laugh at me now. You know they're real. We just saw one." She murmured to herself, "I was right all along."

Leena sighed. She looked at her friend and shook her head. "I'm not laughing. But, Meeryle, you sound like a child. We can't stay here. I'm not going to argue with you about whether or not we saw a dragon."

"We did," interrupted Meeryle. "Don't even try to deny it."

Leena clenched her jaw and her fists. "Just... just listen, will you? Dragon or not, we were attacked by something that could very well be on our track right now. You're hurt; I'm not in much better shape, so we need to get out of here!"

"We were not attacked."

Leena threw her hands up. "How can you say that? If we weren't attacked, then why did you run?"

"When a tree becomes a huge dragon, I get scared. So I run. I wasn't expecting anything like that. My reaction was normal." She sounded childish

10

and she didn't care. For the first time in her life, Meeryle had seen a dragon. She wasn't going to let Leena diminish the experience in any way. "You ran too. Right past me, as a matter of fact."

"I didn't want to get eaten by that thing! Of course I ran."

"I'll have you know that dragons don't eat people. Or even meat, I think."

Leena sat down on the ground with a loud thump. She covered her face with her hands and shook her head. "You're getting on my nerves, Meeryle."

"Oh, I'm *so* sorry." She sighed as she took her time sitting beside the apprentice-Healer, mindful of her sore ankle. "Look, forget I just said that. But really think about it. The dragon did not try to hurt us at all. From what I learned, they never do. It just looked at us. I'm actually wondering if we didn't surprise it as much as it surprised us." She put her hand on Leena's shoulder. "Don't you think this encounter is special?"

Leena looked up, her expression unreadable. Meeryle wanted her friend to understand and feel her passion about the creatures. She didn't want to be scorned once again, after so long, especially not by her best friend.

The tall girl looked into Meeryle's cycs, then up at the sky, looking for words. "It was special." Meeryle closed her eyes and sighed with relief. "But Meeryle, what exactly do you know about dragons and how much of the information you've gathered can you really trust?"

"I... Well, it's only written records and reports of people who have seen them. Most is actually speculation, but it makes sense when you look at the dragons' behavior. Like the fact that they never attack. So far, no one has *ever* been attacked by a dragon. They just leave when they see a human. And the people who have been able to watch them for a while without being seen say they've never seen them eat animals, even though they sometimes are very near them. The only conclusion I've ever drawn from all this was that dragons are afraid of people."

"Where did you get all this information?"

Meeryle looked down, embarrassed. "In the books we have here, at the school. But mostly travelers who came through here."

"Oh, Meeryle, this is so naive."

The chubby girl knew her sources weren't the greatest, but what could she do? The village's little library didn't get updated very often; she had only the words of rare passers-by who had been patient enough to answer a dreamy girl's questions. Leena, ever the disciplined researcher, needed tangible documentation, not hearsay.

Meeryle waited as her friend stared out, not looking at anything in particular. Leena suddenly turned and gazed into her friend's eyes with an ardor that surprised Meeryle. "But in everything you've heard and read, did you ever see something about dragons talking?"

"What? It talked to you?"

"Just answer the question, will you?"

Meeryle chewed her lip, trying to remember everything she knew about dragons. It had been years since the last time she'd thought about them. "Well, I don't think so. But I never read anything about a green dragon either, so it doesn't mean anything."

"So what color are they, then?"

"Purple and brown. Why do you ask about talking?"

"Because I think it talked to me." Leena's eyes were shut tight. "I definitely heard something say, 'Don't be afraid.' Only it wasn't as if you or anyone else had said it. It was inside my head." She opened her eyes and looked at Meeryle. "That thing talked to me in my head. That's what made me run. It got inside my head."

Meeryle's mind was in upheaval. It talked. So dragons might even be more than the books said they were; dragons could be creatures with intellect.

"Leena, we have to go back. We have to talk to it."

"Are you crazy?" Meeryle's face must have shown her elation, because Leena stared at her with disbelief. "You're serious, aren't you? You want to go back to that creature. And what if the books were wrong? What if they do attack and eat people? What then? You'll just let yourself be eaten alive and sing praises? Meeryle, snap out of it!"

"Don't be stupid! It told you not to be afraid, so we'll be safe."

"Oh, Meeryle, by all the powers that be, how can you be so naive! Why is it, do you think, that our hunters imitate the love cries of animals? So they'll come close enough to be caught and killed. That dragon of yours is probably licking and smacking its lips right now, thinking its plan will bring a fine meal."

As Meeryle's anger rose with Leena's unwillingness to believe her, her sight blurred with an orange tinge. Her friend was just like everyone else: she feared the unknown. Leena had to see how important this was. "Leena, you can't just go," she said through clenched teeth. "I need you to find the dragon." As she spoke, the orange tinge filtering her sight intensified briefly before dispersing and surrounding Leena in the form of a diffuse and distorting light. Meeryle blinked and the light was gone, her sight once more normal.

Leena stared, a dreamy look on her face. "All right," she whispered. "Let's find that dragon of yours."

Meeryle wasn't sure if she had heard right. "What?"

Leena took in a deep breath, the dreamy look gone. "I don't believe I'm saying this. I'll take you to...."

"You will?"

"Don't interrupt! I don't want to do this because it's really a stupid idea, all right? But," she sighed and shook her head. "I've never seen you like this, Meeryle. You usually just let things go and move on. This is the first time I've seen you get so upset since... well, since Tarkin stole your sweetcake all those years ago!" Both girls smiled.

"Well, it was the last one. He had no right."

"But this is more than that dumb sweetcake. It's obviously something you've yearned after for a long, long time. What baffles me is that you've never mentioned it to me!"

"Do you really tell me or anyone else everything? Really everything?"

Leena blinked and paused. "No, you're right. Some things are always best never said." As the tall girl stared ahead for a few moments, it dawned on Meeryle that Leena might be thinking of some secret of her own. But before she could find the words to ask her best friend what she'd been hiding, Leena shook her head as if clearing her thoughts. "Now, come on, let's find your dragon."

Meeryle flinched as she got up and once again straightened her skirt. The poor thing was in a very sad state. Her blouse was worse, though. The sleeves were ripped, and the left one looked to be beyond repair. Her mother would not be pleased. Meeryle would have to make amends by preparing her best dishes yet.

She stretched very slowly, mindful of every scrape and bruise. In the meantime, Leena had taken out all the burrs from her hair.

"You should wear breeches and a tunic like I do, you know. They're much more practical for walking." Leena frowned. "Your blouse is gone. It looks awful."

"Never mind. And I don't fit in breeches, all right? Forget about my clothes and let's go."

Leena shrugged as she pointed and started walking. "This way. Actually, it shouldn't be too hard to find the place. All we have to do is follow our trail; we left plenty of broken shrubs and twigs."

Meeryle followed without saying a word, still stunned by Leena's agreement. Did she truly believe her or was she simply humoring her? Meeryle decided she didn't care. Now that she knew they existed for sure, the dragon was much more important. She smiled tightly to herself and remembered the last thought she'd had about dragons years ago. If dragons weren't real, then why waste time writing books on their habits? She had been a ten-year-old whose dream had been shattered.

Luckily, that was the time when Leena's parents had just arrived at the village, giving Meeryle a new friend. Meeryle had immediately felt a kinship with her when Leena expressed an interest in books. And since they became friends, Teerane, the village bully, instantly disliked the tall, thin, serious girl.

For some reason, Teerane had hated Meeryle with a passion since childhood. Once, when Meeryle was just six years old, Teerane had managed to corner her briefly, out of anyone else's sight, and grab a handful of her hair. Twisting and pulling it viciously until Meeryle cried in pain, the older girl continued her torment as long as she dared. Only when someone called for Meeryle did she let go, whispering harshly: "My mother died because of you, I just know it! No one believes me, they all tell me to leave you alone, but I know you're responsible. I'll find out how one day, I swear."

The words had triggered a deep fear in Meeryle, a terror she couldn't comprehend, a dread that stopped her from trying to think about the other girl's accusation, let alone ask anyone about it. Not only did she not understand what Teerane meant, but somehow, she just knew that something bad would happen to her if she brought it up. Of course, she had no idea at all what that might be, and as the years went by, she dismissed the feeling as some silly and childish fear induced by the older girl's threats or her constantly menacing attitude, which became more and more discreet as Teerane was scolded for it over the years. Yet Meeryle never dwelt on the thought or even dared to question anyone about this. She simply accepted that Teerane blamed her and borne the girl's barbs without any comment.

Anyone who befriended her got the same treatment, so Meeryle didn't have many friends. Leena was no exception, but the serious girl's attitude had a way to cool tempers. Teerane's sneers were also cut short when Leena's father, Parin, very quickly became the village's leader. His worldly experience, his standing as a hunter, and his big stature and booming voice were exactly what the small and isolated village needed. Teerane was intimidated by the big man and quit her remarks, limiting herself to dirty looks.

Meeryle and Leena became inseparable. Leena was already very interested in the Healing arts and had later been tested for the Healing gift. She was as passionate about Healing as Meeryle had been about dragons. Meeryle followed Leena in her studies when she could, trying to forget dragons and to learn about something new. Healing wasn't for her, though. So when Leena took on her official apprenticeship and had less and less time for her friend, Meeryle had to find another activity. She developed a taste for cooking.

Her mother had been quite surprised to discover that her daughter was better than she was around the stove. Surprised, but pleased. She was a seamstress and her daughter's trials in that field were disasters. If cooking was her gift, it would simply add to the family's welfare.

17

Therefore, Meeryle was given the responsibility of preparing everything that came out of the oven. The breads and pastries were always baked to perfection; Meeryle just knew when to take them out. As a result, her family's breads were the most sought after in the village. Meeryle had become a respected cook, albeit too young for her opinion to really matter with some of the older women. The dragons had faded away and Meeryle no longer saw them in the clouds or the flames.

Until today.

Meeryle was so far lost in her thoughts that she didn't realize Leena had stopped, and bumped into her. Her arms burning from the pain of that brief contact, she jumped back and yelped. "Warn me when you stop, will you?"

"Sorry. I think this is it." Leena looked back at her friend. "This is the clearing. What do you want to do now?"

Meeryle peered around, but all the trees looked the same. "Are you sure?"

"Yes, I'm sure. I know how to find my way around the forest." Leena was glaring at her.

"That's not what I meant. I just don't recognize any of this."

"I'm sure. We have to find the exact place where that dragon of yours was standing, then we'll know for sure what it was."

"What do you mean?"

"The tracks will tell us."

Meeryle blinked a few times. It had never occurred to her that a dragon would leave tracks. Or any animal, for that matter. "Village girl, that's me," she muttered.

Meeryle looked again at the clearing. One spot seemed stranger than the rest. She stared at it for a while and realized that it was empty compared to the rest of the clearing. "I think this is where the dragon had been standing. This spot should have a tree on it," she said, pointing.

Leena squinted. "It did have a tree on it. It just became a dragon. Now it's gone. No tree, no dragon. At least this shows we didn't dream it."

Meeryle rubbed her arms lightly and winced. A dream didn't make one panic and hurt like this.

She joined Leena, who was squatting by the spot in question. Meeryle didn't even attempt to squat; she bent down. She sucked in her breath sharply at the sight of a footprint. A very, very large footprint.

"Leena, what's this?"

"I don't know, Meeryle, I just don't know. This doesn't look like anything I've ever seen."

The print was three times the size of Meeryle's hand. It was elongated and ended with three toes. "What are these strange holes in front of the toe mark?"

"Claws."

"Leena, they're almost two inches away from the toe mark."

"I know." Leena looked at her and licked her lips. "This thing is huge, Meeryle."

"I guess." She felt short of breath. "This can't be a bear, can it?"

"No. We were shown bear tracks, remember? They have four toes and like a thumb. The tracks were also a lot rounder. And much, much smaller."

The girls were silent for a while. Meeryle's heart calmed down a little. She looked at the tracks again and noticed a mark behind the footprints. "What is that?" She pointed at a sinuous dent in the ground that circled the footprints.

"Well, all I can do is guess. A tail track?"

"A tail? Did you see the track? It must be huge!"

"It's probably proportionate to the feet and the rest of the body."

"Leena, that thing seems bigger than five horses put together."

The apprentice-Healer sighed. "I know. Are you sure you want to stay and see it again?"

Meeryle didn't have to think about it. "Yes. I want to see the dragon."

CHAPTER TWO

Meeryle sat by the tracks, unable to tear her eyes away. Trying to recall the dragon in detail proved fruitless, as her memory was already playing tricks on her. The footprints didn't match the size of the dragon she recalled. The absurd image of a small dragon with huge feet popped into her mind. Shaking her head to clear the strange idea, Meeryle concentrated on the track presumably left by the tail. She couldn't remember seeing a tail at all; the only things she remembered vividly were the green scales and the ruby eyes. Those were imprinted in her mind like two bright suns.

A movement seen at the corner of her eye startled her. She turned to see a little black fox sitting by a tree, staring intently at her. The girl stared back with a smile, without making a sound or moving. She'd seen the animal several times on previous trips into the forest with Leena, but in all the excitement she'd never even thought about it. This time, she was able to see clearly the white tips of its ears, paws, and muzzle, as well as the white that flecked its tail. The unusually dark coat was shiny and healthy. The piercing black eyes almost seemed to be trying to relay a message, making the encounter very strange.

The fox suddenly threw back its ears and bolted, startling Meeryle. Her heart skipped a few beats and her breath caught in her throat. She hadn't moved or done anything to frighten it, yet it ran as if terrified. Meeryle shook her head, telling her heart to calm down, and shrugged at the jumpiness of wild animals, dismissing the little creature. She had much more interesting and important things on her mind than scared foxes.

Returning to her initial examination, Meeryle peered closely at the claw marks. The hole in the ground was the size of her thumb, and the space between the hole and the actual footprint almost the size of her flat hand, fingers tight together.

"That's one big dragon," she muttered. "Leena, how big did it seem to you when we first saw it?" She turned to her friend, who was sitting against a tree, as far from the tracks as possible. "Leena, what are you doing back there? Don't you want to see this?"

"No! I've seen enough. You look all you want."

Meeryle stood very slowly. She had only been sitting down for a little while, but her legs were very, very cramped and her ankle seemed stuck in the wrong position. She stretched each leg carefully and made her way to Leena. "What's the matter?"

"I can't believe I went along with this," mumbled the apprentice-Healer. "I mean, how long are we going to wait here? How can you be sure it'll come back?" she asked, making a face.

"I'm not. I'm really hoping it will. And if you're right and it spoke to you to tell you not to be afraid, can't it mean that it's also curious?" She was elated by the very thought of seeing this dragon once again. While she still wondered at how easily Leena had agreed to come with her, and while she understood why someone as practical as her friend wouldn't be all that eager to sit around waiting for a mystical creature to show, something inside Meeryle was filling every part of her body with excitement, dismissing any misgiving of Leena's. It was silly; she was too old for this. But dragons were real!

"I just feel really, really tired, Meeryle. And hungry. And sore. Very sore. Even worse, I lost my scarf."

Remorse tried to make its way into Meeryle's elation; after all, they were both in a sad state. But her happiness quashed it down quickly; for once, they were doing something for *her*, rather than seeing to one of Leena's tasks or errands. For once, even if it didn't make any sense, Leena had agreed to do something deemed frivolous. Meeryle wasn't going to let anything get in the way, especially not remorse. While Leena didn't usually go back on her word, it wouldn't be wise to give her the opportunity to do so.

Instead, Meeryle decided to remind her friend that she wasn't the only one in poor shape right now. "If you feel sore, how do you think I feel? It took me forever to get up." Meeryle's conscience made another appearance, and this time, the girl hesitated. "You can make another scarf, can't you?"

Leena looked at Meeryle, shook her head and smiled. "Yes, I can get another scarf. This was my third, actually. I lost the others in the woods, too. And you do look terrible, you know. You just might scare the dragon away."

Meeryle stuck her tongue out, relieved. Maybe Leena, underneath it all, found this situation just as exciting as she did. Leena didn't respond, though. She stared past the plump girl. "You were right, Meeryle. You were right," she whispered. "Here it comes."

Meeryle turned and looked up, focusing on what her friend was seeing. The general shape was a bird's, but a long tail, which matched the tracks, broke the illusion. The appendage trailed behind the dragon, following the flow of the wind and the air. The creature approached on an angle and changed direction twice, displaying its majestic wings and gracious neck and letting the graceful tail undulate.

"You know, it almost looks like it's showing off." Meeryle couldn't take her eyes off the dragon. It was even more beautiful than she remembered.

"I think it is. It wants us to see it."

"Why?"

"Because it knows we're here? Because it's vain? How should I know, Meeryle? You ask the strangest questions."

"Well, you always seem to know so much. And I'm not really asking you in particular, I'm just asking." Meeryle was losing patience again, but she didn't let anger surface. She drank in the extraordinary sight of the fast-approaching dragon.

Its wings were fully unfolded as it made its way down. The sun glared through what looked to be a thin membrane. It had no feathers like a bird, but the flight movements were the same. The light displayed the fine bones running through the skin, thick close to the body and thin at the tips. The shadow generated by the dragon had a greenish tint where the wings were translucent.

As the creature drew nearer and lower, both girls backed away, eyes towards the sky, so Meeryle didn't see the rock. The heel of her sore foot bumped on it. Pain flared in her ankle, making Meeryle utter a strange squeak. Her ankle refused to move and she fell on her rear end. Pain or not, she felt ridiculous. Thankfully, Leena didn't seem to notice her friend's troubles. She was staring in rapture at the landing dragon.

It had stretched itself out, hind legs down, tail curled up. The left hind paw touched the ground, then the right. The front paws touched down almost at the same time. The tail curled around the body and wrapped itself around the front legs.

The dragon looked down at the girls. It matched the size of the tracks. The scales differed completely from those of a lizard or a snake. They were large and shaped in half-circles on the chest and belly, arranged in two rows, and smaller, more numerous, and more randomly arranged on the legs and tail. The front feet looked like three-fingered hands. The dragon puffed its chest, effectively hiding its folded wings.

The creature was not the same green all over. Each scale was a different shade, ranging from forest green to a green so pale it seemed yellow, and when the sun hit them, they sparkled and took on a golden tinge.

Meeryle stared at the dragon, drinking in its beauty. The creature was the most beautiful living being she had ever seen.

It cocked its head and looked at her. Meeryle held her breath, at a complete loss for words. Would a wave of the hand mean anything to a dragon? The dragon turned its head to look at Leena. The tall girl gulped noisily, her hands shaking. She quickly clasped them behind her back and stood taller, clearly bracing herself. For what, Meeryle wasn't sure. She probably still thought the dragon was going to eat her. Being honest with herself, Meeryle had to admit that it could still be a possibility. She stubbornly refused to give in to fear and squared her own shoulders.

The dragon moved its head forward and huffed in Leena's hair. The apprentice-Healer squeaked, both surprised and terrified. The noise was so unlike Leena that Meeryle chuckled.

The laughter shifted the dragon's attention. As it turned its head towards Meeryle, it stretched its long neck, almost touching Meeryle's face with its nose. The plump girl tensed and automatically shut her eyes. She forced herself to relax and to look into the dragon's eyes. She slowly opened her eyes and found herself staring into ruby orbs. The black pupils slowly disappeared, leaving only a shining red light that beckoned Meeryle and enveloped her, sending a warm sensation throughout her body. She felt completely at ease and safe in the depths of those eyes. Then the dragon blinked and the spell was broken.

Meeryle abruptly came back to reality and found she was looking cross-eyed at the tip of the dragon's nose. She backed her head up without moving the rest of her body. She was rooted in place, unable to quite believe what she was experiencing. Emotions were succeeding one another with blinding speed. Meeryle was in turn elated, terrified, fascinated, and incredulous. She could hardly feel the ground beneath her feet.

Meeryle and the dragon were looking each other up and down without daring to move too much and scare the other away. The dragon's scales were very small and supple-looking on its face. Its nostrils were opening and closing as it moved its head very slowly up and down, taking in the girl's scent. It didn't sniff like a dog, but rather huffed, moving her wavy hair slightly every time. The spikes on the top of its head moved up and down as it inspected her.

She relaxed slightly and dared to break the silence. "Ah, hello. My name is Meeryle."

The dragon moved its head back at the sound of Meeryle's voice. It leaned its head to the right and looked at Meeryle, eyes squinting slightly. Meeryle wasn't sure of its intent, but didn't dare to break eye contact to consult Leena. As she opened her mouth to whisper a question to her friend, Meeryle suddenly felt something in her head. She couldn't define it; however, it somehow felt familiar. When the dragon opened its eyes wide, Meeryle identified the feeling: curiosity. The dragon was asking her a question.

She turned to Leena. "I think it wants to know something," she whispered. "I don't know what it is, though. Leena?"

Her friend wasn't listening to her. She didn't even acknowledge her. Leena was immobile, staring at the dragon, who was now looking at her. Meeryle sighed. "Leena! Snap out of it! It's not going to eat you."

Leena started. The apprentice-Healer turned toward her friend, eyes unfocused.

"Leena? What is it?"

She still wasn't responding. Panic slowly uncoiled in Meeryle's belly. The dragon had done something to her friend and somehow taken hold of her. What had it done and how could Meeryle possibly free her friend from the enormous creature?

27

Her head didn't even come close to its shoulder. Granted, she was short, but the dragon was much taller than a horse. When its long neck was fully stretched out, the creature looked down from a distance almost three times Meeryle's height, making it impossible for her to overpower it physically-even if she had been in a state to do so. A sting might break its gaze, free Leena for a few seconds, and allow her to run, though. As Meeryle gathered courage to approach the dragon close enough to slap it, Leena spoke. "Meeryle, her name is Tikid. She wants to know what we are." Leena's tone was flat, expressionless. When she looked at Meeryle, her eyes had a haunted look. "You wanted to see the dragon, so you talk to her."

Meeryle blinked. And blinked again. She? The dragon was a female? How could Leena know? However, Leena's look quelled any questions. She seemed deeply troubled and not herself. Before Meeryle could say or do anything, the dragon's gaze turned to her once again. The same sensation of curiosity as before filled her, except it was now tainted with frustration. The dragon wasn't the only one. Meeryle's cheeks were slowly warming up with her own feeling of helpless frustration.

"Look, Tikid. What did you do to Leena? She's not normal, and she became that way after you looked at her. So take it back," she said using her older brother's tone when he was at his rudest.

The dragon jumped back at Meeryle's tone. The girl felt surprise and... pain? The creature was hurt by her words! Now she was sure the feelings that kept intruding in her head came from the dragon. Walking toward the creature, she displayed an expression she hoped was menacing. It felt rather silly, but it seemed to work. The dragon was moving back as Meeryle was moving forward. Fear was now emanating from the dragon. Triumph welled up in Meeryle's heart as she made the dragon stand down.

The moment didn't last and came crashing down when the dragon stepped on the tip of its tail, yelped in pain, and tried to sidestep in order to avoid the rest of the tail. At that point, it had backed up into a tangle of bushes, where the tail got stuck in the branches, and it stepped on it again. The dragon made another noise and twisted to get out of the tangle the long tail had become. Of course, it was trying to move the tail at same time, so the tail came loose from the branches, whipping the dragon on the nose. The creature squawked with indignation at its appendage and moved to the side, only to trip on a root. The dragon fell on its side, clearly insulted.

Meeryle could not believe her eyes. How could such a graceful creature look so ridiculous? She stood, gaping, unsure whether to laugh or to cry. Leena, however, didn't hesitate and laughed outright. The incident had taken her out of her daze. Meeryle couldn't help a giggle.

The dragon was radiating disbelief. Meeryle suddenly felt sorry; she'd had her fair share of clumsiness, and hated being mocked when incidents occurred. She schooled her expression and came towards the dragon. "Sorry, we shouldn't have laughed. You have to admit, though, seeing a dragon stepping on its tail is rather funny."

Leena was still giggling. "She says she really feels stupid. These things always seem to happen to her at the worst times."

Meeryle gaped at her friend. "She says? You can hear her?"

"Yes. You can't, though." Leena was frowning, deep in thought. "It doesn't make sense."

"All I get are feelings. Like now, it's... she's relieved, I think."

"Yes. She says you looked very angry and ready to blast her to pieces."

"Well, I was. I mean, do you have any idea how out of it you were? I thought she had wiped out your mind or something."

"I know. When I heard her voice in my head... I think I panicked. No one is meant to hear voices inside their heads. It just doesn't feel right."

"Why can't I hear her, though?"

Leena turned to the dragon, who had finally untangled her tail. She was sitting on her haunches, wiping her stomach with her right front paw, mustering as much dignity as she could. Leena and Meeryle exchanged a look and tried not to burst out laughing again. The dragon truly looked like someone whose pride had taken a blow.

"So, Tikid, why is it that I can hear your voice and your words, but not Meeryle?" The dragon turned her unblinking gaze towards Leena. She briefly looked at Meeryle and resumed brushing off imaginary dust. "She says it's because you're too powerful. You're blocking out true thoughts. Only emotions can get through."

The words triggered something deep inside Meeryle's mind, something that had to remain hidden at all costs. The thought was quelled before it could become clear, and the emerging fear subsided quickly. Meeryle blinked once, trying to forget about the sudden uneasiness, and looked at Leena in puzzlement. The tall girl shook her head in response. Neither knew what the dragon meant, so they both shrugged.

"How did she know we were back?" asked Meeryle, her curiosity erasing all memory of that flash of fear.

As Leena was "listening" to Tikid, her eyes opened wide in astonishment. "She asked the birds and the trees."

"What?"

Leena shook her head and threw her hands up. "You heard me! It seems your dragons talk to the flora and fauna! Meeryle, this is getting really strange."

Meeryle sighed and got a feeling of amusement from the dragon. "And what do you find so funny?"

Leena paused. "Apparently, we are. It seems we look quite funny, especially you, and weird because *we* don't talk to animals and plants." Tikid came near and pushed Meeryle's skirt with her nose. Meeryle jumped back. "Yes, your dress is hilarious, apparently," explained Leena with a smile.

The dragon made a strange noise. A rumble resonated in her chest and vibrated in her throat. The wings briefly flapped and the dragon's entire chest was contracted. Meeryle couldn't believe her ears: Tikid was laughing. Anger flared up. "Listen, dragon. You didn't like it when we laughed at you when you fell. My clothes are ripped and our hair is so tangled from all the twigs and branches because you scared us to death. I've hurt myself and it's your fault. So quit it!"

31

"Meeryle, calm down! What's the matter with you?"

"She's making fun of us!"

"Well, we do look grubby. And we are the first humans she's ever seen. We're not what she expected."

Taken aback, Meeryle turned to Tikid. "You've never seen people before? How come?"

"Well, really, Meeryle, she's the first dragon we've ever seen, isn't she?"

"Ah.... Yes, I guess. But what about the books on dragons?"

The pause was longer this time. Leena was frowning, listening to Tikid. Just as Meeryle was losing patience, Leena explained. "They were probably written by people who saw dragons from afar, only once in a while. She swears she doesn't know of a Green who ever met humans."

"A Green? A Green what?"

Pause. "A Green dragon." Leena smiled. "Well, you're going to get your share of dragons. It seems there are different sorts of dragons."

"Like what?" Leena had stopped just when the explanations were becoming interesting.

"Meeryle, you'll have to calm down, all right? First I have to listen to what she says; then I can tell you."

"Sorry," she mumbled.

The dragon gave a frustrated grunt and huffed into Leena's hair.

"Yes, yes, I'll tell her." Another pause, this one long enough to make Meeryle want to scream her impatience.

Finally, Leena spoke. "Well, so you have Green, Purple, Brown, White, and Red dragons. It seems that the only dragons who have reported seeing humans were the Purples and the Browns. Your information wasn't completely wrong, then. Tikid is a Green and this type of dragon lives in the forest and takes care of the trees."

Meeryle looked at her friend, speechless. She stared at the beautiful green creature in front of her, imagining trees waving their branches at the dragon. The situation was getting stranger by the minute.

***

Much, much later, after a long three-way conversation, when the sun was nearly setting, Leena insisted on leaving. "I won't be able to find my way back to the village in the dark, Meeryle. Let's go."

After reluctantly agreeing, Meeryle wanted to know if Tikid would meet them again-she hoped the dragon was as happy as she was to have made the encounter. "We can come back, if you want." The dragon nodded once, sending a warm feeling that could only be the creature's way of expressing happiness. Meeryle smiled, glad to know she seemed to have made a friend. "How do we know when we can see you again? We don't know where you live."

Tikid looked up and a bright blue bird landed on her extended claw. After a few moments of silence where both girls exchanged puzzled glances, the dragon gave an explanation to Leena.

"Well, it seems we only need to feed the bird and tell it to get Tikid when we want to meet. This is getting so weird. She gave it instructions, she says. And the bird likes bread crumbs, not seeds." Leena was shaking her head. "All right. Follow us, little fellow."

Meeryle waved goodbye to her new friend as the dragon lifted off and flew away. "We will see you another day, Tikid."

Leena tore Meeryle from her daze. "Come on, let's go home," she said.

They slowly made their way to the village. They were both weary, tired, and sore. Neither felt like talking.

As the bird was fluttering above her, Meeryle tried to wrap her mind around everything she had learned about dragons. The books had been right only in their descriptions and the fact that dragons ate neither humans nor meat. Otherwise, she now knew the privileged people who had seen dragons did not know what the creatures really were.

Luckily, Leena had geared the conversation in the right direction and asked Tikid all the right questions, making the hours spent with the dragon very informative: Dragons were part of their environment. They could use the essence of their environment to become part of it superficially, so anyone but their own Color would only see a tree, a fish, a rock, ice, etc. They did not actually transform, so Tikid's tree disguise had disappeared when Meeryle touched the dragon-as-a-tree. She had surprised the dragon, making it move, thus breaking the spell.

As dragons were physically part of their environment, they naturally took care of it. The Green dragons made sure the trees and plants of the forest were healthy. If a tree died, they removed it and put it in a place where the rotting wood would feed needy soil.

They also had good relations with other living things. Animals would tell them if a disease affected some plants, point out sources of unclean water, and report on the general health of the forest.

However, the more dragons had observed humans, the further they had moved away from them. The Greens only had the reports of the other Colors, but humans did not seem to respect their environment and were quite destructive. For the sensitive Greens, the best solution had been to retire to the middle of the greatest forests and to avoid such creatures. They had trusted the Purples and the Browns and had never sought humans to verify the negative comments. To the Greens, humans had become a legend, just as dragons were to humans.

The situation was going to change, though. Tikid had told them that she would make a full report of their encounter as soon as she flew home. The dragon was now very happy to have gone beyond the boundary that she called the Great Rift; meeting creatures out of legends had been well worth the transgression. Meeryle didn't know what that rift was, but Leena, after thinking about it, recalled her father's description of a huge chasm, extremely long and wide, much further out within the forest. It had taken him and his wife, Jetyaa, Leena's stepmother, more than half a day at running pace to reach the rift. According to them-and they were experts in the matter-it was impassable. Villagers seldom ventured that far into the forest, so the obstacle had never caused any problems for hunters. For the dragons, the rift was a natural barrier protecting them from humans. Tikid was finding out that humans were not what she had been taught. She told her new friends she wanted to continue the relationship, but she wasn't sure how the adults would react to her crossing the official boundary of dragon country.

Meeryle's mind had to encompass that particular bit of information. Tikid was a young dragon, probably the equivalent of her age, and she wasn't fully grown yet. The size of an adult dragon was unfathomable.

Lost in her thoughts, Meeryle didn't realize they were out of the woods. The bark of a dog brought her back to the present, just in time to see that Leena had stopped and to avoid bumping into her. "Leena, I told you not to stop like that. I almost walked right into you." When her friend didn't react, Meeryle looked around her. Leena's parents and her own were standing in the middle of the street, arms crossed, and a few other people hovered in the back. She winced at the voices, which seemed shrill after the quiet of the forest.

"Where have you girls been?" Parin's deep voice resonated in Meeryle's very bones. The man downright scared her at times. The only resemblance Leena bore to her father was her height. Otherwise, father and daughter were almost opposites. Where Leena was thin, delicate, and graceful, Parin was wide, thick, and strong. His hair was a curly mess, due to be cut, whereas Leena's was straight and silky. Leena had inherited her almond-shaped eyes from her mother, just as she had her milky skin. Her father was deeply tanned, though in the dark, his features were hidden. All that remained was a massive, looming shape.

A much shorter shape moved forward, gesticulating. "It's almost dark out!" cried Meeryle's mother.

Then, another voice quieted them all. "Meeryle, what in the great powers happened to you? You're a mess, girl! Let me have a look at you."

She looked into the concerned eyes of the Healer. Her parents were fussing and yelling at the same time, demanding an explanation. When she spotted Teerane smiling mockingly, Meeryle's heart sank. The elation of the encounter with the dragon completely disappeared as she came back to the hard reality of life in the village. She hoped Tikid's kindred would be more receptive than her own. She was sure her dragon story, which was feeling less and less real by the second, would not be well received among humans.

CHAPTER THREE

Corvin, the Healer, forestalled any comment from parents and youths alike with a quelling glare, and dragged Meeryle and Leena to his cottage. Parin grunted and left, letting the Healer take care of the situation. Parin liked to organize, not chastise, at least not in public. From what Meeryle had seen over the years, she was sure Leena would undoubtedly hear about it later, but in private. The rest didn't even try to protest; the Healer had too much authority. In a way, Meeryle was glad for the older man's interruption. She'd never thought her absence-and Leena's-would be noticed, and she certainly hadn't thought about how to explain their encounter, either. Tikid had seemed confident in telling her story, but as soon as she saw her mother's face and Teerane's, Meeryle was certain she couldn't simply describe her meeting with Tikid. Her mother would dismiss dragon stories as the fruit of her daughter's overactive imagination, and Teerane.... Why add fuel to her fire? The older girl would seize the opportunity to harass Meeryle further. Her obvious pleasure in Meeryle's shame when her mother expressed loudly her displeasure with the state of Meeryle's clothes was enough.

Leena's closed expression told Meeryle that her friend wouldn't mention the dragon. While Leena wasn't all that worried about her reputation-she didn't care what anybody thought about her, really-she was nevertheless always extremely serious about her future and never really did anything frivolous, like seeking mystical dragons. Meeryle was still surprised that Leena had agreed to wait for the dragon, but she didn't dwell on it; what was done was done.

"You girls go on in. I'll get wood for the fire." Corvin's tone brooked no argument.

Well over sixty, Corvin was of middle height, thin, and frail-looking. His white and wispy hair was usually held in place by his hat, which stood straight on his head. At first glance, he seemed a doddering and charming old man, but his piercing gaze and stiff posture soon broke the illusion. The Healer was ensconced in his position and craft, and was, after Parin, the unofficial leader of the small community. His words were final and very rarely challenged. His voice, which he never raised, could be as gentle as a lullaby when he tended to the sick, or as sharp as a razor when he reprimanded someone. Corvin was not on Meeryle's list of favorite people.

Yet since she didn't know what else to do, Meeryle meekly followed Leena inside.

The first floor of the Healer's cottage was separated into two parts: the first a large room where he received his patients, and the second, behind the first, his living quarters. The second floor was reserved for patients who had to be monitored by the Healer during the night. Such patients were very few, but since bad accidents happened even when all precautions were taken, Corvin was always ready to accommodate anyone needing his day-and-night care. While using the second floor allowed for more privacy for patients and Healer, getting them there was always difficult. Whether no one had ever had the courage to tell the Healer so, or whether it was truly worthwhile, when the time came, the villagers carried up the unfortunates using the stairs designed for that very purpose.

The receiving room had three alcoves separated by screens, which ensured a bit of privacy. Each bone-weary girl sat with some relief in one of the five chairs lining the entrance.

The room was dark; the Healer hadn't lit any candles yet. Meeryle couldn't see things clearly in the half light. Hope stirred. "Leena, I just thought of something. I look like a mess, right?" Leena nodded. "But it's because of my dress. It's too dark to see my arms and to notice that I was limping. Heal me. That way, we'll just say that we were racing and got lost."

"Meeryle, stop. First of all, I can't Heal you. I'm not allowed yet. Second, what does it matter whether the Healer sees your injuries or not? We were gone too long and on top of it, I forgot my basket with the plants I picked. Anyway, I think they all fell out when we were running."

"I just want... I don't want to have to explain why I would run to the point of hurting myself and why we didn't come back right away after I fell. I don't want to tell anyone about Tikid yet. I just have a bad feeling. If we tell, they might laugh at us or something."

"I guess it makes sense. But I still can't Heal you. I haven't come into real power yet and something might go wrong."

"Like what?"

"Like I put in too much power and kill you? Gee, now, wouldn't that be nice! And guess who would lose her apprenticeship. 'Now, killing friends just isn't done, young lady.' Is that what you want? I

40

wouldn't know what I'm doing, Meeryle. In a way, I never did. You don't want to mention Tikid, fine. But you're the one who basically got us into this mess, so you think of something. My brain is closed for the day."

Meeryle gaped. "What do you mean, you've never known what you're doing?"

"I.... Let's just say I'm not what I want to be and leave it at that, all right?"

"What? You don't want to be a Healer?"

"I said, let it be!" snapped Leena.

The day was getting stranger by the minute. First the dragon, and now Leena was expressing doubts about her chosen path. Meeryle shook her head, suddenly overwhelmed. Life was normally so simple; finding out her childhood dreams were true was already quite the life-changing thing, but now to learn that her best friend's self-assurance might not be what it seemed was too much. She would think about it later.

The words that took up all her attention now were *You think of something*. Leena was making her deal with the consequences of her decision, something to which Meeryle was not accustomed at all.

The truth was, Meeryle didn't want to be near the Healer. She had the impression Corvin might get an insight from her and suddenly know about the dragons simply by touching her with his gift. Shaking her head, she reminded herself that Healing didn't allow anyone to read another person's thoughts. Instead, she concentrated on trying to concoct a story to explain her sorry state.

41

Corvin came in loaded with logs. He put them down in a neat pile in the bin by the fireplace before adding a log to the dying fire and reviving it with his small bellows. He then proceeded to light the room. Since he needed to see properly day and night, the Healer had many candles and oil lamps, which took him a long time to light. Meeryle didn't mind. The longer she could put off the examination and the explanation, the better.

However, the moment came sooner than she expected.

"Well, come on. Let's see the damage. Meeryle, sit here; Leena, in the other alcove."

Meeryle got up and winced. Her legs and ankle had cramped again. Her eyes were also starting to feel gritty. There was only one lamp by the chairs in the entrance; she had been sitting in semidarkness all that time. The brightly lit alcove made her blink.

The Healer's eyebrows sprung up. "What happened to you? You look like you've been dragged behind a horse through an entire field."

Leena snorted on the other side of the screen. The Healer gave Meeryle a questioning look.

"I fell," she mumbled.

"And quite some fall it must have been. Can you take off your blouse without hurting your arms too much or do I have to cut it off?"

"I... Just cut it off. It's ruined, anyway."

The Healer smiled wryly, shaking his head. "Ruined isn't the word," he muttered. He took his scissors and with precise cuts, he removed the blouse. Meeryle closed her eyes when he got near her arms, but felt nothing other than the cool metal of the scissors against her skin. She was glad he had revived the fire; her under-chemise didn't do anything to keep her warm. Maybe it was the older man's scrutiny. His piercing gaze was going right through her, chilling her to the bone.

For some reason she couldn't fathom, Corvin always gave her strange looks. One day, he'd even tested her for the Healing gift, which she of course didn't have. Had he bothered to ask her instead of bossing her around, she would have told him. Since that day, Meeryle's dislike for Corvin had intensified to the point where she avoided him whenever she could. However, today she didn't have a choice; she was in too much pain.

"Now relax and don't move. I need to see if these are infected yet and if there is any damage elsewhere." His hands hovered over Meeryle's forearms. He closed his eyes in concentration. Meeryle watched with fascination as the Healer's hands started to glow with a dull brown and green light. The hands moved up to her shoulders, then her head. They briefly hovered over her stomach and thighs, and lingered at her ankles and feet. The Healer opened his eyes. "Nothing's broken. The skin on your forearms is bad, but nothing that can't be cleaned and bandaged. I can't understand how you were able to walk on that ankle of yours, though. The muscle is in very bad shape. I can Heal it, or you can wear a splint and use crutches for a while."

Although she was grateful the Healer had to offer the choice of a magical or natural healing-and any other time, she would have refused the magical solution-Meeryle had to accept the magical alternative. "I don't want to have to use crutches," she said. For the first time in her life, she needed

Healing. Waiting for her ankle to heal naturally would confine her to the village for weeks, if not months, and would delay contact with Tikid.

She smiled briefly at the thought of the dragon. Tikid somehow made the pain bearable. Meeryle tried to imagine how the creature would hover over the Healer's implements and question their every use. The dragon's curiosity didn't seem to have any limits.

She was wrenched back to reality when the Healer started to salve and bandage her arms. They stung deeply, but it was nothing compared to her ankle. When the Healer took it in both hands, she gasped in pain. She had been able to ignore all her aches thanks to the dragon, even on her way back to the village. Now, however, her body refused to ignore the unusual hardships it had suffered. The ankle was not the only part of her body hurting. Her arms were suddenly throbbing and her legs felt like jelly. She was glad to be sitting down.

"Don't move, Meeryle. Movement could make the muscle turn the wrong way, which would not be a good thing during a Healing. The muscle would heal in the wrong shape and I would need to tear it again to set it right. Close your eyes and relax."

Meeryle obeyed. With her eyes shut, her other senses were much more alert. The fire was crackling and the air was heavy with the scent of medicines. The hands on her ankle were suddenly very warm. The pain flared up, then disappeared as quickly as it had broken out. She opened her eyes as soon as the Healer removed his hands.

"I'm done. You stay here while I tend to Leena."

Feeling completely drained of energy, Meeryle gladly remained where she was. She closed her eyes and listened to the Healer. The quiet sound of his voice, the fire's crackling, and the warmth of the room got the better of her, and she fell asleep.

***

"Come on, sleepy! Wake up."

A none-too-gentle hand shook her awake. For a moment, Meeryle wondered why her mother would want to wake her in the middle of the night. When she managed to open her eyes, they focused on Leena's thin face rather than her mother's round one. Meeryle blinked and her mind ran through the day's events at an astonishing speed. Everything came back to her at once. The forest, the dragon, her ankle.... She moved it tentatively and found it only a bit stiff.

"Meeryle, I'm going home." The apprentice-Healer paused, biting her lips as she looked at her friend. "I'll see you tomorrow," was all she said before she left.

His student gone, Corvin turned his attention to Meeryle. "Well, how about an explanation? Leena wasn't very forthcoming about your misadventure. She kept on repeating that you would explain. I have to admit I'm a bit surprised. This is the first time I've ever heard Leena deferring to someone else. She's usually more... commanding."

Meeryle didn't know whether to thank Leena or curse her. On one hand, silence was a sure way of not contradicting Meeryle's story, but on the other, Leena had given her friend the entire responsibility.

It had never happened before. Either Leena was much angrier with her than she had originally thought, or the apprentice-Healer simply hadn't a clue on how to remedy the problem.

"Well, this was basically all my fault. I think Leena's not too happy with me."

"I see. But why not give me an explanation at all?"

"Ah.... Because she didn't want me to sound too clumsy? I don't know. We raced and I fell, then we realized we were lost."

"Really." The Healer gave her a dose of his penetrating gaze, making Meeryle squirm inside. She tried very much not to show it and thought she had succeeded until the Healer made a very quiet snort. "Go home, Meeryle. Come back tomorrow if the ankle is still stiff."

He turned to clear the table of the ointment and leftover bandages. Thus dismissed, Meeryle got out and started home.

The fresh air of the night dispersed the rest of her sleepiness. She tried to guess the time and gave up. Her arms were thankfully rendered numb by the salve Corvin had applied under the bandages and her ankle didn't bother her much. She clutched the blanket the Healer had given her to replace her ruined blouse tightly against the cold wind. It had been a warm spring day, but the nights were still cold. By the time she arrived home, Meeryle knew she'd be chilled to the bone.

"Psst! Meeryle."

The girl jumped, barely holding in a shriek of pain as a tall shadow detached itself from the side of the Healer's cottage and grabbed her arm. Trying to disengage her arm-the salve didn't numb her skin completely after all-Meeryle took in a calming breath and turned to scold Rokin. However, when she saw the look of concern on the older boy's beautiful face, her words died in her mouth.

"Will you look at your arms! Meeryle, what happened to you? And to Leena? She wouldn't say anything to me."

"Of course not, because, as you can see, it's very embarrassing and painful for me."

"You don't understand. She completely ignored me," he whined.

"Oh, Rokin. Just.... She's tired and so am I. Can I go home now?" She tugged her arm slowly, mindful of the bandages.

"Sorry," he said with a contrite face. "Tell her I asked, all right?"

Meeryle nodded and Rokin smiled his thanks before running home. The girl sighed. Like every girl in the village, Meeryle was smitten with the handsome boy. Like every girl in the village, Meeryle knew she didn't have a chance since Rokin had set his heart on Leena. Unlike every girl in the village, Meeryle's own heart wasn't broken. Rokin was nice to her, but he had always made it clear he had never been interested in Meeryle romantically. Between her girth and her self-effacing attitude, Meeryle wasn't surprised. When she had failed to choose an apprenticeship the previous summer, her mother's allusions to marriage had also discouraged the girl from seeking relationships with the opposite sex. Aside from Rokin, none of the village boys seemed interesting. When the dark-haired boy had declared his feelings for the apprentice-Healer,

47

Meeryle had brushed aside romance and concentrated on food.

She was happy for Leena; Rokin was nice, serious, and an already accomplished hunter. However, for some reason Meeryle couldn't understand, Leena had no interest whatsoever in Rokin. When asked why, Leena would answer with a puzzled look. "He's not right, that's all. No one is, at least for now." The tall girl would dismiss him and change the subject. Her reaction drove the other girls mad, particularly Teerane. But since the pretty girl was afraid of Leena's stern stare, she settled for occasionally glaring at her. Meeryle found it funny. It gave her the opportunity to gloat at Teerane's discomfiture and to tease her friend once in a while.

Putting Teerane, Rokin, and Leena's lack of interest in romance out of her mind, Meeryle started back home. She didn't go in right away, but stopped in front of the door to think. What would she say? How would her parents react? She tried to make her hair a bit more presentable, but soon gave up. The tight curls were a lost cause without a comb and her appearance would not matter in the least. Her parents would probably be angry with her whether she looked tidy or not.

The spring night cut short her hesitation. The constant breeze-and the fatigue finally setting in-made her teeth chatter. She really couldn't stay outside anymore. Taking in a deep breath, she pushed the door open.

The members of her family were all lounging at the table, which bore the remnants of dinner. The talking stopped and all eyes turned to her. Her mind drew a complete blank. All the things she had thought to say, the arguments and the explanations were gone. Her father was shaking his head slightly. Alvyl was as quiet as his wife was loud. He enjoyed a close and wordless relationship with his daughter, always encouraging her with only a look and a smile. The even-tempered man's small rebuke hurt Meeryle more than her brothers' smirks and her mother's exasperated sigh. Meeryle looked at the floor and brushed past them, muttering that she needed to get changed.

"What did you do with your clothes, Meeryle? Your boyfriend got rough with you?" sneered Tarkin, her older brother. Marvyl, younger than Tarkin by two years but older than her by a year, burst out laughing and added a comment.

She missed his remark as she slammed the door of her room shut. She heard her mother's muffled voice scolding the boys, but it didn't stop them from laughing. Meeryle knew the comments would continue for days.

She threw the blanket on the floor and went through her clothes chest. As she took all her blouses out one after another, her sight blurred. When the first tear plopped on her hand, she sat on the floor and hugged her knees. It hurt her legs to do it, but the pain distracted her a bit. Another wave of male laughter came through the door. Meeryle clenched her hands into fists. It was all they could ever do: make fun of anything she ever did, whether it was good or not. Their mere presence seemed to make her clumsier. Even when she prepared her best meals, they found ways to belittle her. Her cheeks were burning and her stomach had twisted in a knot.

Letting her anger loose, she unclenched her fists and pushed fire from her fingers, burning the blanket.

She stared at the little pile of ashes and sighed. She really shouldn't let her anger get the better of her. Every time she did, she destroyed something, usually a useful object, though never anything around it. When was the last time she had burned something for fun, like she used to do as a young child? She couldn't remember, which made things even worse.

Lately, it seemed her strange ability to burn things had been manifesting itself with anger, sometimes to the point that things took on that frightening red tinge. It happened so often these days, she hardly noticed anymore. Earlier today, before Leena had agreed to wait for the dragon's return, the red tinge had manifested. Good thing she hadn't set her friend on fire.

The very thought filled Meeryle with fear. She mustn't think such things; they only brought on an uncontrollable dread. What she had to do was keep her temper under control; otherwise, she got nauseated with unexplainable terror. The endless teasing from her brothers and Teerane's bullying were constantly threatening to break the hold she had on her anger, though. The other day, she had reduced her father's axe handle to cinders. Luckily-as usual-she had managed to clean it up without anyone being the wiser. She had never told anyone about this skill; somehow she knew it had to remain a secret. This ability and the underlying fear associated with it had been with her for so long it was second nature to her. It could become a really annoying ability at times, though.

Meeryle rubbed her temples, got up, picked a blouse from the pile without looking, and put it on. She then prepared herself to go back to the common room: she had to get the dustpan and the broom to clean up her mess.

If she wanted to meet Tikid and keep it a secret, she would have to control herself. No matter what her brothers said, no matter how her mother would sigh or her father disapprove, she would go back to the forest and meet with her new friend. The thought of the little bird flashing through the branches made her smile briefly. She could do this.

Armed with these resolutions, she took in a deep breath and opened the door.

***

Meeryle had learned her lesson that day and put it to good use. She went back to the forest many times without repeating the fiasco of the first visit. She had prepared a nest for the bird dispatched by Tikid in an old wooden box that she had lined with twigs and grass, and placed it on the roof of her father's workshop, which was hidden underneath the village's biggest oak. The bird was easily accessible, yet discreetly out of the way of curious children-or inquisitive parents.

At first, Meeryle's mother questioned her daughter's comings and goings, but she eventually stopped noticing that her daughter was spending a lot more time than usual out in the forest. The summer harvest would soon be upon them, followed by sowing in preparation for the fall harvest, meaning Meeryle's parents would be needed everywhere in the village. Meeryle's mother was much in demand for her expertise in sewing anything from sturdy work clothes to any type of canvas for the grain sacks. Meeryle's father was the resident expert on leatherwork. His skills were an absolute necessity during sowing and harvest, and he had mastered the repair of broken harnesses; in his hands it was an art. As long as Meeryle was around to do her main chore, the mandatory boiling to make water drinkable, the couple didn't mention her absences.

Leena always came along, of course. Meeryle would send out the little blue bird to let Tikid know they would come, then tell Leena when to be ready to leave. After two tries, they found out that they needed to wait about three candlemarks after the bird had left before they set out.

As soon as they were out of sight of the village, the little black fox would appear, each time becoming bolder, to the point where Leena noticed it.

"Now, this is the strangest fox I've ever seen. And you say you've seen it before?"

"Yes. Ever since.... Well, ever since I've been coming out here to help you with your dumb plant-picking, really. You don't know this kind of fox?"

"Dumb plant-picking indeed. Meeryle, you know these plants are a necessity." Leena glared at her friend, but didn't continue with the old argument. "To answer your questions, no. I only know of red and white foxes. This one's pretty, though."

The little creature's appearances were always brief, but the anticipation of seeing Tikid wiped any disappointment Meeryle felt when the fox ran quickly away.

She followed Leena briskly: the apprentice-Healer always led the way, although Meeryle was pretty sure she could now find her own way. Tikid also made quite a bit of noise when she landed, which made it easy to get one's bearings. The conversations were becoming increasingly irritating, however, and Meeryle's frustration grew every time she met with her new friend. The dragon had become much more than a legend come to life. She had quite a sense of humor, which could lean toward sarcasm, if Meeryle could trust what she felt emanating from Tikid. She was also very curious about humans, and asked incessant questions about the village and its inhabitants. When the girls were finally able to make the dragon understand that their village was nothing compared to the cities, Tikid was beside herself with curiosity and excitement. They had to calm her down and point out that she couldn't fly over a city without becoming a perfect target.

The fact that humans would be afraid of a dragon was a very difficult thing for the young dragon to accept, and conversations on that subject were numerous. One-way conversations, that is. Meeryle would grind her teeth every time her efforts were thwarted. Tikid could hear her just fine, either aloud or in her mind, but all Meeryle could hear from the dragon were emotions.

Yet it never stopped her from wanting to learn more about the creature. Tikid's life was fascinating: she could converse with all the animals and the plants around her. With that gift came responsibilities foreign to Meeryle. Every dragon had the obligation to listen to the forest and its inhabitants, mobile or not, and report any problems in its balance. Tikid was not quite yet of age to be able to fix major problems, but she could take care of minor, common ones. Meeryle and Leena didn't completely understand exactly how Tikid would go about it, but it seemed her very presence brought balance to the forest's equilibrium, and that without the dragons, the forests would die.

Today, Meeryle wanted to find out exactly how the dragons maintained the forest's energy. She wasn't even sure if she fully understood what this energy was in the first place. It didn't matter. Whenever the subject of the forest was broached, Tikid's mind projected warm feelings of love and passion for her environment. That alone was worth it, as when she communicated them, the dragon filled Meeryle with a warmth she had never felt on her own. The short girl didn't have anything about which she felt so intense-aside from dragons.

Today, the girls had set out right after the blue bird. Since the Healer needed herbs, Leena wanted to take advantage of the opportunity and combine the two outings. When Meeryle had pulled a face, Leena had shaken her head. "For once, we'll be doing something legitimate in the forest. And you could look for that rare herb you need for the special dish you want to make for the festival."

Meeryle had quietly demurred. She had to be honest and admit she wanted to forget altogether about this important village event. Yet how could she? She had been given the responsibility of setting up the food area, which was an unheard-of honor for

54

someone her age. The position recognized that she was the best cook of the village, and as such, she was expected to present a stunning dish. Meeryle was slowly coming to realize the festival had lost some-if not most-of its appeal. What had seemed like such an honor weeks ago had soon become a chore. Having to organize the food section of the festival was taking a lot of her time, time she could so easily have spent with Tikid. Today's outing was the first free time she'd had in the past six days. The day before had been spent from dawn to dusk running from one end of the village to the other, trying to finalize the entries for the pie contest. By dinnertime, her feet had been so sore her mother almost had to send for the Healer.

She also found Teerane's attitude more taxing than usual. The pretty girl was undermining Meeryle's authority in any way she could, bringing confusion to anything Meeryle had managed to organize in such a way that no one other than Meeryle seemed to notice it. The plump girl therefore had to spend a lot of time going back to fix Teerane's mayhem.

Meeryle had found the trek into the forest very hard physically, but good for her mood. The thought of meeting with Tikid dispersed the last of her stress. However, Meeryle found she didn't have the energy to look for the cooking herb she needed, and had to sit down for a well-deserved rest. She found a comfortable spot against the trunk of an oak. Moss made the ground soft and a bit bouncy, making it a perfect place to doze off in the sun. It turned out, however, that despite her efforts, Meeryle wasn't going to sleep. Her mind wandered and she wondered what the birds were really saying when they chirped. Was the tree happy to have someone leaning against it? Tikid would know. All she had to do was ask.

The black fox came running out of the bushes and stopped in front of Meeryle, staring intently at her. She smiled.

"Well, you're a brave one, aren't you?" she asked quietly. "I thought I wouldn't see you today. We're waiting for Tikid. I wonder if you've ever talked to her."

Admiring the fox's gleaming coat, Meeryle absent-mindedly trailed the pattern of the tiny flowers lining the moss with her finger. She looked from the corner of her eye and for the first time in a long time, carefully lit the first one, allowing the next one to burn only once the preceding flower had burned itself out. Every flame lit a spark of bubbly pleasure in Meeryle's heart. It felt so good to control her ability rather than letting it surrender to anger all the time. Surprisingly, the little fox seemed to enjoy what she was doing. It stood mesmerized, unafraid of the flames. Within fire, Meeryle found a small echo of Tikid's passion for the forest, a passion found for some reason in the strange animal standing in front of her. The more the girl concentrated on her skill, the stronger the feeling became, the more fascinated the fox seemed. Lighting flowers in such a way took a lot of concentration, as the flowers were very close to each other and the fire could spread so easily. Meeryle plunged herself in the exercise, finally relaxing, the fox forgotten. As the eleventh flower disappeared, Meeryle was interrupted by a gasp.

56

"What are you doing?" Leena's eyes were wide open in shock.

"Hem.... Having fun. Waiting for you."

"Meeryle, you were setting fire to the moss. That's very dangerous."

"Not the moss, the flowers. And I know what I'm doing; don't worry." She looked away, uncomfortable under Leena's gaze. She looked for the fox, but the animal was gone.

Leena knelt in front of her and stared at her friend as if she had never seen her. "Meeryle, how do you light the flowers?" Her tone was unreadable.

"I... don't really know. With my fingers, I guess."

"With your fingers." Leena licked her lips. "Meeryle, you do know that normally, people can't light a fire with their fingers, right?"

"Well... yes."

"Then don't you think it's a bit strange that you can?" Leena was trying to get her to say something, but Meeryle didn't want to. That old fear resurfaced, squeezing her heart. Cold sweat trickled down her back as Meeryle tried to push the rising thought away. As the silence lengthened, the apprentice-Healer sighed. "How long have you been able to do this?"

Teeth clenched, Meeryle fought away the terror. Her friend had asked a simple question; she could answer it, nothing would happen to her. It was so silly. "I always have," she said after taking a shaky breath. Since no tree fell on her after saying the words, Meeryle relaxed somewhat.

"That's impossible. You should only have been able to do it since puberty."

The matter-of-fact reaction from her best friend threw Meeryle off. Where the underlying fear had led her to believe this secret of hers would be an extremely uncomfortable subject for anyone, Leena was treating it as something normal.

"Leena, the very fact that we can talk about this is very, very strange. I have never dared mention it to anybody and for some reason, no one ever noticed. It's always been this way. I just... create fire. It does what I want it to do. Well, most of the time, anyway. What does that have to do with puberty?"

"Because that's usually when the affinity with fire manifests itself."

"Huh?"

Leena had a very strange look on her face. Her almond-shaped eyes were wide and her upper lip was trembling slightly. She stared past Meeryle. "That's what Tikid meant," she whispered hoarsely. Her eyes bored into Meeryle's. "Do you remember the first day we spoke with Tikid?" Meeryle nodded. "She said you couldn't hear her because your power was blocking her off."

"She did?" The terror had returned, twofold, rooting Meeryle on the spot, almost choking her. Leena was delving into something that had to remain unsaid; otherwise, she could die. Meeryle's mind shut itself down to the implications of Leena's words, denying the conversation was happening.

But Leena was pushing on. "You've been able to play with fire for as long as you can remember. You can't hear dragons because your power is too strong." She shook her head. When she spoke, her voice was breaking with tears. "Why you?"

"Leena, I'm scared," she managed to whisper. But she wanted the fear to go away; she was no longer a child, she could face this. "What are you talking about?"

"The affinity with fire is the first sign of the Mage-gift. The fact that you've always had it means that you're probably something no one has ever seen before."

Meeryle was bewildered. She didn't want to hear what Leena was saying, yet she knew. She had always known, but for some reason, she had never wanted to admit to herself. She was a Mage, and if what Leena was saying was true, she was a very special Mage indeed.

CHAPTER FOUR

Tikid saved Meeryle from having to respond in any way. The dragon landed with the usual flurry of leaves and dust, but she soon stopped what Meeryle thought of as the dragon's "greeting dance"-making a graceful show of folding her wings and settling herself in a majestic way. Tikid seemed to want to make up for her initial clumsiness every time she landed to meet her human friends. This time however, she quickly curled on the ground, leaned her head on her forelegs, and stared in turn at each of the girls, who were both silently sitting on the ground. Tikid was projecting feelings of concerned curiosity; Meeryle guessed the dragon could feel the tension between the two girls.

Tikid moved her head and nudged Meeryle's shoulder. The girl looked into the ruby eyes and wished she could drown in them. If only she could stay in this moment and not think of what Leena had said, of the fear choking her.

The dragon was sending concern and sorrow. "Sorry, Tikid. We're just...."

"We're just discussing that Meeryle's a Mage and never said anything about it, not even to me." Leena was no longer crying, but her face was still blotchy from the tears. "But you knew, Tikid, didn't you? You said her power stopped her from hearing you." The dragon nodded. "I just didn't listen. Meeryle, you should have known what she meant. Why didn't you say anything then?"

"Leena, you're making a big deal out of nothing," she whispered. Couldn't Leena see that it was wrong to discuss this?

"Out of nothing? How can you say that?" Leena yelled as she stood; she paced in front of Meeryle and Tikid, the dragon's head following her every move. "Being a Mage is the greatest thing of all. It was all I ever wanted to be. All I got was a flimsy Healing gift that I can't trust."

"Leena...."

"Stop. Don't say anything. I... I...." Tears welled up again in her green eyes, and she ran, sobbing, out of the clearing, passing Tikid, who jumped back in surprise.

Overwhelmed by Leena's extreme behavior-she was leaving her alone in the forest!-and the sudden confrontation of something she had long ignored, Meeryle's sight blurred. As she blinked to clear it, tears ran down her cheeks. A Mage. She was a Mage. Leena was right; she had always known, and something-or someone-had prevented her from even acknowledging it. Whatever it was had made sure she'd want nothing of the kind, and made her believe even now that the Mage-gift could only be a curse. In a way, it was true, as it hindered proper communication with the dragon and was costing her the only true friend she'd ever had.

Meeryle's thoughts veered towards Leena's confession. Could it be what she had mentioned the other day-why she wasn't sure of her path? Yet she seemed so proud of her position with the Healer.

Magic in general and Mages in particular had never come up in any of their discussions, or even during the normal course of the village's activities.

The village had never been graced by a Mage; it was much too remote. The villagers managed to purify the drinking water without one of these personages. And as far as Meeryle knew, that was all Mages ever did: clean the water so people could drink it. Why anyone would need a Mage for that, Meeryle didn't understand. All one had to do was to boil the water. The animals fared well on untreated water; only people needed to do something to it. How long could boiling water for a household take? Why bother with a Mage at all? And what was so special about being a Mage, then? That Leena could keep quiet about something so important to her baffled Meeryle. The girl snorted and reminded herself how surprised Leena had been when she herself had been so adamant about wanting to meet a dragon.

"I guess we all have our secret longings," she said, wiping the tears away with the back of her hand. When she turned toward the dragon, Tikid was gazing intensely at her, broadcasting concern. "This is a mess. And now I can't even hear what you have to say! This is so stupid!"

Another wave of tears washed over Meeryle as she sat down on the ground. Her best friend wanted nothing to do with her and any advice her new friend could give her would literally fall on deaf ears. She wanted things to go back to the way they were. Could she do something like that with that dratted gift of hers?

The girl frowned, tears forgotten. For once, thinking of the Mage-gift didn't trigger the terror. The fear was there, just not as intense. What did it mean?

Meeryle shook her head and sighed. "I'm wishing for the impossible. And the worst thing is, I'm wishing I could make my gift go away with magic! I am making no sense. And it's no use asking you what you think, either."

She sighed and put her forehead on her knees. Despair threatened to crush her. She wished for anger, if not to help her find a solution, at least to stimulate her, but she never felt its heat triggered by something she had done, only by other people's actions. This time, she couldn't blame anyone but herself for her predicament. The best solution was to wait for Leena for a while, then seek her out, in case the apprentice-Healer was lost. Meeryle snorted. As if Leena would get lost.

Tikid's nudge on her shoulder jerked her out of her thoughts. She felt concern and frustration from the dragon, who blew in her hair. Meeryle wasn't sure what Tikid wanted. She got up and looked into the ruby eyes. "What?"

Tikid moved forward until the tip of her snout touched Meeryle's nose. Surprised, the girl jumped back. The dragon snorted in frustration and moved forward once again, renewing the awkward contact. Meeryle stood still, curiosity winning over fear. Never before had she dared to touch the dragon. Although she was a friend, Tikid was physically imposing, and notwithstanding her enthusiasm about dragons, Meeryle hadn't been able to bring herself to touch her new friend yet. The intelligence gleaming in her eyes made Meeryle forget she was not dealing with a human. Physical contact was an abrupt reminder the girl was facing a big creature that could easily crush her. Reminding herself that Tikid could not possibly wish her harm, Meeryle kept still and stared into the dragon's eyes, not daring to breathe. Tikid was trying something; she just didn't know what. Meeryle was getting dizzy from staring and not breathing. She took in a deep breath and relaxed slightly.

"...*you hear me now?*"

Meeryle yelled, took a step back, and tripped on a rock. She fell heavily on her behind, the shock making her teeth rattle. She hadn't stopped looking at Tikid.

"Was... was that you?" The dragon nodded eagerly. "I heard you! Tikid, this is wonderful. How did you manage?"

The dragon moved her front leg and rested her "hand" on Meeryle's shoulder. The girl tensed. The paw was huge and intimidating, and the claws extremely pointy. Tikid snuffed in frustration. She took in a deep breath and closed her eyes. Meeryle gulped and did the same, forcing herself to relax.

"*You have to calm down. When you tense up the way you just did, your power surrounds you and forms a shield that blocks my words.*"

Meeryle's face broke into a wide smile. "I can hear you." Then she turned away and burst into tears of relief. "I'm sorry, Tikid. I know it's kind of dumb to be crying, but I just can't help it."

The dragon cocked her head. She was obviously answering, but Meeryle couldn't hear her. She panicked. The dragon's strange voice was gone from her head. "Tikid, it's gone. I can't hear you." Her tone was getting frantic. "I was relaxed!"

The dragon shook her head and broadcasted scorn. She extended her neck and Meeryle

understood. "You were touching me both times."
Tikid nodded. "So we have to touch and I have to relax."

She moved and hugged the dragon's neck. She forgot everything in that instant. The sensation of the warm scales was unlike anything she had imagined. Unlike a lizard's or a snake's, they were smooth and dry, almost fuzzy. She slowly stroked the neck, feeling the bump of every scale. They overlapped each other so tightly, she couldn't fit a fingernail between them. And the smell! The dragon emanated an odor completely different from that of an animal. It seemed familiar, but she couldn't quite place it. Meeryle closed her eyes and took in a deep breath. The odor intensified and she pictured... the forest. Tikid smelled of the forest-of the sweet sap from the pines, of the dried leaves warmed by the sun, of the ripe underbrush berries, of the fresh moss full of dew, of the blooming wildflowers, even of the fresh running water from a small creek. An earthy and spicy undertone wove itself within the images.

"*Are you having fun?*"

Startled, Meeryle jumped back, breaking the physical contact. "Sorry. I'm just not used to hearing things in my head rather than with my ears."

The dragon chuckled. It was such an odd sound coming from such a creature. It rumbled from the base of the neck and trickled out her nostrils, making them vibrate. Meeryle could not help smiling.

Tikid butted her head against Meeryle's chest. "*I do not know what I find funnier: your description of hearing me or the fact that you were stroking my neck as if I were one of those pets you described to me.*"

Embarrassed, Meeryle blushed. The dragon had found it very curious that humans would keep animals for no other reason than to enjoy their company. The last thing she wanted was for Tikid to think Meeryle thought of her as an animal. She backed out to look Tikid in the eyes and put her hand on the dragon's muzzle. Once again, she marveled at the feeling. "I was not petting you. In fact, you feel nothing like a pet. But you do feel different. I've held snakes in my hand before, but your scales are completely different. You're also warm and you smell... like the forest."

"*It is normal. The forest is my environment. In reality, I am part of the forest. It is only natural that I should smell of it.*"

"Ah. Right." Once again, Meeryle didn't know what to make of the dragon's comment. More than once, Tikid had explained herself, but she only confused Leena, who in turn tried to relay the messages. Meeryle hadn't fared any better. She was beginning to suspect that Tikid might not be the best teacher in dragon affairs. Then again, things that humans took for granted seemed just as baffling to the dragon.

"So, Tikid, what do I do about the Mage-gift?"

"You train it, you dolt."

Meeryle jumped and squawked in surprise. Leena stood, much more composed than she was when she had stormed away, her hands on her hips and her lips tight. Her eyes went straight to Meeryle's hand on Tikid's snout. She did not comment on it, however. Anger flared for a brief moment. The Mage-gift was much more important to Leena than a mere dragon. The underlying fear brought on by the word "Mage" quickly calmed Meeryle down. She also chastised herself; she was hardly being fair to her friend. They were each passionate about something and in a different way. Leena's eyes looked almost feverish with their intensity.

"You have to train your gift. There's no way around it."

The words took all of the day's warmth out of Meeryle. "But... I can't," she finally managed to say, as the terror made her shiver.

"What do you mean, you can't? Meeryle, you can't just leave a gift alone! What if it turns rogue? Or what if you can't control it?"

"I can control it just fine, thank you. I obviously have for all these years. Leave it be." She had to stop even thinking about this before the shivers started to wrack her body.

Leena was not really listening to her, or even paying her any attention. Her eyes shifted dreamily and a brief smile crossed her lips. "Just think how wonderful it will be to go to Sharitown to study.... The city, the library...."

The words shocked Meeryle out of her shivers. That Leena could even propose that Meeryle leave the village was unthinkable. "What do you mean, go to Sharitown?"

"Well, we don't have a Mage with us. We're lucky to have a Healer at all."

This time, it wasn't fear that took her over, but an irrational anger. "So? I told you I don't want to train. You've been trying to get me to apprentice with the Healer along with you, and now it has to be with a Mage." Fury exploded, leaving a hot feeling in her stomach. It just seemed as if Leena had always been trying to tell her what to do. Now she knew why: Leena was jealous. "Oh, but wait! It just wouldn't do if I trained with the Mage, would it? I have the gift you want and you can't handle it, so it's better that I get out of your sight, right?" She stared at Leena, lips quivering. The tall girl stood, eyes wide open in surprise. Her mouth opened and closed without making a sound.

The lack of response from Leena was an admission; Meeryle was right. The chubby girl ran out of the clearing, tears running down her cheeks. The betrayal hurt, then quickly enraged her. Her anger was such that her tears evaporated from her skin. Her sight was becoming orange and the first pangs of nausea stirred. She knew from experience that if she didn't get the smoldering heat out of her, she would be sick. She stopped and willed the heat to move to her fingers. Once they were burning hot, she let all the fire go and blasted a bush to cinder.

"I have perfect control. She has no clue what she's talking about."

The destruction of the bush eased her anger somewhat. It was renewed by the sound of footsteps. Could Leena not leave her alone? That was always her way: she pushed and prodded until everyone agreed with her. Not this time. Meeryle would decide what she would do with her gift. Just because Leena had always wanted it didn't mean that she would get to control it.

Meeryle turned, ready to throw a scathing comment. But Leena hadn't followed her; Tikid had.

Her anger vanished, leaving only relief, and eventually, puzzlement. She didn't want to fight with Leena anymore. Why even do it in the first place? What was wrong with her?

"Oh, Tikid, I messed up again, didn't I?" This time, the tears were cool on her cheeks. She reached out and hugged the dragon's neck. She breathed in the dragon's wonderful scent and felt a bit better. "What am I going to do?"

"Well, to start, stop burning innocent plants. They do not like it and it hurts the other ones."

Meeryle was taken completely aback. To her, plants were objects. But by definition, plants were alive and a live thing wouldn't like to be burned.

"I can understand why they don't like it, but how do you know that it hurts the other ones?"

"They tell me."

Meeryle pressed her cheek against the dragon's neck. She had never been too sure what to make of the fact that Tikid could communicate with plants. Did the plants volunteer this information, or did they wait until Tikid asked them? The concept was just too strange, so Meeryle didn't press the matter.

"Tell them I'm sorry. I'll try to clear my anger with dead wood instead."

"But that would not be appropriate, either. The dead plants become part of the forest as they break down. If you burn them, they will not become part of it and will just disappear with no purpose."

"I... I don't really understand any of this."

"Everything is connected. You do not want to upset the balance."

Meeryle squeezed her eyes shut. This was obviously extremely important to the dragon, but it was beyond her comprehension for some reason. Maybe it was Tikid's lack of clear explanations, or maybe it was just her wariness.

"Let's just drop the matter of plants complaining, all right?"

"Right. Let's talk about training your gift."

Meeryle started and turned, letting go of Tikid. Leena had caught up with her. Gone were her scathing words. She looked at her friend, unsure of what to feel. Was Leena really so jealous that she wished Meeryle gone from her life? It didn't make any sense! Where did she even get this idea?

"Leena, I'm sorry. You don't want me as far from you as possible, do you?"

"No. I can't believe you would think that I could possibly want to do this to you. I'm your friend, remember? I want to help. Yes, it does grate that you have the most wonderful gift possible but that you don't seem to want anything to do with it. But it doesn't mean that I hate you for it! And I don't want to see you hurt because you lose control of your gift, either."

At the mention of training, Meeryle's shivers resumed. This time, Leena was paying close attention.

"Meeryle, what's wrong? Are you afraid or something?"

The chubby girl burst in tears once again and dropped to the ground. "Yes, yes, I am and I don't know why! Something inside me is saying that I'll... I don't know, die or something if I even mention the word 'Mage.' The thought of training my gift just makes it even worse."

Leena sat down beside her friend and put a gentle hand on her shoulder. "We'll figure this out, all right? This reaction of yours reminds me of people who went through a trauma."

"What is that?" asked Meeryle, thankful for the momentary distraction.

"Remember when Lornyl fell off that big horse and how afraid of it he was for the longest time?"

"Yes. He got teased for it, too, especially by the ones who didn't know about the accident."

"Exactly. I think you're going through something similar, so we need to figure out what it is so you can face it. Then you should be fine."

"Oh...." was all Meeryle could say. Yet Leena was right: she couldn't continue like this. She was now wondering if the earlier anger with her best friend hadn't been triggered by that same thing. Could the mind replace fear with anger?

"All right, let's think about this. You said you've been able to summon fire for as long as you can remember, right?"

"Right," answered Meeryle with a gulp. She could do this; she mustn't let the fear get to her.

"So, this might mean that you were a child when whatever happened to you occurred. Hmm.... Do you mind if I try and put you into a trance?"

"A what?"

"A trance. It's a semiconscious state that will allow me to guide you into your memories without interference. Well, at least, I hope."

At the thought of delving into her memories, Meeryle started to shake uncontrollably. She held her hands together, hoping Leena wouldn't have noticed, but to no avail.

"Meeryle, this is worse than I thought. We absolutely need the trance; otherwise, I'm not sure how you'll react. So sit down and relax."

She obeyed, a strange numbness overcoming her. Even if all the nerves in her body screamed to her to run away from this, even if cold sweat trickled down her back, she didn't hesitate. Only now did she realize how much whatever had happened to her had affected her life. No more.

"I want you to close your eyes," said Leena, as she moved her hands.

Meeryle complied and soon found herself in a state close to sleep. The forest sounds were all muted; Tikid's movement seemed far away and Leena's words incomprehensible. Yet she felt safe in this muffled darkness. Leena's voice droned on, giving unintelligible instructions, until Meeryle caught a few words, which pulled her out of the darkness.

"... are back before you used fire."

***

Meeryle was standing in a strange house, gazing up at a familiar-looking woman. She had to look up so far to see her that Meeryle realized she was a child again. Who was this woman? The house wasn't familiar at all, yet she had been in all the village's houses at one point in her life.

The woman beckoned and crouched to Meeryle's eye level. As the little girl came forward, the woman put her hands on her head. Her eyes widened and her mouth hardened. "You have the gift, I know it. You felt me wield the water." She

72

straightened and paced in the room. "What am I going to do with her?" the woman said to herself.

Meeryle gave the door a longing look; she wanted to leave. This woman scared her; she had seen her do something, something both wonderful and scary, with the carafe she always carried with her. Why would anyone carry such a thing? The woman would dip her fingers in the carafe and flick the water to people, who would writhe in pain.

Now Meeryle knew she had to leave; otherwise, this woman was going to hurt her with the water. She made for the door at a run.

"Stop, you little brat!"

Meeryle managed to open the door, but the woman grabbed her by the hair and pulled her back. While the young Meeryle didn't know it, the gesture told the older girl reliving the memory who this woman was: Teerane's mother. But she had died before Meeryle was born, hadn't she?

The little girl struggled, trying to escape the woman's tight grip. "I won't let you go until you swear to me you won't say a word about this."

"I won't, I won't!" she screamed, in pain and fear.

The grip relented and the woman grabbed Meeryle's shoulders so tightly, the girl cried out. "How can I believe you? You're just a brat, always in the way of your betters. You're just like your mother; you'll blabber away." She reached for the carafe, but instead of putting her hand into it, she grabbed the handle and flung the water it contained at Meeryle's face. The liquid splashed her face and after the woman gestured, it stopped splashing down and enveloped the girl's face. Meeryle opened her mouth to scream, but the water gushed into her mouth and her nose, choking her. As the water unnaturally crept up her face and made its way into her eyes, Meeryle panicked. She didn't want to die; she wanted to see her mother, her father, her brother. It wasn't fair; she didn't do anything wrong. This woman was the one who was bad, not Meeryle!

As her lungs burned, demanding air, Meeryle screamed as loud as she could. While her throat couldn't make any sound, somehow her mind did. The woman collapsed to her knees, holding her head in her hands, shrieking in pain.

The water lost its hold on Meeryle and the girl was able to take in a ragged breath. As soon as she could, she yelled as loud as she could. "I won't tell, I promise, I won't tell! No one will know, no one!" She repeated the words over and over, both with her mouth and her mind.

The woman managed to contain her own pain and lifted her hand. At the gesture, the water on the floor moved up slowly towards Meeryle.

"No!" screamed the little girl. The water wasn't going to get her again, it just couldn't. The moving drops terrified Meeryle, and that terror sought something deep inside the girl. She needed to protect herself against this water. What was the opposite of water, if not fire? Meeryle thought very hard where she could find fire; she needed it right now! The hearth was behind the woman. Reaching with her hands, Meeryle wished for the fire to come to her. It didn't make any sense, but the water obeyed the woman, so why couldn't she call the fire?

The terror and the panic ruled Meeryle's frantic thoughts and fire did indeed burst out of the hearth.

It also came out of her hands, making the now-near water evaporate. The woman screamed in pain as the fire banished the water and leaped onto her.

The child was mute with fear. The water was now all gone, but the woman and the house were on fire. Meeryle ran out of the house, still screaming that she wouldn't say anything, that no one would know....

***

Meeryle opened her eyes with a gasp. She was safe, unhurt, and dry.

"What did you see?" asked Leena.

"Teerane's mother was a Mage," she answered, then explained what she had remembered during the trance.

"Wow. So she tried to kill you so you wouldn't tell that she was abusing her powers. And you probably noticed her in the first place because you have the gift."

"But no one ever said anything about Teerane's mother being a Mage or dying in a fire." Although it turned her stomach to think about it, Meeryle had to accept that the fire she had started had killed the woman.

"Yes, but don't forget that you reacted in fcar. You said you were repeating over and over that no one would know. A Mage can influence other people under certain conditions, if I recall. A child's mind can be very powerful; I think you projected that thought and that the entire village was induced into thinking that nothing had happened, that there wasn't anything they needed to know."

"So they just... forgot she had even existed?"

"No, they just knew she had died. They forgot about the fire. I'd be curious to know where the house was and if anything was built over it."

Meeryle dug into her memory; it was vague, but hadn't there been a house hiding in the edge of the forest on the far side of the village at one point?

"It's so fuzzy, Leena, but I think Teerane moved in with her aunt after her mother died, so...."

"So the house that burned down was simply forgotten too."

"That is so sad! Somehow, Teerane knows that I had something to do with her mother's death and she's right. But how?"

"I don't know. Maybe she was connected to her mother? Her mother said something about you to Teerane before she died and it stuck? Teerane has a bit of the Mage gift too? It could be anything, Meeryle, I'm just guessing."

"Well, she blames me. She just forgot how her mother died, just like everyone else, but something makes her hold a grudge against me."

"And you made yourself forget too. That woman scared you so much that you can't even hear the word 'Mage' without shaking in fear."

Meeryle could only nod. Now that she knew the source of her fear, would it stop? Could she control it enough to train this gift of hers? Did she want to train it? The memory of the fire surrounding her left a sour taste in her mouth. The cold sweat resumed trickling down and she clenched her hands into fists to try and stop the shaking.

"Oh, Meeryle, you can't possible leave to train with a stranger. Look at you!"

Tears filled Meeryle's eyes. "I'm just so afraid, Leena."

The apprentice-Healer bit her lip. "I will try to train you."

"What?" Meeryle couldn't believe her ears. Reason told her that an apprentice-Healer, no matter how talented or disciplined, had no business training anyone else, especially someone with a different gift than Healing. At the same time, she was glad she wouldn't have to leave the village, or even disclose her secret to anyone. If people knew about her gift, they would know that she had killed Teerane's mother. "But how could you possibly train me?"

"Well, I guess we would begin with my training exercises. They would be the same for basically all gifts. Then I would research it as much as possible." She smiled. "Maybe I could get the Healer to send me to Sharitown so I could plunder the library. Would you trust me enough to do this?"

Meeryle was relieved. Yet the fear still had a hold over her. "You will tell no one about this. People can't know I killed someone." Meeryle made it a statement. "I don't want everyone to look at me like I'm a freak. They already do, anyway, because I'm so big. I just don't want it to get worse."

Leena clenched her jaw. "Having the Mage-gift does not make you a freak."

"Sure it does."

"Then what does it make me? The Healing gift is in the same category, you know."

Meeryle realized what she had said. "I didn't mean it like that. For someone like you, it's fine. No, it's fitting. You know stuff, you're smart, you understand and remember everything. For me, it just makes me a really strange cook."

Leena laughed, shaking her head. "You have the strangest ideas. It doesn't matter. I won't tell. You did what you did out of self-preservation, so I don't think anyone would blame you. We'll try this training thing on our own anyway. But I warn you, if it doesn't work, we will have to find another solution, all right?"

Meeryle sighed. The underlying fear didn't want her to agree, but Leena was right. She could do this; she could beat the terror that was still gripping her insides.

As if the dragon had heard her thoughts, Tikid put her paw on Meeryle's shoulder. *I will help if I can. But I am afraid I am not one who knows a thing about Mages.*

"Thanks, Tikid. Knowing you're there for me helps."

Leena gasped. "You can hear her? How can that be?"

Meeryle grinned with pleasure. "Let me explain. It was the neatest thing, really...."

As the girls made their way back to the village, Meeryle told Leena about Tikid's discovery. Tikid accompanied them for a while and gladly demonstrated the newfound skill to a fascinated Leena, who tried to understand the mechanics of the process. Eventually, as Meeryle and Tikid tired of the questioning, the dragon declined a more thorough experiment and bid her friends goodbye.

The girls moved on, Leena mumbling to herself and Meeryle smiling at her friend's single-mindedness.

The apprentice-Healer stopped abruptly, lifting a hand to warn Meeryle to do the same and to stay quiet. The short girl stopped just behind Leena and tilted her head to the side to peer around Leena. The little black fox was sitting on its haunches in the middle of the trail, as if it were waiting for them.

"There it is again," whispered Leena. "Why is it always around? And I'm sure it's the same fox."

Meeryle shrugged. "I don't know. Maybe it likes us."

Leena turned and snorted. "It's a wild animal. They don't usually like people, Meeryle."

Leena was no longer whispering and the fox's ears twitched, but it remained sitting still. Meeryle suddenly felt the urge to pet the soft-looking head. She slowly moved past Leena and crouched down, hand forward, beckoning the fox. The animal wriggled its nose and came hesitantly towards the girls. Strangely, it kept looking at Leena, as if fearing the tall girl, and slowly made its way to Meeryle. The fox stopped and sat down just below the crouched girl's hand. Without pausing to think, Meeryle stroked the dark head. The animal moved to meet the hand, pushing into the caress. Meeryle giggled with pleasure. She kept on petting the fox, much to its pleasure.

Leena gasped. "I don't believe this! You just tamed her."

"Her? How do you know it's a female?"

"Really, Meeryle, this close, it's easy to tell."

Annoyed, Meeryle looked up at her friend and rolled her eyes. "For you, maybe. I like her. And I think she likes me too."

"Now, that's an understatement. If foxes could purr, I think she would," replied Leena with a smile.

The little animal was rubbing herself against Meeryle to the point where the girl almost lost her balance. Laughing, Meeryle stood with a wince. "Well, then, if you like me so much, maybe I should adopt you. What do you think?"

The fox's gaze bored into Meeryle's. The black eyes were trying to convey a message, but Meeryle couldn't grasp it. The meaning was tantalizingly close and kept frustratingly evading her.

Leena grabbed her shoulder, breaking her trance. "What is it? You're both staring at each other. Don't tell me she's trying to speak to you."

"Well, that's the thing. I think she is, but I just can't seem to get it."

"Meeryle, animals don't speak," said Leena hesitantly. "Do they?"

"They speak to Tikid, right?"

"But not to people."

"Normal animals, no. But you have to admit this fox is not really like other animals."

Leena nodded. "True. I've never heard of a black fox before."

They looked at each other indecisively, while the fox leaned happily against Meeryle's leg. The plump girl came to a decision. "Well, then, how about I give you a name?" The fox stopped and looked up at her. "I will call you..." Meeryle blinked, feeling dizzy for second. "Suqi. Your name is Suqi." The fox jumped and turned, as if dancing.

Leena gave Meeryle a baffled look. "I guess she likes the name."

"No, you don't understand. That's her name. I didn't make it up."

"How do you know?"

"I... I'm not sure. Almost as if she told me, but I didn't hear any words."

"Meeryle, this makes no sense."

"I know. Look, let's just forget about it for now, all right? My head is starting to hurt. We'll ask Tikid about it next time. She should be able to talk to Suqi and give us one of her very confusing explanations."

Leena laughed in agreement. "Let's go home, then."

The fox lead the way, stopping regularly and turning to check on the girls. She boldly made her way into the village, where everyone present followed her progress open-mouthed. A group of children gathered in her path, forcing her to stop and wait for Leena and Meeryle. Once they had caught up, Meeryle was bombarded by questions. She started to answer them, but was cut short by an approaching group of older youths. Her heart sank when she realized Teerane was leading them. Leena forestalled any confrontation by asking the little crowd to give them space in order not to frighten Suqi.

Meeryle hid a sigh of relief and motioned Suqi on, only to find the way blocked by Corvin. Why did he have to be there? Didn't he have anyone to look after? Meeryle reprimanded herself; he was probably looking for his apprentice. She took in a discreet breath to calm herself. She just hoped Corvin wouldn't scare Suqi away. Her fear was unfounded: the fox was staring at the Healer, challenging him.

"Why, there's a bold animal. Where did you find it, Meeryle?"

She was bothered by his assumption. How could he know that Suqi had been interested in her rather than in Leena? She didn't dare to ask him, as his piercing gaze made her uncomfortable. She was beginning to suspect Suqi had something to do with her gift and she didn't want to even think about it in the Healer's presence, lest he notice the effects of her unnatural fear. "In the woods," she mumbled. "She followed us around for a while and I called her Suqi." Corvin raised an eyebrow. "If she wants to come home with me, I can keep a pet. Others have cats or dogs," she said defensively. "Don't worry, I'll watch her," she called reassuringly as she made her way around the Healer. He watched her go in silence, while the gathered children followed her from a distance, asking to pet the fox.

Meeryle sighed with relief when the Healer left. She stopped and tried to get Suqi to sit and be petted by the youngest child, but the fox gave her an offended look and bounded away, much to the disappointment of the children.

"Don't worry, I'm sure she'll be back," said Leena. "Now, go. Meeryle and I have things to discuss." Once they were alone, she repeated her statement. "I am sure she'll come back, you know. I just don't think she's ready to allow anyone but you to touch her, though. Don't forget that she's a wild animal. She'll probably never react like a dog."

"I just wish I could have taken her home," answered Meeryle.

"Give her time."

CHAPTER FIVE

Leena had been partially right. The little fox came back, but it never followed Meeryle inside the house. It would wait for her outside, then follow her everywhere she went. Meeryle wasn't sure where the fox hid during the night, but invariably, in the morning, the black animal would be sitting by the side of the door, tail swishing, looking expectantly at her every time she stepped outside.

Leena was also true to her word. She avoided discussing the Mage-gift with Meeryle unless she was sure they were completely alone, and she did not mention Meeryle's gift to anyone - not that many people would volunteer a question in that direction, since Meeryle's gift had gone unnoticed all these years, thanks to the fateful events she now remembered. Whenever Meeryle did come into the conversation, the topics were her cooking skills and speculations on what she would present at the Festival. Meeryle had to admire her friend's integrity; she'd caught her once, when Leena didn't know Meeryle was around, clearly about to disclose the information, then changing her mind at the last minute. Meeryle had sighed in relief and debated whether to thank her friend. She'd refrained, afraid to anger her. When Leena gave her word, she kept faith and resented it if questioned.

Meeryle wasn't so glad about her friend's integrity when the apprentice-Healer started to plan for the training. Leena dragged her to the small library adjacent to the school and questioned her exhaustively about her gift, writing the answers down with astonishing speed. When Leena ran out of questions, she went into deep thought, barely acknowledging Meeryle's presence. She suddenly headed to the Healing section, where she proceeded to take every book off its shelf and search them all. When over twenty opened books covered the floor, Meeryle, drained by the questioning and irritated by Leena's intense focus, quietly excused herself and left. She doubted Leena had heard her.

She was beginning to hope Leena hadn't found anything when she didn't see her friend for two days. Her hopes were crushed when Leena swept into her house, took Meeryle by the hand and dragged her out of the kitchen in front of Meeryle's mother, who could only gape.

Once outside, Leena made for her own house. Meeryle, her hand still in Leena's, stumbled behind her, bewildered. Suqi had followed them, ears perked up, eyes bright with pleasure. The fox stopped at the doorstep and sat, looking pleased. Leena didn't give Meeryle the chance to think on the animal's attitude.

"My parents are out hunting, so the house is ours. I have your training schedule," said Leena. Inside, Meeryle stood by the entrance, weighing her chances of bolting. Anticipating Meeryle, Leena gave her a sharp look and pointed at the kitchen table. "Just sit here. I'll be right back."

Leena went up the ladder to her room. Meeryle was glad her parents had a one-story home. She couldn't picture herself making her way up a ladder at all, let alone as nimbly as Leena.

She shuddered when the tall girl came back down, facing her, clutching papers in her left hand. "Don't you ever fall, doing that?"

Leena gave her a blank look. "Fall? From where?" She shook her head. "Anyway, here's your schedule. I wrote down...."

"Don't," interrupted Meeryle. She tried to grab the papers, but Leena backed up.

"What are you going to do with these? I spent two days modifying Healer exercises for you."

"You can't write them down. What if someone found them and read them? Then they would know about me."

"But... how will you know what to do?"

"Just tell me, I'll remember."

Leena frowned. "Are you sure?"

"When did I ever forget something?"

Leena could only agree. She reluctantly read her instructions and Meeryle repeated them word for word. Satisfied, Leena motioned her friend out, making her promise to do the exercises regularly. Meeryle's answer was noncommittal, but under the piercing gaze of Leena's large eyes, the big girl promised with a sigh.

When she stepped outside, Suqi wriggled her nose questioningly at Meeryle, who smiled and crouched down beside what the villagers called her pet. "Well, I now have a program. I know it by heart and I really, really don't feel like doing it, Suqi." The fox's ears fell back. The girl giggled. "You seem disappointed. If I didn't know better, I'd say you're in this with Leena." She ruffled the soft hair on the animal's head and went back home, leaving her "pet" to its own devices.

Once ensconced in her kitchen, after mumbling an excuse for her abrupt departure to her mother, Meeryle wondered if her acute memory was a side effect of the Mage-gift. She had never questioned her faith in her memory. In school, she had always been able to repeat word for word the lessons taught, even if she couldn't make heads or tails of them. She tucked into her mind any recipe she heard, absorbed instructions instantly, and recalled the words for all the songs she had ever heard (when the singer's pronunciation was good). Meeryle smiled, realizing her memory was trustworthy only when she heard things, not when she read them. Hence, any lesson she needed to learn by herself at home was a lost cause, she couldn't tell in which direction Sharitown lay, and she still didn't know by heart old Teere's leek soup recipe; the elderly cook had written it down for all the women in the village. In the end, she dismissed the thought as irrelevant, especially during the preparation of bread.

***

The first part of the lessons was to be done alone in her room, just before going to sleep at night and again in the morning, just after she woke up. She tried it reluctantly the third night after Leena had given her the instructions. She felt silly and thought the whole thing a waste of time, but she wanted to please her friend and, more important, keep her word.

The first thing she had to learn was to listen. As a Healer, Leena had been taught to listen to the life force that infused everything, but a Mage had to listen to the elements. When Meeryle had given her a disbelieving look, Leena had been adamant: all the books she had ever consulted said the same thing. A Mage had to be able to manipulate all the elements and the first step toward that goal was to hear the elements themselves.

Meeryle thought that hearing any element was foolish and impossible. She was tearing apart the meat on her plate during supper without eating it, trying to wrap her mind around the exercise she had to perform that evening. The fire in the hearth popped at that very moment, bringing suddenly to memory the sounds the wind and the river made. Her task suddenly didn't seem as foolish.

What did still seem foolish was to do this exercise inside. Outdoors would make more sense. However, she couldn't see herself going out this late at night or just after waking up without raising attention. She also decided such an exercise would be more successfully accomplished if she was dry and warm. Presently, sitting cross-legged on her bed in her nightshift, Meeryle closed her eyes and took in a deep breath, forcing her muscles to relax.

She could hear her parents talking in the next room. The words often came out as a mumble, but they seemed to be discussing the day's events. She shifted her attention and tried her brothers. Muffled laughter confirmed that the two boys were in their room speculating on one of their favorite subjects, dog races. They had their own dog, the only one of its kind in the village. It seemed to be built for running, if the number of races it had won were any indication. The bigger dogs never stood a chance against the lithe little beast. The dog was her brothers' pride and joy. This year, they were aiming toward winning all the races at the Festival.

Meeryle forced her thoughts away from the subject; whenever it came up, she felt sorry for the poor thing, always tied up when it longed to run. Now was not the time to think of the skinny animal. She took in another deep breath and listened to the house, which always creaked on its own. The wind and the rain made it worse, but tonight, the weather was calm. The floor squeaked under her parents' feet and the roof thumped when a night bird landed on it. The door of her parents' bedroom closed gently, making the walls vibrate ever so slightly. One of her brothers threw himself on his bed, making a resonating crack, immediately followed by her father's outraged bellow.

During the next few minutes, she heard the familiar sounds of the household settling for the night. She had never realized before how much she had become used to them and how reassuring these sounds could be. She also had never noticed how loud everyone in her family was.

Finally, the only sounds left were those of sleepers shifting in their beds and the natural sounds of the house. Meeryle paid close attention, as this was supposed to be the best time for her to listen to the elements. Eventually, she should be able to hear them regardless of the sounds around her.

She focused her attention on the element that was the most familiar to her, fire. While she briefly regretted snuffing out the candle in her room, it didn't seem worth breaking her concentration to get up and light it again. Instead, she sought the hearth, where the fire had been banked for the night and would no longer make its usual physical sounds. She pictured the fireplace with the blackened back and side walls, the hearthstone with its worn-out spots, and visualized the embers glowing, their fiery red pulsating through the ashes. She smiled. Embers were the best for cooking stew.

All was so quiet that Meeryle could hear her own heartbeat. She slowly realized that it was beating to the rhythm of the embers' pulse. Could she control the fire so? Frowning as she listened harder, another beat made itself heard: thump-thump, thump-thump. It was familiar, like another heartbeat, but she couldn't place it. Concentrating even more, she listened to the two beats and tried to separate them.

The house creaked, startling her. One of the beats, the second one, became a lot quicker for a few seconds.

It was her heart.

The first beat was still constant, without the irregular thumps of her own heart. Meeryle blinked in astonishment. The sound was the fire's beat.

She had to test her theory to make sure she was indeed hearing the fire in the hearth, and not something else. Her nose wrinkled in her effort to think of another source of fire. Rolling her eyes, she recalled the obvious: all the neighbors had hearths. All she had to do was pick one. She decided on the neighbor closest to her parent's house, the one on the right. Slowing her breathing, she pictured the outside of the house and "walked" up to the neighbor's door. She then realized that she couldn't remember if their hearth was on the left side of the main room, or on the right side. She resolutely decided to try both.

Meeryle "entered" the house and sought the same beat she had heard coming from the embers. For some reason, she didn't feel drawn to the left or right of the imagined room, but toward the floor. It was odd. The neighbors certainly did not light a fire on their floor. She nonetheless let herself be drawn and found herself going down, below the floor, past the dirt basement, down deep inside the earth. She was aware of the rocks supporting the foundation of the house, of the clayey earth beneath the rocks, of sand and of a strange liquid substance, and more rocks, solid and massive. Her descent was accelerating and she lost track of the different environments she felt, until she heard the beating again. It had the same rhythm as her embers, but it was a hundred times louder. She was surrounded by the beat and she wallowed in it. Meeryle could not remember ever feeling so good. She opened her eyes and found herself in a glowing orange and red light. As it shifted around her, shades of orange and yellow danced in her eyes. The beating didn't change. It was strong and constant, surrounding Meeryle in a blanket of security. She was safe there and would always be. She closed her eyes, the warm feeling making her smile. The beat was slowly growing quieter.

When she opened her eyes again, she was in the darkness of her room. A bit of orange and red still remained, but the colors were fading away. Full of wonder, she rubbed her eyes to get rid of the last visions of color. Her cheeks were burning and her arms felt hot, even through the shift. She wasn't sweating, though. Shrugging it all away, unwilling to spoil the feeling of well-being, Meeryle rolled up in her bed, pulling the covers over her, even if she didn't need them. She fell asleep suffused in heat and happiness.

***

Meeryle woke slowly, basking in the warmth of the sun. She stretched in contentment and abruptly sat up when she recalled her room didn't have a window. A brief once-over showed that she wasn't flushed. While she felt hot to the touch, like she was feverish, she was not feeling sick at all.

Quite the opposite, in fact.

The previous night's experience rushed back to her. She had heard-and touched-a great source of fire who had welcomed her.

Giggling with giddiness, Meeryle got up and dressed as fast as she could. She couldn't wait to tell Leena about her success. The whole Mage-gift business might not be so bad after all.

When she opened her bedroom's door, her mother curbed her enthusiasm abruptly. Meera was standing with her hands on her hips, obviously displeased about something. "So, you're finally up, are you?"

"Ah... yes, I am."

Meeryle's mother frowned. "Are you all right? You're looking a bit off."

"Oh, I'm fine, just fine. Did I oversleep a lot?"

"She asks if she overslept by much! Girl, it's well past dawn. What about the preparations for the festival? You're expected to check if everything will be ready for this evening, remember?"

"Oh.... The festival!"

"Yes, the festival. Everyone's already there. You'll be the last one to arrive. Leena's already asked about you, but when I told her you were asleep, she said not to wake you, that you'd need your sleep. Are you sick and you didn't tell me?"

Meeryle's thoughts were a jumble. How could she have slept in like that? It wasn't in her habits. Yet Leena had seemed to expect it. Could communing with the fire have brought this on?

She was brought back to reality by her mother's cool hand on her forehead. "You're burning up! You get back to bed right this instant. I'll call the Healer."

"Mother, get Leena instead." Meera gave her a searching look. Meeryle winced as she lied. "I might have taken too much sun yesterday. We spent a long time planning for the square's layout." She stifled a sigh of relief when her mother nodded.

"Get back to bed. I'll fetch her." Meera grabbed a shawl against the still-cool morning and walked out of the house.

Meeryle was startled by the growling of her stomach. She was ravenous, which was never the case when she was sick. After she grabbed some bread and cheese from the kitchen and brought it with her to her room, she put the food down on the floor on the side of the bed opposite to the door and stripped. She found she was still very hot to the touch, but not sweaty. Since she didn't feel too warm, she put her nightshift back on before attacking her food in a way that surprised her. She couldn't remember ever being so hungry.

When she heard the front door of the house open, Meeryle hastily hid the little that remained of her breakfast under the bed and slid under her sheets. The walls muffled her mother's voice and Leena's while they made their way to Meeryle's room. A brief knock preceded their entrance.

"Hello, Meeryle. Your mother tells me you have a fever." She gave her friend a questioning and hopeful look.

"Yes, well, I guess yesterday's sun was too much for me." Leena touched Meeryle's forehead and cheeks. Her eyes widened in surprise. She turned her back to Meera and mouthed: "What happened?" Meeryle answered in the same way that she would tell her about it later.

"Meeryle will be fine. I actually would suggest fresh air."

"But her fever!"

"It's not actually a fever. It's an aftereffect of the sun. Nothing to worry about."

Meera harrumphed and left the room, shaking her head.

As soon as she had closed the door, Leena turned expectantly to Meeryle. "Well?"

"I tried to hear fire last night. I heard it, Leena! It was amazing!"

"But why are you hot like this? You look fine, but when I touch you, you feel like you have a very bad fever."

"I'm not sure. At one point, I was inside the fire." Leena blinked in confusion. "It's hard to explain. I was looking for fire outside the house and I was pulled under the ground, until I was surrounded by the light and the sound of fire."

93

"Under the ground?"

"Yes! I've never felt anything of the kind before."

"The only underground fire I know about is the lava from the volcanoes."

"There're no volcanoes here."

Leena shrugged. "I'll look into it. In the meantime, I told your mother you'd need fresh air, so get to it!"

Meeryle sighed. "This will be the second time I get dressed within less than a candlemark."

"Well, I don't know if your... heat warms you, but it's cool out today, so dress warmly. Everyone was asking for you. Your presence is absolutely necessary, don't you know. Teerane's been trying to convince everyone she can do a better job than you, but it's just not going her way."

"So they did notice she was undermining my efforts, huh? Well, if you can believe it, I almost wish I could give her the job. I feel so bad about her mother, plus it's turning out to be a lot more work than I anticipated. People suddenly can't decide anything on their own, and Teerane's meddling didn't help either. Since Tikid and that Mage business, the festival just doesn't seem as appealing or important. My life is completely upside down," she said with a rueful smile.

"Life doesn't stand still because you meet a dragon, you know. Anyway, I'll see you there. I was given the much-sought-after task of making bouquets for the tables with Navee."

"Go on, I won't be long."

Once Leena left, Meeryle got dressed once again and suddenly remembered she was supposed

94

to repeat the exercise in the morning. She debated whether she should. Leena hadn't reminded her-which was strange, as the tall girl had been so adamant-and she wasn't sure if her mother would walk in on her. Meera seemed to have her doubts about her daughter's health, so Meeryle decided not to take the chance.

The sky was overcast, but the sun was managing its way through some of the clouds. Meeryle quickly made her way, with Suqi in tow, to the village square where the tables were being set for the evening feast. Everyone still looked twice at her, but the comments were becoming rarer as the villagers were getting used to the presence of the unusual fox. Since Rokin had expressed an interest in Suqi from the very beginning, Teerane had never teased Meeryle openly about her pet. It did not stop her from taking the opportunity to glare at her, which she did as soon as she spotted her across the square where the festivities would take place. Now that Meeryle knew the truth, she was finding it harder and harder to ignore the other girl. She managed once again and made for the roaring open fires that were keeping the nearby organizers warm.

Meeryle stopped by the first one and listened to it. A few moments later, the now familiar beat made itself heard. She smiled, proud of the fact that she could now hear fire at will. "Listening" to the spitted pig that was slowly cooking, she was instinctively sure the meat was still raw. How did she always know when things were cooked? Could she have been unconsciously hearing the fire within the food? After a moment of concentration, her question was answered: the meat was slightly emitting the beat of the fire, more so at the bottom. The top was silent. The pig needed to be turned.

Leena found her doing just that. "Already? They just put it up less than a candlemark ago!"

"Well, the fire is very strong. Too much, actually. They should have waited before spitting the pig." Leena's face was split by a huge grin. "What?"

"Meeryle, the greatest cook in the world! Now I know why. And I'm sure you'll get better at it with time and practice. Did you try it again this morning?" Meeryle shook her head. "Well, in a way, I'm glad you shirked that lesson. I'm not sure if this much contact with an element is good. Try it again tonight."

Meeryle smiled. "Leena, it felt great. Really, really great. I feel almost in tune with everything that touches fire now. And the best thing is that I don't really have to concentrate that much, not like I had to last night!"

"Well, my guess is that if you've been playing with fire for all your life, you're definitely attuned to it. All you needed was the one exercise to consciously do what you've always done automatically. It's the other elements you have to master now."

"Which one should I try next?"

"So you're fine? No more shaking?"

Meeryle blinked in surprise. "Well.... No! I just did it without really thinking about it." The question cooled her enthusiasm. Would she truly ever be free of the fear? The breeze was suddenly colder on her skin. When she briefly touched her cheek, it was normally cool and the magical heat of the fire she had heard was gone.

96

She changed the subject. "We have to tell Tikid about this." The dragon had been very keen on knowing the progress of Meeryle's training. The girl was eager to share the news with her friend.

"Well, go ahead. You don't need me to relay her words anymore and don't tell me you'd get lost without me."

"No, but it just seems wrong to go there alone. I still don't like the forest, you know. It gives me the creeps. And now that I know that the trees talk to Tikid, it's even worse. I feel like they're watching me."

"Maybe they are," teased Leena. "But really, Meeryle, you don't need me. Besides, Tikid's starting to take too much of my time. The Healer's bound to notice something is amiss. So far, I've managed to give him plausible excuses, but I'm running out."

"Just this once?" Meeryle's face was pleading. The thought of being alone among the whispering trees formed a coldness in the pit of her stomach.

Leena sighed. "All right. Just because all these visits have actually allowed me to stock up on plants a lot more than I ever thought possible. I got complimented for it the other day."

Meeryle gave a relieved sigh. "Good. Let's make it right now, before the celebration starts. I'll see if I can answer all the questions and get my sweetcakes going, then we'll leave. It should give the bird and Tikid enough time."

Leena nodded. "I'm almost finished with the flowers and no one will need me for the moment."

As she turned to leave, the apprentice-Healer fully collided with Navee, the girl who was helping her with the flower arrangements. Navee was so surprised, she landed heavily on her rear end. Leena apologized and helped the girl to her feet. "Really, Navee, you shouldn't creep up on people like that. Cough or say something! Now your skirt is full of dirt. What did you want?"

The girl, eyes wide, managed to stammer an answer. "We.... We need you for the extra tables."

"I'll be right there."

Navee left hurryingly, glancing back toward Meeryle and Leena twice. Once she was out of eye- and earshot, Meeryle turned to her friend. "How much do you think she heard?"

"I don't know. Anyway, it doesn't matter. We didn't say anything all that strange. What can she say and to whom? Don't worry about it. I'll send the bird and see you in a candlemark."

Leena left Meeryle just as the big girl was accosted by three women, all talking at once. Deciding that she'd had enough and much more interesting things to do than to tell these women how to set tables, Meeryle called an astonished Teerane and put her in charge of that task. Satisfied that she had killed two birds with one stone-getting rid of at least some of her guilt toward Teerane and the gaggle of annoying women-Meeryle made for one of the fires to prepare her entry for the contest. She had decided to make her favorite sweetcakes. Meeryle had come to realize that she liked them so much, she had never shared them with anyone. They were bound to be a surprise and probably a winning entry. She was welcomed by two women who were preparing meat pies.

"We've kept you a space, Meeryle. We were afraid you would not have time! Oh, and that little pet of yours is with you. What do you call it again?"

"Her name is Suqi," repeated Meeryle for the hundredth time.

"Well, keep her away. We don't want her to get into the meat, now, do we? I mean, all the dogs are tied up. Maybe you should tie her up too, don't you think?"

Meeryle laughed as Suqi bared her teeth in outrage. "That won't be necessary. She'll stay with me."

The woman sniffed with disapproval. "If you say so. Don't let her get you distracted. You're late, you know."

"Not to worry! There's always time to prepare something special for the festival," responded Meeryle with a forced smile. The women shooed her to work. While she immersed herself in the preparation of her dish, Meeryle pondered the encounter with Navee.

As one of the youngest teenagers of the village, Navee always tried to please everyone. She gossiped a lot in order to keep up, but had never become part of Teerane's entourage, probably because she made sure she didn't offend anyone. However, Meeryle didn't know if Navee was one to tell tales. Leena seemed confident she wouldn't, but one never knew. The girls had so far been able to keep their friendship with the dragon a secret and Meeryle didn't want one of the village gossips to ruin it.

For some reason, Meeryle's absences from home had remained unnoticed and Leena always had the Healer's tasks as an excuse. Leena's parents were hunters, so they were out more often than not. Their daughter was therefore used to being on her own and very independent. It had been a few years since Leena had had to answer for her whereabouts, unless of course she came home after dark without prior notice. Meeryle's case was a different story. As the only daughter of the house, she was expected to pull her share under her mother's watchful eye, especially since most of the cooking had been delegated to her over the years. Looking back, Meeryle realized the way she had managed to skirt her duties and get away with it did not make sense.

She pursued the thought and tried to remember how she had always done it. She recalled an incident during the winter, when the sun had managed to break through the clouds at the end of a particularly bleak day. Meeryle had been sewing and become sorely sick of it. As the sun was calling to her, she had simply put down her work and told her mother she was going out. For some reason, Meera hadn't asked where Meeryle was going or how long she would be gone. All her children and even her husband had to answer such questions when they left the house. So why had Meeryle escaped the interrogation?

She frowned in concentration. She distinctly remembered thinking she wished she could just leave without her mother noticing her absence. What if her wish had come true? Could it be another part of the Mage-gift? If she assumed it was, then every one of her absences going unnoticed made sense. It would also explain why Leena had agreed to stay with her to meet Tikid on that first day.

The thought that she could influence people this way made her giddy for a moment. However, she could well imagine Leena's disapproval if she ever abused it. Meeryle wasn't even sure if she should mention it to her friend.

She resolutely put away the thought, giving her sweetcakes the attention they deserved. Cooking in general was very soothing to her, but preparing her sweetcakes-the very ones that Leena blamed in part for her girth-was pure bliss. The dough smelled sweet and was smooth beneath her fingers. Rolling it into leaf shapes was challenging, as she normally made them round, but she wanted them to look special, so she took the necessary time to perfect her technique. She became engrossed in her task, but not as much as usual. The dragon was in the back of her mind, which inadvertently made her prepare her pastries in record time. In her desire to meet with Tikid, she forced the fire to burn harder. She arranged the sweetcakes on a platter on the table and covered them with an anonymous cloth before excusing herself with a mutter and making her way quickly to the outskirts of the village, Suqi trotting behind her.

Leena was already waiting with her basket. "Hurry, we won't have long. We have to be back before nightfall."

Meeryle nodded. They both started at a quick pace into the forest.

As soon as they were a few furlongs in the forest proper, Meeryle felt the trees closing on them. She shuddered and tried to ignore them. Every time the wind moved a leaf, every time a branch cracked, she jumped. They were whispering, hovering over her, telling each other who knew what about her. They probably resented her burning moss and twigs. She truly felt like someone was watching her.

Leena's voice brought her out of her gloomy thoughts. "We're the first ones here. I don't really need anything, so I guess we can just sit and wait."

"Why did you bring the basket, then?"

"Out of habit, I suppose. I never go into the forest without it. And you never know, I could find something of interest."

Meeryle and Leena sat against a tree trunk. With a frown, Meeryle noticed that Suqi was nowhere to be seen. She was about to mention it to Leena when she spotted Tikid spiraling down. The dragon seemed to want to crash to the ground, but at the last minute, she swooped up.

Leena shook her head. "What a showoff." Meeryle opened her mouth to argue, but Leena forestalled her. "Well, she is. What's the point of doing this?"

"You don't fly. How can you know? Maybe it feels good on the wings. Ask her."

Leena snorted. They both stood up and waited for the dragon to land. Tikid's descent had slowed dramatically. She stopped beating her wings and left them wide open, letting them carry her to the ground. Once her hind feet were firmly landed, she folded her wings and posed for a moment. As Meeryle and Leena burst out laughing at their friend's vainness, a scream startled them.

Behind them, Meeryle's brother, Tarkin, and Navee were staring at the dragon with terror. Navee's mouth was still opened, but no longer making any sounds. Stunned by their presence and

Navee's scream, Leena and Meeryle were rooted on the spot, unable to say anything. Then Tikid put her two front feet down and projected a questioning thought to the newcomers. As if jolted awake by the dragon's mindtouch, Tarkin and Navee turned and ran back screaming toward the village.

CHAPTER SIX

The screams echoed in the otherwise silent forest. The three friends looked at each other, eyes wide and mouths gaping. Leena shook her head, biting her bottom lip. Meeryle felt her legs weaken and fold underneath her. Tikid caught her just in time and allowed her to sit without falling.

"*They did not listen to me, yet I told them I was not dangerous.*" The dragon's feelings were hurt.

Leena snorted. "At least you were able to say something. Meeryle and I just stood and stared like two idiots."

"They took us by surprise," protested Meeryle. Leena shrugged and kept quiet. Meeryle closed her eyes, discouraged. "So what are we going to do about this?"

The girls and the dragon tried to pool ideas. The fear that made Meeryle want to renounce her gift was back, this time telling her that she shouldn't return to the village. To her surprise, Leena reluctantly agreed it might become an option. It all depended on Tarkin and Navee's report. They would certainly be hysterical and raise the village, but would they be incoherent enough and dismissed? Or would they be taken seriously, without any questions? Meeryle's brother liked to embellish anything he told and the entire village knew about it; however, he wasn't the type to make up stories about dragons. Navee had the reputation of a proper girl in every way, so her word would carry a lot of weight.

They concluded that everyone would believe the frightened youths.

The more they spoke, the more Meeryle wanted to hide in the smallest hole she could find. Leena was seriously talking about staying away from the village. In the end, Tikid made the decision for them. The dragon had rested her chin on Meeryle's lap to avoid interruptions in the discussion.

"You cannot stay in the forest. You have no means of survival."

"But could we not come with you and live among the dragons?" Meeryle asked hopefully.

Tikid closed her eyes, projecting embarrassment. *"No. It may not be safe."*

Meeryle and Leena exchanged a look. Meeryle felt her stomach churn and had to swallow before asking her question. "Why not? I thought you'd said your... family would be thrilled."

"They.... They scorn humans. Say they are irresponsible creatures, that dragons should have nothing to do with them. I was actually forbidden to come to you. You have become very close friends, and yet, because of this prejudice, I can do nothing to help you." The dragon lifted her head and looked away, her body trembling and her throat constricting. She emitted a choking sound resembling a hiccup and lay limp, shaking and hiccupping for a few minutes before Meeryle understood that Tikid was crying without shedding tears. When the dragon turned to Meeryle and leaned her chin on the girl's shoulder, the sorrow she projected almost drowned the human.

Leena cleared her throat, allowing Meeryle to disengage herself from Tikid's intense emotion. The apprentice-Healer stood and wiped her clothes clean of twigs and leaves. "Well, it seems we don't have much choice. We never told anyone and it was a mistake. Now we have to fix it and try to explain as rationally as possible."

"Can't we stay here?" asked Meeryle plaintively.

"Don't be silly, Meeryle. Tikid's right. I know my way around the forest, but I wouldn't be able to survive in it for very long. We'd need to build some sort of shelter and hunt."

"Well, once I have a dead animal, I would know how to prepare it," Meeryle argued. She smiled weakly. "And fire wouldn't be a problem." Leena gave her a reproachful look. Meeryle sighed and gave in. "All right, all right. But still, it is an idea. Tikid could hunt for us."

"*I would certainly not! Dragons do not kill!*" Meeryle jumped at Tikid's vehemence. "*Only in extreme situations do dragons harm another living being. To protect themselves and only as an extreme last resort.*"

Leena stared from the dragon to Meeryle, baffled. She opened her mouth to ask a question, but Meeryle stopped her with a look and tried to stammer an apology. Unfortunately, before the words were out of her mouth, the dragon had already stood on all fours, turned away and taken off, shooting Meeryle an offended look. The wings moved leaves and dust, forcing Meeryle and Leena to turn their faces away and close their eyes. When they looked back up, Tikid was a dot in the sky.

"Great! We made Tarkin and Navee run away screaming and we offended Tikid. This day is

106

getting better and better. Some Festival. Come on, Meeryle, let's go home and see how much damage these two ninnies made."

***

The damage was extensive. All the inhabitants of the village were standing at the village entrance by the outskirts of the forest, muttering amongst themselves. They were all garbed in festival garments, bright and colorful. This year, the peddler had told them that many-colored scarves were the rage in the cities and the younger adults had competed to have the brightest and most outrageous scarf, worn around the waist by the men and on the shoulders by the women. The garments were flapping in the breeze, cheerful spots in a serious crowd. The mood was not celebratory; some even had bows and arrows in hand.

Meeryle's heart clenched. Sorting the misunderstanding would not be easy. Realizing that if they got in trouble, it would be her fault, Meeryle avoided looking at Leena. She had forced her friend into all this and so Leena might have to bear the consequences with Meeryle. For a second, Meeryle was glad for her friend's presence. It was wrong, but she didn't know what she would say, whereas Leena certainly would. The apprentice-Healer was quick and intelligent, and she always found a way out of awkward situations. Meeryle gave herself a mental shake and reminded herself that she couldn't leave everything up to Leena. She would have to do the explaining and try to make everyone see that dragons were not dangerous. Tikid's earlier reaction to the suggestion of hunting reinforced that fact.

Someone spotted them and yelled. The crowd turned as one, scowling at both girls. The collective gaze stopped Meeryle in her tracks. She quickly scanned the crowd and caught a glimpse of Rokin's concerned face trying to make eye contact with Leena, but the tall girl did not see him and moved on slowly, back straight and head high. However, when she saw her father, the apprentice-Healer stopped.

Parin moved forward to stand before the crowd, arms crossed, frowning at his daughter. "Well, it would seem you haven't been very honest with your activities. I thought you were training to be a Healer. Now I learn that you're playing with dangerous animals."

"But the dragon's..." Meeryle was cut off by Navee's voice.

"See, see, she admits it! We didn't imagine anything, we saw what we saw. It was a huge green beast, I tell you. It was going to eat us!" The girl had elbowed her way to the front; her eyes were too wide and her skin white. She was eyeing Meeryle and Leena in turns, glaring with anger and fear.

Meeryle had not expected such an outburst. She should have, but she had hoped... she wasn't too sure what she had expected. Navee's glare made her very, very uncomfortable. Her mind was blank. Navee hadn't given her the chance to finish her sentence, and now saying that dragons weren't animals seemed out of place.

Leena, however, perked up at the other girl's voice. "And how exactly did you know it was going to eat you?"

Navee jerked her chin up. "It wanted to be left alone with you."

Leena and Meeryle exchanged a look.

"How could you possibly know that, Navee?" The girl hesitated. Leena pushed on. "Did it tell you, by any chance?" Startled, Navee shook her head and turned away. Leena tried to catch her arm to turn her around and make her admit she had heard the dragon's voice in her head, but the Healer stopped her with his hand on her shoulder, his face flushed with anger.

"Leave her be. She isn't just scared, she's terrified. She may never recover. Her mind refuses to accept what she saw. You know more than anyone what an injured mind can do to the body."

"But she heard the dragon. That's what's bothering her so much. If only she would..."

"Enough!" The Healer was livid. "You knew about this... dragon and yet told no one. You obviously know how it can affect people, but you're talking about Navee as if she were the one who was unreasonable. I tell you she may be scarred for life and all you can do is scorn her! As for you, Meeryle, your brother is so afraid, he locked himself up in the wine cellar. Your parents can't coax him out and he's screaming about strange voices threatening him. I hope you two are proud of yourselves. You managed to ruin the festival for everyone. Meeryle, I will leave your parents to deal with you. Leena, same thing, but before, I would like to say that in the light of this event, you have proven to be unworthy of being a Healer."

Leena gasped. "How can you possibly...."

"You withheld information about a beast lurking in our vicinity, and your negligence caused the mind-wound of two people. Hurting anyone except to defend your own life is strictly forbidden to Healers and you know it. You've just broken that rule, and for no good reason! There are precedents where such an act could be forgiven, but not in this case. You are therefore no longer my apprentice. Be glad that I do not take the steps to make your gift latent. If you want to resume your apprenticeship, you will have to find another Healer."

The Healer nodded to Leena's father and left, followed by most of the crowd, including Teerane, who was shaking her head disapprovingly, a smirk on her face. Meeryle thought bitterly that they considered the show to be over.

Not everyone left, though. Rokin was hovering, unsure if he should approach Leena and speak to her. The tall girl was completely unaware of the concerned young man. She usually smiled or nodded, but in this case, she didn't even acknowledge him. Unable to get Leena's attention, Rokin gave up and withdrew, clearly disturbed by Leena's reaction.

Navee's mother was also still standing, glaring at her and Leena. Meeryle refused to meet her eyes. She didn't want the woman to rant at her. She felt so miserable, she wanted the ground to open and gobble her down. This was her fault; she couldn't be angry at anyone except herself. Just because she was fascinated by dragons, it didn't mean everyone else would be. Meeryle suddenly remembered the absolute fear that had engulfed her the first time she had seen Tikid. She should have planned for this....

A rough hand on her arm interrupted her thoughts. Leena's father was holding her with one hand and his daughter with the other. The big man dragged them with him, making Meeryle stumble. His grip prevented her from falling, but it was so tight around her arm, it hurt as much as if she had fallen.

Meeryle glanced at Leena, but her friend was staring ahead, not seeing anything. The normally nimble girl tripped on every rock. Only her father's firm grip kept her from sprawling.

The girls were brought to the barn. Leena's father pushed them in roughly and shut the door behind them. Meeryle gulped when the bar slid in its hooks. The last person to have been locked in the barn was a murderer. He had posed as a hunter-a credible identity, as the only travelers to come so far out were indeed hunters and two or three peddlers-and succeeded in killing one of the oldest couples of the village while ransacking their house in hopes of finding gold. As crime was usually limited to petty theft, a dedicated jail had never been necessary; the only real criminal-the fake hunter-had simply been tied up and thrown in the barn, out of sight, until the proper authorities had taken care of him. Meeryle took some reassurance in the fact that they hadn't been tied up; nonetheless, to be treated like the murderer was terrifying. And unfair. They hadn't done anything remotely dangerous, yet they were given the harshest treatment.

The barn was already dark this late in the afternoon, as the only window was small and dirty, and would get even darker as the sun set. Meeryle squinted until she found the lantern. She lit it with a spark from her finger, the small flame boosting her spirits a little.

Leena's silence frightened her. The tall girl hadn't said a word since the Healer had revoked her apprenticeship. It had happened so fast that Meeryle didn't quite believe it. She had not even been able to try to defend her friend. She felt alone.

"Leena.... I... I'm sorry just doesn't seem enough. I tried to tell them, but Navee's rambling cut me off and the Healer never gave me a chance." Leena was staring ahead, eyes empty. A tear rolled down Meeryle's cheek. "Please, Leena, say something."

Leena slowly turned her head and gave Meeryle a bone-chilling look. "Shut up, Meeryle. This is all your fault."

"But...."

"Shut up!" she screamed. Stunned, Meeryle gaped. She had never heard Leena scream. The tall girl faced her, fury in her eyes. "You tried? You barely said three words. All you did was stand like an idiot! You got me into this mess, Meeryle. You didn't want anyone to know about your precious dragon. And now, not only does everyone know about it, I've been completely disgraced because of her!"

"But...."

"Shut. Your. Mouth. You are the most selfish person I've ever known. From now on, you're on your own with your stupid dragon. Oh. I forgot. And your Mage-gift." Meeryle's stomach churned. "You understand me. I will no longer keep any secrets for you. Now you go stand at the back so I can't see or hear you."

112

Meeryle was shaking. The light of the lantern was a blur. Leena was standing still, pointing at the back of the barn. Her teeth were so tight with rage they were grinding. Meeryle turned and stumbled in the direction of Leena's finger. She didn't really see anything through her tears. She hit things, not knowing what they were and not caring. When she could no longer see the light of the lantern, Meeryle sat on the ground and hugged her knees. The tears had stopped. She had never felt so empty in her life.

She didn't dare make a sound, as she didn't want to set off Leena again. She had never seen her friend that way. Meeryle wasn't even sure she could call Leena a friend anymore, as their friendship might be completely ruined. Since Leena would have to leave the village to find another Healer to take her on as an apprentice, they might never reconcile.

She recalled that Leena wanted to send her to Sharitown to study with a Mage, because she was envious of Meeryle's gift. Well, it seemed she would get her wish and finally see the world. Meeryle would stay at the village; she'd be fine without Leena, since she still had Tikid.

New tears welled up at the thought of the dragon. If they had locked them up, it probably meant they would keep a close eye on them when, and if, they let them out. They couldn't call in the King's men, could they? She hadn't killed anyone. Yet she was still treated like a criminal. They would probably make her work her way into paying her wrongly perceived debt. No more tromping in the forest, no more clapping at Tikid's antics in the sky. Despair swallowed Meeryle as she realized she had lost her only two real friends. Some festival, indeed.

CHAPTER SEVEN

At one point, Meeryle fell asleep. When she woke with a start, panic rose as she tried to understand where she was. It only took two breaths to remember and wish she could once again forget.

Meeryle stretched her stiff legs and got up, trying to gauge how long she had slept. The darkness indicated it had been a while. She rubbed her gritty eyes and allowed herself the luxury of a full stretch.

Feeling a bit refreshed, Meeryle now wanted to see how Leena was doing, but she wasn't sure how to proceed. She moved quietly toward the front of the barn-or so she thought-relying on the lantern. Leena's voice made her jump.

"You can come, you know. No need for stealth."

"How did you know?"

"I'm sorry to have to tell you this, but you're as quiet as a horse when you walk. And breathe."

Meeryle was hurt. While others were free with their comments about her weight, Leena had always been tactful until now. The comment rankled, but Meeryle bit her lip and let it pass. "Ah. Well, my parents aren't hunters."

"No, they're not. They didn't treat you like a freak, either," replied Leena bitterly. Meeryle forgot her anger. Leena had much more to worry about than watching her words. She was a serious girl whose opinion had counted, at least in Healing matters. It seemed her word was worth nothing when it came to dragons. The Healer had forestalled anyone who could have supported them by stripping Leena of her apprenticeship. Meeryle knew that Parin had been beaming with pride when his daughter put on her scarf for the first time. He had started to treat her like an adult that day. Leena treasured her father's approval and today, not only had she lost it, but she also lost his trust.

Meeryle sat beside her friend, feeling awkward. Anything she said would hurt Leena's feelings, yet she just couldn't stay quiet. "Leena, I...."

"It's all right. Well, it's not, but it was wrong of me to get so angry with you. I'm as much to blame as you." She gave Meeryle a weak smile. "I like Tikid too. I think she's funny. I'm going to miss her." Her voice broke with the last words as she finally let her anger and pain out. She put her forehead on her knees, her entire body shaking with sobs. Meeryle knelt behind Leena and hugged her, leaning her head on her back.

Finally, Leena stopped crying. Meeryle let her go and scrambled on her knees to sit facing her friend. "Better?"

"Yes. It doesn't change anything, but I feel better."

"What are we going to do?" asked Meeryle. "I mean, being locked up in here is bad, isn't it? Do you think they'll banish us?"

"In your case I don't know, but I think I will have to leave and find another Healer. I was bound to leave the village, anyway. I just thought I would have done so as a full Healer."

"Leave? Since when?"

"Well, since the beginning. I knew the village was too small for two Healers. Besides, Corvin had mentioned it to me. My parents have always moved around, so I'm used to it. Didn't you ever want to leave? I mean, this place is kind of isolated, you know."

"I was born here. No, I can't say I want to leave."

"Well, it's up to you, Meeryle. What is it that you want to do?"

"The only thing I know for sure is that I want to keep on seeing Tikid. The rest doesn't really matter."

"Aren't you forgetting something?" Meeryle stared at her blankly. Leena let out an exasperated sigh. "You're a Mage, remember?"

"Oh, that." Meeryle shook her head. How quickly she forgot! "I'm... getting used to it."

"You still don't look comfortable at all talking about it, but is the fear still there?"

"Yes, kind of."

"Meeryle, you need to fight this. Doing the exercises will help, you know."

She was right, of course. However, the thought of knowingly using her gift-her *Mage*-gift-still brought cold sweat. "I don't know, Leena. I'm not sure I should be doing any...."

"Promise me you will do these exercises."

"Leena...."

"Promise!"

"All right, all right. I'll continue with my... studies." Leena snorted. "Well, I think it's a good description."

"I know it's hard, Meeryle. But trust me, it'll make your life easier in the long run. You have to control it; otherwise, something bad might happen."

"Yeah, I remember what you said." Meeryle simply wasn't looking forward to experiencing the fear once again.

"Why don't you do the exercises now?" suggested Leena in a gentle voice.

"Right now?" Meeryle asked.

"You're supposed to do them in the morning and at night. You certainly didn't do them this morning."

Meeryle shook her head. She had a hard time believing she had been wallowing in the after-effects of the contact with fire only that morning. Years seemed to have gone by. "No, I didn't listen to fire this morning."

"Go ahead, then. Take your time. You can do this. If anyone comes, I'll warn you."

They were interrupted by a scratch on the door. "*Psst*. Leena, are you there?"

"Rokin?"

"Yes, of course! Are you both all right?" Meeryle's throat tightened. For some reason, the fact that he remembered her touched her deeply. "Are you hungry? Thirsty? Cold?"

"Just plain sad, Rokin. Thanks for asking," answered Leena with a smile.

"You have food with you?" asked Meeryle, hopeful. "Oh, and have you seen Suqi?"

"No, Meeryle. I thought she'd be here, but didn't see her. Mind you, it's dark, so she could be around; I'm just not seeing her."

Meeryle sighed. "I guess she can take care of herself. Go back to the food part, will you?"

Rokin chuckled. "Well, we ate the stuff prepared for the feast and the contests and all. We just took some and ate it at home. No festival this year. Not that I felt like celebrating at all after what happened. But your sweetcakes were the best, Meeryle. Here, I saved as many as I could." He pushed a small bundle underneath the barn's door. The gap was not very wide and the sweetcakes suffered, but they nonetheless tasted very good. Meeryle ate hers while Leena spoke to Rokin. She missed part of the conversation, but she assumed Leena was giving details on Tikid and dragons in general. Meeryle paid attention again once she had licked the last crumbs off her fingers.

"...so I will need to find another Healer to finish my apprenticeship."

"I will go with you, then. You can't leave on your own."

Leena sighed. "Rokin, I need to do this by myself. You're a hunter and the village needs you. They don't need me-and they don't want me, anyway."

"Nonsense! I will...."

"Rokin, enough. Thank you for your concern, but now, go, before you get in trouble."

"I won't. No one has seen me," protested the young man.

"And probably no one will. However, I'd feel really bad if you did get caught."

"All right, then. I will see you tomorrow," answered Rokin, mollified.

Meeryle didn't hear him leave. Leena shook her head and rolled her eyes. "Why won't he let me be? I can take care of myself."

"He's in love, you ninny. You're the only one who doesn't see it."

"I do, but... I just don't feel that way about him, that's all. I know he means well, but he just seems...."

"Eager?"

"Too much of a gentleman. Too nice. Did you notice he's always so nice to everyone?"

"So you want someone who's mean?"

"No! Oh, forget it. This isn't the time to discuss the ideal mate. It's time for you to practice your gift."

"Are you sure? Wouldn't you rather be trying to get out of here?" For a few moments, Meeryle wondered if she was only delaying knowingly practicing with her gift or if she truly did want to try escaping. The fear was there, on the verge of digging in its claws, but it hadn't taken hold. So she wasn't postponing the exercise; the feeling lifted her spirits. For the first time, Meeryle was confident she could beat this awful fear.

Leena answered her question with a shrug. "Rokin would help, too. I think he was disappointed I didn't ask him to open the door. No, I'm not going to break out of here. It wouldn't be worth anything. When I leave the village, I want to be ready to travel. I don't want to escape like a thief. So doing your exercise is the only constructive thing to do. Go on."

Meeryle nodded. "Let's go in the back of the barn. I don't want to be too close to the door. Bring the lantern with you."

Both girls got up and found a comfortable spot in the back. Leena sat on the ground, leaning on the wall, legs stretched out in front of her. The lantern was beside her, making the area a cozy refuge from the rest of the dark barn.

Meeryle sat cross-legged, as she had the evening before. She closed her eyes and opened her mind, willing the fear to let her be. She heard the flame of the lantern right away. Its beat was faint, but just as regular as that of the huge fire presence she had felt. She focused completely on it, ignoring the mild panic threatening to grip her insides, and analyzed the heat the flame produced and the sound it made-aside from the beat. Curiosity quashed the anxiety: she noticed a sound she hadn't heard before. It was regular, but it wasn't a heartbeat. She frowned, trying to grasp its likeness.

Leena cleared her throat, breaking Meeryle's concentration. Frowning, she kept her eyes closed and took in a deep breath before continuing to listen for the lantern's flame. She cocked her head and found the other noise again. It was still there, but rougher. Then Leena coughed once. The sound changed and became regular.

She was listening to the sound of Leena breathing.

"Leena, I can hear you through the lantern."

Leena stared at her. "I'm sorry?"

"When I listen to the flame of the lantern, I can hear you."

"Hmm, it must be a mix of fire and air." Leena frowned and made a face. "How much can you hear? Only the breathing, or would you hear me if I spoke?"

"I don't know. Let's try. Move to the front of the barn."

Leena got up and left with the lantern. Meeryle waited a little while for Leena to settle. As soon as her friend stopped making noise, she went back into her trance and quickly found the sound of the lantern's flame. She concentrated and heard Leena's breathing, but faintly. Suddenly, within the breathing, she heard words.

"Can you hear me?"

It was barely a whisper and it was completely different from hearing Tikid's voice in her head, but she was hearing Leena through the fire.

Meeryle whooped in glee. "Yes! I can hear you!"

Leena came back running with the lantern. She set it down carefully and stared intensely at her friend. "If you could hear me this close but whispering, do you think you could hear someone talking farther away?"

"Actually, I'm not sure distance has anything to do with it. The fire presence I felt was deep in the earth. I think it has to do with the intensity of the fire. The lantern only has a tiny flame. If the flame had been bigger, I might have heard you breathing, like before, as well as you talking. Why?"

"You could try to listen and find out what they're planning on doing with us."

Meeryle was stunned: her unwanted powers could actually be useful. She looked at Leena and giggled. "I can try. It's just that I never thought I would be eavesdropping in the fire."

Leena returned her smile. "Do you want me to douse the lantern?"

"Yes. It could interfere. I'm not that good at this yet."

Leena opened the small door and blew out the flame. The darkness was so thick it was almost physical. Finding the darkness disturbing, Meeryle closed her eyes.

She went back into her trance, seeking fire. She immediately felt the call of the huge fire presence deep in the earth, but she ignored it. As much as she wanted to touch it again, now was not the time. Instead, she went up, hovering over the barn. She was able to feel all the hearths of the village. She singled out the inn's-it would be the most likely place for the village's most important members to gather.

Meeryle was dizzy for a moment. The fire roaring in the inn had pulled her in at an incredible speed. She shook her head slightly and took in a deep breath. The fire's regular beat was all Meeryle could hear. Once she had waited for the beat to become part of the background noise, she heard the voices.

"...decided what to do with these girls. What about the dragon?"

"What about it?"

"We can't just let a dragon hunt around the village! When will it start eating our sheep? And when it's done with the sheep, will it go for the children?"

"Don't be a fool! That so-called dragon didn't come crashing after Tarkin and Navee. Leena seemed to think it was friendly."

"You'd still trust her word?"

"Ah...."

"I wouldn't. If this were about a bear, no one here would be hesitating."

"But it's not a bear."

"No, it's worse."

"What would you propose?"

"Let's hunt."

"All right, let's hunt."

Meeryle gasped. She lost her contact with the inn's hearth.

"What is it?" asked Leena as she relit the lantern.

"They want to hunt Tikid," she whispered. She looked at Leena, full of despair. "They're going to kill her!"

"Who?"

"I don't know. The voices all sounded the same. I couldn't even tell if it was a man or a woman talking."

"What did they say exactly?"

"That they've reached a decision about us." She lifted her hand to forestall any question from Leena. "I don't know what it is, they were done and they didn't repeat themselves. It didn't take long for them to decide to hunt, though. Mind you, they didn't say exactly when they'd go."

Leena shook her head. "There's nothing we can do."

"What do you mean?"

"I mean exactly that. We've been too involved. We should let it go and get on with our lives. Let the dragons take care of themselves."

Meeryle felt like the barn had come crashing down on her. Leena didn't care. She truly didn't care. She was going to let Tikid die.

Fury engulfed Meeryle. Her cheeks burned and everything took on an orange glare. Her stomach clenched, but the usual nausea didn't appear. Something strange must have shown on her face, as Leena stared at her, eyes wide. "Meeryle, think. How can you stop a group of hunters?" Her voice was quivering.

The sound of her friend's voice full of fear was a cold bucket of water on her head. All anger left. "I don't know, Leena, but I will at least try. I think I will go find Tikid instead and warn the dragons to hide." She stood and straightened her skirt. "Seeing as you won't help the dragons, can you help me out of here?"

Leena gulped and nodded. "Use the side window. You should go unnoticed. It's tight, but you should be all right."

Meeryle made her way to the dirty window and turned to Leena. "Can you help me up? It's too high and I can't pull myself up there."

Leena ran to her side and locked her hands. She motioned for Meeryle to put her foot in them.

"Leena?"

"Yes?"

"Don't tell them anything you know about the dragons. They didn't seem to want to know anything about them, but they may change their minds. It might help for the hunt." Leena nodded, eyes still wide.

Meeryle opened the widow and listened. Aside from the wind, the night was silent. She grabbed the windowsill, put her foot in Leena's hands and braced herself.

"Meeryle?"

She stopped and turned to Leena. "What?"

"I'm... I'm sorry I made you angry."

"It's not the first time."

"This time was different."

"What do you mean?"

"Your eyes were orange."

Meeryle bit her lips and shook her head. "You imagined it. Get ready; I'm out of here."

She stepped up, pulled herself onto the window ledge, and lay uncomfortably across the window on her stomach. Bracing herself, she grabbed the side of the window and pulled herself further out, the ground looming in her face. From this position, her options were limited to falling on her face or putting her hands out. As she slid further out, she soon realized her arms were still too far from the ground to catch herself with her hands without breaking a wrist. She grunted and slid completely out of the window, and turned at the last minute, letting her shoulder take the brunt of the fall.

Meeryle bit her lips to refrain from crying out in pain. Leena whispered something, but the plump girl ignored her. She stood up slowly, wincing at the thought of the bruise bound to appear. Meeryle shook her head and rubbed her shoulder. It didn't matter. Tikid's life was worth a thousand bruises.

A cold nose bumped her ankle. Meeryle bit back a yelp and looked into Suqi's black eyes. "Oh, it's you," she whispered. "Well, I'm going to find the dragons. Want to come?" She could have sworn that the fox nodded. Meeryle decided her imagination needed some dampening. She rolled her eyes at herself and started towards the forest, fox in tow.

Meeryle kept to the back of the houses. The village was deserted, but she didn't want to take a chance. She neither met nor heard anyone. She almost expected to bump into Rokin, but Leena's would-be suitor hadn't come back. Meeryle was a bit surprised; she thought he'd have seized the opportunity to become some sort of hero going to his lady's rescue. Leena must really have discouraged him.

When she finally reached the outskirts of the village, Meeryle resolutely squared her good shoulder and started on the path to the forest. Once the trees were looming over her, she closed her eyes and shuddered. If the forest was scary during the day, its very edge was truly frightening at night. Thankful for Suqi's presence, Meeryle took in a deep breath and set off into the woods.

CHAPTER EIGHT

The experience proved to be much worse than she had imagined. The night had given trees a new life; the wind made the branches move in a threatening way, its noise sounding like malevolent whispers. The darkness also hid hundreds of insects, whose drone covered the rustling of nocturnal animals. Every step Meeryle took seemed to awaken or frighten *something*. She nearly tripped on an animal whose scream was echoed by Meeryle's shriek. When she stepped on a snake, panic gripped her and she ran blindly ahead. Every step made her shoulder throb. When the pain became unbearable, Meeryle stopped and rubbed her shoulder. The fact that she could actually touch it probably meant it wasn't badly damaged. Trying to tell herself she'd be fine and that she hadn't permanently lost movement in that part of her body, Meeryle looked around, trying to get her bearings in the dark, only to realize she was lost.

Despair set in; Meeryle dropped to the ground, startling yet another little animal. "Oh, go away! If I scared you, well, you scared me too. Serves you right."

A wet nose prodded her hand, triggering a scream she barely stifled when she realized it was only Suqi, who had faithfully kept up with her. The moon was bleeding light through the branches, allowing Meeryle to see Suqi sitting, staring intently at her. "Thanks for being here with me, Suqi. I know this is your kind of home, but it scares me silly," she said with a smile.

Meeryle blinked in astonishment: she had felt an emotion, just like she did with Tikid when she wasn't touching the dragon. Elation pushed away all her fears; this could only mean that her friend was close to her, probably looking for her.

Calling out Tikid's name as she got up, Meeryle was unnerved by the instant hush. Her loud voice had scared all the nocturnal insects immediately around her, making the forest eerily silent. Yet her calls went unanswered. She closed her eyes as her heart sank, and sighed. Her imagination was playing dirty tricks on her.

Another emotion made her heart skip. This time, she was able to identify it: scorn. Puzzled and elated, the girl looked around and scratched her head. It was very unlike Tikid to feel scorn towards her. Unless it was another dragon....

A small bark drew her attention. Meeryle looked down into Suqi's mocking eyes. "You... You're the one I'm feeling. How can that be? Can I hear animals, just like Tikid?" She felt a mix of amusement and mockery. "Just you, then?" To her astonishment, she clearly saw the fox nod. "I'm dreaming. My weird fox just nodded at me." Suqi snorted. "All right, if I touch you, will I be able to hear you in my mind, just like with Tikid?" No sooner said than done, Meeryle reached out and stroked the soft head. The feeling of amusement intensified, but no words formed in her head. "Nope, you can't talk to me like this. But you understand me, right?" This time, Suqi cocked her head and projected mockery. "Yes, well, I guess a fox is cunning and would understand anything anyone said, but it's kind of strange to me. Can you help me find the dragons?" The fox stared, emotions suddenly blank. Meeryle sighed. "Ah, well. Just thought I'd ask."

The sound of her own voice and Suqi's presence reassured her. She wasn't in any immediate danger. Even if the trees looked threatening, they weren't about to eat her, and neither were the animals she had encountered so far. Taking in a deep breath, she forced herself to think rationally: this was the same forest where she came to meet with Tikid. Being a bit off course here was the equivalent of being in a different room in a stranger's house. However, no matter how she tried to reassure herself, the thought that she was alone for the first time among the trees threatened to make her panic again.

Suqi used her nose once again, comforting Meeryle. The little animal's presence helped, but the girl had to take in another deep breath and remind herself why she was doing this. Tikid and her kind needed to know that people were about to hunt them down like animals. "Dragons are not animals." Once again, the sound of her voice heartened her. It also seemed to frighten away some of the animals, who scurried in the underbrush. "That's right! I'm a human, much bigger than any of you. If you don't move out of my way, I just may step on you. So shoo!" She looked at Suqi, who once again projected amusement.

She squared her shoulders and brushed off her skirt. Even if she didn't know if any dust or dirt had clung to the fabric while she had been sitting, she didn't actually really care as she was alone. The dragons-if she found them-probably wouldn't mind either. However, the gesture allowed her to calm down and prepare herself to continue with her search.

Meeryle wanted Suqi to precede her and guide her steps, and as soon as the fox realized what the human was about, Suqi's ears perked up and she led the way. However, it quickly became obvious that the animal had never guided anyone or anything as big as Meeryle. The little creature went underneath fallen branches on which Meeryle would have tripped if she hadn't seen them just in time, and avoided holes or rocks at the last second, making Meeryle jump awkwardly and painfully at times. Once she followed Suqi around the same tree twice, the girl gave up. For some reason, the fox was having fun at her expense.

Ignoring Suqi, the girl started slowly on her own. The fox went ahead and came back once in a while, as if to check on her. Meeryle's eyes had become accustomed to the night and the winking moonlight, and she was now able to make out details. She could tell where the tree trunks stopped and the underbrush started and she could see deadfall just before she tripped on it.

Her progress was nonetheless very slow. She couldn't tell time; the trees hid the stars and she didn't know how to read the time according to the moon. Normally, at night she slept; she didn't moon-gaze.

After what felt like candlemarks, the girl stopped, discouraged and frightened. "Who are you kidding, Meeryle? You're so lost, even in daylight you couldn't find your way back." An owl hooted at her, startling her. "Well, you can talk all you want, bird! Why don't you make yourself useful and tell the dragons I'm looking for them?"

The owl didn't answer. She listened to find out if it had flown away or if it was still near her, but she remembered owls made no sounds when flying. She sighed. "I have to go about this another way. Suqi, if you have any suggestions, now would be a good time." The fox sat and stared, projecting a feeling of expectancy. "I didn't think so. I need light."

Mindful of Tikid's comments about burning things uselessly, Meeryle blindly gathered a few twigs and lit them. The little fire didn't help: it only made the trees look taller, darker and more threatening.

"Suqi, do you know if dragons use fires? Because if they did, I could find them that way for sure." Her own statement stunned her. She had finally found a solution, once again thanks to her gift. However, they had never asked Tikid if she had a hearth in her... lair. The young dragon was familiar with fire, but she hadn't mentioned it otherwise. Did dragons need its heat? Meeryle was willing to take the chance.

She snuffed out the burning twigs with a thought and was soon back in the dark. Sitting down and eyes closed, Meeryle was once again in her listening trance, seeking the familiar beat of fire. Her Mage-sense roamed the forest, looking for the sound of fire. Nothing. She was about to give up when a faint beat caught her attention. Her hopes were dashed when she heard voices discussing the upcoming hunt: she was once again listening to the inn's hearth. The exercise heartened her; it meant that she could listen to fire at a much greater distance than she had thought possible. While she didn't know exactly where she was in the forest, it was definitely farther than she had ever been. Unless, of course, she had been going in circles, which was doubtful. She was convinced Suqi would have tried to correct her if she had been doing so. Also, without knowing why, she was sure she hadn't been retracing her steps. Maybe an effect of her Mage-sense.

Meeryle frowned at the thought. How could her Mage-gift allow her not to get lost? Leena had wanted her to listen to the other elements, so she could be listening to the earth without being aware of it. She cocked her head, blocked the fire's beat out and let her Mage-sense seek her trail. Sure enough, she heard a faint murmur just behind her, where she and Suqi had last stepped. It was barely detectable; in fact, she had to strain her sense so much in order to hear the murmur that her head started to hurt.

She opened her eyes and shook her head, dispersing the odd pain. Earth was much more difficult to hear than fire. "But why? Fire is so easy to find." Her voice scared yet another unseen animal. Suqi only moved her ears. Meeryle wondered how long she'd been sitting, listening to both fire and earth. "That's it! Earth is opposite to fire. I'm just too used to fire." The black fox moved her tail. "Water is also an opposite." She smiled at the sound of the rustling leaves. "Air. Air is close to fire." She recalled Leena's comment. Her friend had mentioned a combination of air and fire when she had heard her through the flame of the lantern for the first time. The air might be what made her able to hear voices from the fire. Since she was most familiar with it, fire was the vehicle, the thing that had allowed her to connect to air, but air was the key and the answer. It was everywhere.

Meeryle closed her eyes again and concentrated on the wind. The breeze was chilling her to her bones, actually. She suddenly felt very tired. The events of the day caught up: the shock of getting found out and locked up, the lack of sleep and the traipsing in the cold forest during the night. Meeryle shook herself out of her sinking mood. "Air. I am listening to the air." The thought of someone hearing that statement made her smile briefly. She sounded stranger and stranger to her own ears. Another person would be ready to brand her as crazy.

As Meeryle emptied her mind of these impeding thoughts, Suqi moved closer and settled against the girl's back. The animal's warmth and presence brought a smile to the girl's face. Concentrating, she once again listened to the wind, trying to hear it with her newfound sense. It didn't take her as long as it had to hear the beat of fire. She was getting the knack of it. Unlike fire, wind didn't have a beat, but sounded more like someone breathing. She chuckled. If she ever heard anyone breathing like that, she would call on the Healer immediately. Air sounded something between a rasp and a groan. It really was like a strange breathing: in, a rasp; out, a groan.

"Almost like snoring," she whispered to herself.

Now that she knew what to seek, she wiggled and tried to make herself a bit more comfortable. It would take her a while to find the dragons while listening to the air. They could be anywhere and the forest was vast. Anchored by the fox's warmth, she let herself be carried by the air's sound.

Meeryle didn't know how long she'd been listening. Air had carried many sounds to her: a river, animals screaming, a branch falling, and even what sounded like people snoring. Some she hadn't been able to identify, some she didn't want to. If she had heard dragons, she didn't know. From what Tikid had told them, dragons seemed to be day creatures, so they would sleep at night, just like humans. What sounds did a dragon make when it slept? Did it snore or whimper from nightmares? Meeryle didn't know, yet she kept on listening, her senses seemingly sweeping the entire forest.

Suddenly, within the rasp and the groan of the air, she heard flapping. It wasn't a bird; this was the sound Tikid made every time she took off. The large leathery wings of a dragon did not beat the air the same way a feathered wing did. Somewhere east of her, a dragon was taking flight.

Sighing with relief, Meeryle opened her eyes. She couldn't believe that dawn was already upon her. "I spent all night looking for them." She stood and stumbled. "I'm tired, Suqi. Why didn't I wait until now to search and sleep before?" The fox sent feelings of concern. Meeryle shook her head. "Because I don't have time. Come on, Suqi, we're going east, toward the sun."

While she sought the rising sun through the trees, her body reminded her that she didn't just lack sleep; sudden thirst gritted her throat. Even if she could push herself to move on despite the fatigue, thirst wouldn't allow her to go very far. If she could find a source of water, she could heat it with her gift, but the nearest was that river she'd heard during the night. It certainly hadn't sounded near.

"Great. For once, I have the means to purify my water, but I don't have water!"

Suqi barked, drawing the girl's attention to a low bush. The fox pulled one of the branches and chewed on it.

Meeryle made a face. "You want me to eat this? It's a branch! I'm not a grazer." Her gritty throat told her this was no time to be picky. Reluctantly, she knelt by the bush and examined a branch. Suqi had chewed on all of it, but the main interest were small dark green berries. Picking them gingerly, Meeryle tried one. The taste was rather bland and it left a raspy feeling on her tongue at first, but the berry was filled with refreshing juice. Once the liquid hit her throat, the craving for more overwhelmed her. She almost had to stop herself from imitating Suqi and chomp on an entire branch. The idea made her smile and reason overcome the instinct.

A few minutes later, the bush almost bare and her thirst slaked, the plump girl was ready move on and started at a slow pace. Even if it was lighter out, her way was hampered by holes, fallen branches, and stumps. Her sore shoulder had become a constant background pain that she ignored to the best of her ability.

Periodically, she stopped and listened to the air, the fox waiting patiently at her feet. Every time, she would hear a dragon noise coming from the same direction. She also made the effort to listen to the murmur of the earth made louder by her steps-that still made no sense to her-to make sure she wasn't going around in circles.

However, the sleepless night and the strain of using her gift suddenly took their toll. Meeryle's knees buckled; she managed to avoid rocks and roots, but she still fell hard enough on her knees to let out a cry of pain.

"Come on, come on! I don't have time for this. I have to get up!" Her body refused to listen. The sun chose that moment to break through the tree tops and bathe her in warmth. With a sigh, Meeryle lay down on her side and fell asleep with Suqi curled up against her back.

***

The insistent chirping of a bird woke her up. Meeryle blinked twice, wondering how come her bed was so hard and why someone had let the bluebird inside the house. The breeze brought her quickly back to reality and she sat up abruptly. The sun wasn't very high yet, so she hadn't slept more than two candlemarks. She sighed in relief. "I won't be too late." Meeryle got up and took a good look at her clothes. "I look like a forest spirit. Mother would not be pleased." She made a face at the thought of her mother's scornful look. "What I do is more important than clothes. If she can't understand that, too bad. I know I'm doing the right thing. Right, Suqi? Suqi?" The little fox was gone. Meeryle bit her lip in dismay. She had come to rely on the animal's presence. "No matter. I can do this on my own."

She resolutely put Suqi out of her mind to shake and brush out as many twigs as she could from her hair and clothes. Closing her eyes, she rolled her stiffened shoulder and sought the dragon sounds. She heard shuffling, wing snapping, grunts, and the grumble of laughter particular to dragons. She was glad she had heard it from Tikid; otherwise, she would never have been able to identify it.

All the noises were still coming from the same general direction. Meeryle started walking eastward and made good progress until she came to a huge chasm, which stretched out as far as the eye could see on both sides. She had reached the rift Tikid had mentioned, the natural boundary of the dragons' territory.

Meeryle was both elated and disheartened. She was on the right track, but she now understood why Parin discouraged anyone from going in that direction. The rift was extremely wide and very deep. As she moved slowly to the edge and peered down, Meeryle gulped. One false step and she would plummet down for what looked like furlongs. She couldn't make out the bottom of the precipice.

She smiled. If that chasm stopped her, it would surely stop the hunters! Hope warmed her belly and she sighed in relief. Tikid was safe. All the dragons were safe from hunters.

Something nagged her in the back of her mind. Although she hadn't been able to recognize the voices she had heard in the fire, their determination had come through very clearly. No, the hunters wouldn't give up. They would cross, no matter the cost.

The warm feeling in her stomach disappeared as quickly as it had come. Numb, Meeryle backed up and sat down. "I wish I could fly." Flight was the only option. She couldn't circumvent the rift or cross it, unless she climbed down, then back up again. "Let's face it, Meeryle, even if you were willing to do it, you couldn't. Maybe Rokin could, or Leena. Just not short, chubby Meeryle." For the first time in her life, Meeryle wished she had exercised. All the trouble and all the exertion seemed worth it now. She realized she was crying when a fat tear splashed on her hand. "Talk about feeling useless." She hugged her knees and pressed her forehead on them, letting the tears of rage and discouragement flow.

Once she had shed the last tear, Meeryle sniffed and wiped her face with the back of her hand. A familiar nose touched her leg. "Well," Meeryle hiccupped, "where have you been?" Suqi projected feelings of encouragement mixed with exasperation. Hope stirred anew. "You know a way?" At Suqi's nod - on which Meeryle refused to dwell - she scrambled to her feet. "Show me!"

Although Meeryle couldn't have said what she had expected, a fallen tree was not on her list. "You can't possibly be serious." She looked into Suqi's earnest eyes and her heart sank. The fox's solution was worse than climbing down and up the huge rift.

Meeryle resolutely closed her hands into fists and forced herself to look at the makeshift bridge. "It's the only way. I have to use it." She took a deep breath and studied the tree objectively. It had been a giant and was now resting straight across the rift. The base was almost three times higher than her own height. As it had fallen a while ago, offshoots had grown, engulfing the base and hiding its true size. The lowest branches had been high up in the tree and were now hanging in the rift, naked and gray. The other side of the rift bore the mark of the fallen tree; part of the facing cliff had caved in, unable to withstand the weight of the tree. The tip, bristled with pointy and smooth-looking branches, continued in the facing forest, creeper plants tying it down in the cradle it had made in its fall. Had it been months or years ago? Meeryle couldn't tell. Leena would have known, probably down to the day.

Meeryle closed her eyes and gulped. The age of the tree was irrelevant. All that mattered was its solidity. The base wouldn't be a problem, but the closer she got to the tip, the higher were the risks of the wood being dry. She refused to think about the possibility of the trunk breaking under her weight. "I can do this. Think positive, Meeryle, think positive."

The first step was to get onto the giant trunk. Suqi had somehow found a way up and was sitting on top, looking down on Meeryle. The only way up for an inexperienced climber was through the roots. The smallest ones had long broken away, leaving only the bigger ones, dressed in creeper plants. The short girl had to fully stretch in order to find and grab a low root that wasn't in an advanced state of decay.

"Ugh!" she yelled, jumping back, as she disturbed crawling insects. She had to gulp down several times before she gathered up enough courage to grab it again.

Once she had the first solid root firmly in hand, Meeryle pulled herself up, feet scrambling to find support. Eventually, her foot found another solid root and she was able to climb up slowly. She came nose to nose with Suqi when she reached the top. The fox guided her to a place where the roots were wide enough to let Meeryle through. The girl crawled to the base of the trunk on her stomach, then slowly stood, holding on to a root.

Meeryle looked around, feeling giddy. She had never undertaken such a task and felt good about its relative ease. When she looked at herself, she snorted. Her appearance was getting worse and worse. Her skirt and blouse had been torn by the roots and were now a uniform dirt brown, highlighted with the green of the plants she had damaged on her way up. She refused to check for scratches on her skin, focusing instead on her footing.

Decay had rendered the bark soft and slippery. Only the very surface was hard, making footing treacherous. Twice her foot broke through the bark and twice she slipped to her hands and knees, panic threatening when she slid near the side. Meeryle decided to proceed on all fours. She bit her lips in disgust at the feel of the spongy rotting wood. The squishy sounds were sometimes accompanied by a crunch when she squashed an insect's shell. Her stomach heaved. It was one thing to flatten a bug with a shoe, but doing it with the flat of the hand or the fingers was just gross.

She kept going, trying to ignore what her hands were feeling. Left hand, then right hand, then left knee, then right knee, over and over, inch by inch. She repeated the words for her movements in her head, then recited them out loud when her hand or knee slipped.

Gradually, the bark disappeared to give way to gray, smooth wood. Meeryle stopped and gauged her progress. She was now over the edge of the cliff, overhanging the rift. The trunk had narrowed, allowing Meeryle to look down. She could barely make out the bottom of the rift. The sun reflected on something, probably the water of a river-maybe the same one she had heard-but she couldn't see its silver ribbon. Meeryle suddenly became aware of her vulnerability. The wind felt stronger, whipping her hair in her face, trying to make her fall over. She felt the tree swing with the wind, which triggered a dizziness that jeopardized her balance. She flattened her body and hugged the dead wood, eyes closed. The wind didn't feel as threatening and the tree had stopped swinging. Meeryle sighed in relief and shook her head. "You know you shouldn't look down, you ninny." The sound of her voice banished the last remnants of her vertigo. She got back up on her hands and knees, and proceeded toward the end of the tree.

Suqi was just ahead of her, sitting, tail swishing. Meeryle could feel encouragement coming from the fox. "You know, you're just too strange. I'm thinking you're not an animal, but one of these mystical creatures that aren't supposed to exist. I mean, dragons weren't supposed to be real, right? So why can't there be some beings that look like foxes?" She slowly continued forward, eyes on the wood. As the trunk narrowed, she wanted to see exactly where to put her hands down. A little bit too much to the right or to the left, and she'd end up feeling empty space. She kept talking to keep her fear under control. "Do you have a family like Tikid? Do you have special powers?"

Her questions were cut short by a new obstacle. As the trunk was getting smaller, so were the naked branches. She had been able to overstep or go around the big ones, but the closer she came to the tip of the fallen tree, the smaller and more condensed the branches became. Suqi had to wriggle through the forest of dead branches. Some snapped as the animal brushed them, but not enough to clear the way for Meeryle.

The girl carefully sat back and spread her legs as widely as she could, straddling the trunk, making a point not to look down. She then broke all the branches within her reach. Some were very thick and needed extra effort, and almost made her lose her balance. Once the way was as clear as she could make it, Meeryle scooted forward, wincing as the remainder of the branches scraped her buttocks and the inside of her thighs.

She continued to move on, straddling the tree and breaking as many branches as she could. By the time she had reached the other side of the chasm, she was weeping. Her entire behind and thighs were burning with pain. She didn't want to look back, afraid to find strips of her flesh on the wood. Instead, when her feet touched the vines growing on the rocks of the cliff, she moved as fast as she could, grinding her teeth. Once she was sure she was on firm land, she dismounted the tree and lay on her side, letting the pain wash over her.

Meeryle yelped as a wet tongue scraped the back of her thigh. She turned and Suqi's concern hit her like a wall. "Oh, it's that bad, huh?" The fox's eyes bore into hers and Meeryle almost heard something. Frustrated, the girl tried to sit, but pain flared. She lay down on her stomach, sobbing. Once again, Suqi licked Meeryle's wounds. This time, the girl could only whimper. She closed her eyes and put her cheek on the cool ground. Twigs dug in, but they felt comfortable compared to her backside. The fox licked her a third time and Meeryle's eyes flew open when she realized the spot where Suqi had licked her hurt less. She twisted and looked at the fox, amazed. "You're Healing me!" Suqi snorted. Meeryle smiled. "I was right. You're not an animal. Well, work your magic, then." She put her head back on the ground and let the fox tend her wounds. At first, pain flared with each lick, but her legs went gradually numb. Meeryle dozed without falling completely asleep, listening to the hum of the insects and the call of the birds.

Opening her eyes when she no longer felt Suqi's tongue, Meeryle looked back at her legs and winced at the sight of her shredded skirt. However, the skin of her buttocks and her thighs was pink and smooth. She carefully got up and touched her legs. They were soft like baby skin. Meeryle smiled and looked for Suqi. The fox was lying down, eyes closed. Panic gripped the girl's heart. Had the effort cost Suqi too much?

She knelt by the animal, gently stroking the fluffy head. Suqi opened her eyes and Meeryle let out a breath she didn't know she had been holding. "Are you all right?" Suqi sighed and closed her eyes. Seconds later, she was asleep, snoring softly. Meeryle smiled and whispered: "Thank you. I think I'll be able to continue on my own. You rest now."

A glance told her she was at the edge of the trees, in a part of the forest where no one had been for a while, if ever. She could see no trails, the underbrush was unbroken and the small animals

143

weren't afraid of her as she made her way through the growth. Some small squirrels actually came down level to her face and chattered questionably at her. She imagined they were asking her who and even maybe what she was.

"I'm looking for the dragons. Can you help me?" She felt rather silly talking to them, but Tikid had said animals spoke to dragons, so she had to take the chance they might understand a human. No luck there, though. The nearest squirrel let out a strange squawk at the sound of her voice and ran up the trunk so fast it became a blur. All the other squirrels followed him and the forest became hauntingly silent.

Meeryle felt oppressed by the trees. They were looming over her again, judging her. The wind brought in clouds that darkened the sky and made the forest even more stifling. Suqi wasn't there to reassure her. She was completely alone. Panic swept her up and she started running.

For some reason, the daylight made her flight worse. At night, she hadn't seen all the obstacles, the near misses, all the things that could go wrong and hurt her. Now, each stump, each hole, each tree she avoided made her heart beat faster as she imagined bumping and falling against them. Her newly healed skin was tight and hurt as it stretched. Unwanted tears welled up, blinding her and making everything blend in one huge greenish curtain. The ground, the trunks, and the branches became one wall into which she ran head first. Leaves whipped her face, bushes scratched her legs, and branches caught her sleeves. She was sure she heard the trees whispering about her, wishing her harm. When she finally tripped on a root, she heard the trees laugh. She barely had the time to see the trunk before she hit her head. Then everything became blissfully black.

***

Meeryle grunted. The top of her head itched terribly. She scratched it and yelped in pain. Everything was green when she opened her eyes. She blinked a few times and the green became moss. The girl carefully sat up, eyeing her blurry surroundings. She touched the top of her head again, but with much more care. Her fingers had blood on them.

Meeryle remembered her flight and her fall. Her head was pounding. She didn't know how badly she'd hurt herself. Her clothes were a tattered mess, her hands and face scratched, and the pain from her shoulder, which she had been able to ignore while crossing the rift, was radiating to her entire arm. Maybe she should have asked Suqi to Heal it.... She dismissed the thought. The poor fox had been exhausted. No, Meeryle had to do without her pet.

She tried to listen to air again, but the pounding in her head blocked out any sound her Mage-sense could pick out. She wanted badly to shake her head to clear out the fuzziness but feared the headache would worsen. All she could do was to sit and wait for her head to clear on its own.

After what felt like an eternity, Meeryle's sight started to clear. The trees and the sky became separate things and the ground was no longer an even green and brown carpet. She was finally able to see everything normally when the sun was right above her.

Meeryle braced herself to get up. Leena had told her once that head injuries could cause someone to lose their balance. She wanted to avoid falling again-it seemed she'd been falling a lot lately. Her body would without any doubt be a nice shade of blue or purple within the next few days. She turned and leaned heavily on a tree stump and got slowly up. The stump shook. Meeryle wavered before landing on her rump. She stared at the stump. It was no longer covered with mushrooms and moss, but with green scales, and it had grown a snout. Two big ruby eyes were staring at her.

Meeryle's heart stopped for a second and a smile of pure joy broke her face: she had found the dragons.

CHAPTER NINE

Elation dampened somewhat as the red eyes pierced her with their gaze. Meeryle didn't dare move. The eyes scrutinizing her were much bigger than Tikid's and definitely unfriendly. The shape of the head was different than her friend's, longer and narrower, and the spikes on the head were much more pronounced. Meeryle's stomach clenched as she realized she was face to face with a seemingly threatening adult dragon.

She gulped, remembering Tikid's comment. Dragons scorned humans, who weren't considered fit company for dragons. Meeryle ground her teeth. She had gone against everyone in her village in order to warn dragons of the coming danger. She wasn't about to let herself by intimidated into silence after all she'd been through.

Still sitting where she had fallen, Meeryle straightened her back and looked defiantly at the dragon. "My name is Meeryle. I've come to warn you...."

The dragon moved. She hadn't realized that its head had been leaning on its forelegs. She had almost been at eye level then, but now, the dragon was rising to sit on its haunches. Meeryle closed her eyes briefly, pushing panic as far down as possible, desperately wishing for Suqi's soothing presence. This dragon was at least twice as big as Tikid. It was looking down at her, projecting feelings of mockery. Meeryle felt tiny and insignificant. She looked at the front feet and bit her lips. Tikid's would wrap around her shoulder like a huge hand; the adult could easily wrap her in its talons and pick her up.

Fear was slowly being replaced by terror. Meeryle understood why anyone would think dragons would make an easy meal out any human. This dragon looked particularly predatory and only Tikid's offended words at the idea of killing stopped the girl from running for her life.

She got up slowly with a confidence she didn't feel and stood squarely in front of the huge creature. "My name is Meeryle. I know Tikid and I know you won't eat me, so you can stop pretending you're choosing which part you'll munch on first." The dragon's eyes opened wide in surprise. "And I can't hear you unless I touch you, so right now, you may be wasting your words."

The dragon's chuckle was very deep and resonated in the trees, making all the plants vibrate. Meeryle's own heartbeat changed briefly to match the sound.

The green creature lowered its head level to Meeryle's and cocked it to one side, daring her to touch it. The girl stopped herself from taking a deep breath; she didn't want to show the dragon how reluctant she was to touch it. Hugging Tikid was one thing, but being so close to this huge creature was quite another. She reached out her hand, waiting for the dragon to indicate where she should touch it. The large creature moved its head even closer to Meeryle, then changed its mind and presented its right front paw, closed fistlike. Meeryle's instincts were telling her to get as far from the claws as possible. She pushed her fear away and resolutely put her hand on the huge fist. Her hand was very small indeed against the smooth green scales.

"*Well, human? What have you got to say?*"

Meeryle started at the deep voice in her head, which was completely different from Tikid's. It also definitely sounded male. "Ah... What's your name?"

The dragon blinked, surprised. "*Korad. I have to admit I did not expect courtesy from a human.*"

Meeryle bristled at the tone. He sounded as bad as some of the villagers. "How many humans have you encountered?"

"*You caught me in an unfairness,*" he apologized. "*You are the first human I have met. I do not fly over areas of the forest where humans live, so I cannot even boast of having seen one from afar. However, all the reports from other dragons who have seen humans were not... flattering.*"

"Well, you are only the second dragon I've met. And you're nothing like Tikid."

"*Ah, yes, our wayward kin.*"

"She did nothing wrong! She became my friend, that's all."

The dragon chuckled once again. "*So much spirit. I would guess you are closer in age with Tikid than with me.*"

Meeryle gaped. She quickly closed her mouth and smiled at the dragon's assumption. He didn't know she was young. If she really thought it through, however, it did make sense. The dragon had admitted she was the first human he had ever seen. He had nothing to which he could compare her. Just like the first time they met Tikid, it had come as a surprise to find she was a young dragon rather than a full-grown one.

"Yes, I am the same age as her. It took us a while to understand that, though. She's not very clear with her explanations, sometimes."

"She would not be. Tikid is a very impulsive youngster who does not spend the time listening to her elders and pondering their words. Hence she cannot express her thoughts as easily as her peers."

"If it makes you feel better, I hate school too." The dragon didn't smile, but he was amused. "I'm not the only one, either. I'm just better at cooking than counting."

"Now that is an odd concept. Why would you need to count?"

"Oh, that would take a long time to explain. Leena and I were never able to explain properly the whole money and bartering thing to Tikid. She just doesn't get it."

The dragon frowned. He cocked his head to the side, troubled. *"I see humans have a culture of their own that is much more complicated than I had thought. This will require some pondering. Follow me; I will take you to your... friend. Then we will discuss your presence here."*

He put his paw down, breaking the mental contact, and turned, twitching his tail. He started at a pace so brisk that Meeryle had no choice but to follow him at a run.

Luckily, they didn't go very far. He slowed to a stop and motioned Meeryle forward with a movement of the head. They were facing a strange clearing rendered dark by the thickness of the leaves above and the density of the surrounding branches. When her eyes had adjusted to the greenish darkness, mounds took shape everywhere. She stepped forward and some of them, the smaller ones, moved. They were dragons.

Meeryle gulped under the scrutiny of so many ruby eyes. A multitude of emotions assaulted her: curiosity, surprise, disdain, and anger. Overwhelmed, she closed her eyes and staggered. Something grabbed her elbow and gently held her upright.

"Are you all right?" asked a familiar voice in her head.

Meeryle sighed with relief and opened her eyes. Tikid's snout was so close, Meeryle went cross-eyed. She took a step back, blinking, and tripped on Tikid's tail. The young dragon sidestepped, yelping in pain. She had coiled herself around her human friend, but had managed to tangle them both in a knot.

When Meeryle had finally unraveled the twist of the long tail, she was red with shame and Tikid wasn't feeling any better. The girl leaned her forehead on the dragon's neck, hiding her frustration. The adult dragons started roaring with laughter. The sound was so unexpected and loud that Meeryle forgot her clumsiness.

She stared in amazement as some dragons started to hiccup, while others were rolling on the ground. One huge dragon was howling, snout toward the sky.

"I hate it when they laugh at me." Meeryle was still touching Tikid. *"Even when I really try, I always manage to look like a fool. Like right now. I was protecting you, but all I really did was to make you look as clumsy as me."*

"Don't worry," she whispered back, hugging the dragon's neck. "I *am* clumsy. This wasn't your fault. At least they're not angry or anything. They're happy."

One of the adult dragons, even bigger than Korad, stepped forward and settled down in front of the two friends. Meeryle realized that she couldn't tell if the dragon was male or female. It leaned its head on its front paws, staring at her.

"Well met, Meeryle." The girl started at the sound of the gentle female voice in her head. She had heard the dragon, but was not touching her. *"Yes, I see you can hear me. It would seem that as long as you are touching one of us, you can hear all of us."* Meeryle was still hugging Tikid's neck. She nodded slowly. *"My name is Larid. I am Tikid's dam."*

Meeryle didn't know how to answer that statement. It did make sense for Tikid to have a mother, but it still surprised her.

"Tikid has told me much about you and Leena, even after she was forbidden any contact with humans. I did not share the information she gave me with the rest of the Kin. It seemed to me she had found true friends. But now this friend is in our lair and I am not sure it is a good thing to have a human know its location." Meeryle stayed silent. She almost said she had found this place by accident, but decided the information was irrelevant.

This dragon was very different from Korad. She didn't have his haughty attitude towards humans; on the contrary, she seemed extremely level-headed. Nevertheless, her knowing eyes seemed to delve inside Meeryle's mind and to know her very thoughts, making the girl feel naked. That stare combined with her great size made Tikid's mother very intimidating. "*Speak, child. I will not tolerate this gaping for very long.*" Her tone, reminding her of Corvin at his worst, chilled Meeryle to the bone.

"I... I came here because... I think you are all in danger."

"*Oh? How so?*" Larid's eye ridge went up questioningly.

"Well, yesterday, two others from my village saw Tikid and... panicked. They told everyone in the village and now they're going to hunt you down."

Larid's eyes opened wide. She reared up and roared in fury. "*They would dare?*" The dragon took flight in a flurry of leaves and dust. Soon, all the other dragons followed her, leaving a very flabbergasted Meeryle behind. Why had her comment generated such a reaction? The fury in Larid's eyes had been frightening. A scary thought crossed Meeryle's mind. Would the dragons seek revenge for what obviously seemed an insult?

"Tikid, where are they going? Not to the village, right?"

"*No, they will first want to meet with all the other Greens at the reunion clearing. Then they might decide to go to your village.*"

"And then what? You said dragons don't kill. Would they attack people, do you think?"

Tikid turned and looked Meeryle in the eyes. "*I do not know, Meeryle, I just do not know. This is a grave insult. Not only do your people threaten us, but they want to hunt us like animals.*"

"Well, to them, you are animals. They're afraid of you. Dragons do look scary, you know."

153

"I know. I remember the look on your faces the first time you and Leena saw me. It was sheer terror. And it hurt me so much!"

"Why?"

"Humans are the only creatures of this world who find us scary."

Meeryle was stunned. "Well, who else is there?"

"All the animals accept us, and so do the elves, the melusins, and all the others. They all know we are essential to the balance of this world. Without us, everything would fare very poorly or die."

"Oh." Meeryle was at a loss. Elves? Melusins? Not only had she never heard of such creatures, but she also wasn't sure she understood her friend. "What do you mean, everything would die? How come?"

"The Greens in particular ensure the health of the forest and the trees. No dragon has been near your village in a long, long time. The trees there are... not well. Look around you. This is where numerous Greens live. Can you not see how much healthier the trees are?"

The trees did look much better than the ones around the village. The trunks were so large, she couldn't circle them with her arms. The foliage was extremely thick and some leaves seemed to glow. Even the moss on the ground was exceptional.

"You should be showing this to Leena. I don't really know plants."

"Yet you do see the difference?"

"Yes. And come to think of it, the clearing where we usually meet looks better. Leena mentioned it."

"My presence is the reason. I renew the essence of the forest. I reestablish its balance. Or at least, I try to. I am still learning. It takes a long time for a full essence replenishment."

"Ah... You lost me, Tikid. But it doesn't matter. What you're telling me is if the hunters kill dragons, the forest will die."

"Yes."

"So they would not just be killing people, but part of the world." The young dragon nodded. It explained Larid's seemingly extreme reaction. Dragons were natural entities, who were, if not worshipped, at least highly respected by everyone-except humans. "This is even worse than I thought. What do we do?"

"I am not sure. What can we do?"

"Well, what it really comes down to is influence. It turns out I have none. And neither does Leena."

"What do you mean?"

"That nobody was even willing to listen to us when we said you weren't animals or dangerous," she answered bitterly.

"Are you sure?"

"What?" Meeryle was a bit miffed by the question. Of course she was sure. She recalled the angry faces and shuddered.

"I asked my question the wrong way. Was Leena's influence discarded when she said dragons were not dangerous? It seems to me from what you have said that one would listen to a Healer, apprentice or otherwise."

Meeryle hesitated. The confrontation had been so overwhelming, its memory was a bit fuzzy.

"Come to think of it, Leena was trying to demonstrate that Navee had heard you, but the Healer would hear nothing of it. The real reason for his anger was that Leena didn't see that Navee was... hurt by the encounter."

"Hurt? I did not hurt her!" Tikid was offended.

"No, not physically, but in her mind. To the Healer, it's a high crime. He held Leena responsible for that and that was the reason for revoking her apprenticeship; not hiding your existence."

"What!" Tikid was so startled, she jumped and lashed her tail. *"Leena is no longer a Healer?"*

"Well, yes, she can be, but she will have to find another teacher. The Healer in our village wants nothing to do with her anymore. He says she's not responsible enough."

"Then he knows nothing. Leena is a great Healer. If he cannot see it, then he is the one who is not worthy."

Meeryle was puzzled by the dragon's comment. "How do you know that?"

"Just like I knew about your power. The best way I can describe it is to call it a glow. You both glow, just differently."

"Ah." She didn't want to get into a discussion on Mage or Healer powers. "I don't think this really matters right now. The question is how do we show humans and dragons that we can get along? And more important, how do we tell everyone that we need dragons, because without them, we wouldn't have trees?"

Tikid blew air out of her nose in frustration. The tip of her tail was twitching. She suddenly started to look Meeryle up and down intently.

"What?"

"*I wonder... I am in no way near my adult size, but I believe I may be big enough to carry you.*"

"Me? In the air?" The dragon nodded. Meeryle's heart skipped. To fly like a dragon and see the world from above.... Many people dreamed of flying, she knew. "I would love to fly. But why?"

"*It would show trust and cooperation.*"

Meeryle slowly nodded. "It would be quite a sight. But are you sure you can carry me?"

"*I am not sure of my strength in general, as I am yet far from my adult size, but the only way we will know is by trying.*"

When she stood on all fours, Tikid's shoulders were as high as a huge plowhorse. The dragon looked nothing like a horse, though. Her body was much longer and sinuous, and her movements were a mix of cat and lizard, both quick and graceful. The always-flickering tail was a bit longer than the body and the head put together, and the neck was long, allowing Tikid to look right over her back if she wanted to. Meeryle now knew that her friend's head would get longer and narrower than it was at the moment and that the spikes crowning her head would expand.

Tikid gave the girl an encouraging nod. Meeryle still had her doubts; she knew she was a heavy girl, but she wasn't sure if Tikid realized it. Though sturdy, the dragon's body looked much too thin to her liking. She wished for Leena's expertise.

"Where do I get on?"

Meeryle guessed from the dragon's frown that her friend probably had never carried anything on her back. Tikid confirmed her suspicion by shrugging her wings.

"This looks wrong, Tikid," said Meeryle as she put a hand on the dragon's neck and the other one between the wings. She frowned as she realized that her hands were above her eyes. "You'll have to bend your legs. This is too high for me."

The dragon complied. *"See if you can sit between my wings, but not too far back. Otherwise, you will get hit when I fly."*

Meeryle sighed in resignation and pushed gently on the dragon's back, testing it. Tikid's muscles tensed under her hands. "Ready?"

"Yes."

The human girl jumped and hoisted herself onto the dragon as far as she could. When Meeryle landed on Tikid's back, she was on her stomach, legs dangling. The dragon had braced herself, but not enough. Maybe if Meeryle had taken a ladder and sat down gently, Tikid would have been able to take her. But the combination of the jump and Meeryle's weight was too much. The young dragon's front legs folded underneath her and she crashed to the ground with a grunt. Meeryle was winded for a moment. Tikid struggled to get back up, but her neck and legs were not strong enough. She wiggled her hind legs and tail, but to no avail.

"Get off."

Meeryle found her breath and sat back on her heels. "I told you." Tikid snorted. "There's nothing wrong with not being able to carry me. You even said you weren't fully grown yet, anyway."

As the dragon moved her neck carefully, a few pops made Tikid wince. She spread her right wing and rotated it slowly, repeating the movement with the left wing.

"Are you all right? Nothing sprained?"

Tikid flicked her tail and coiled it around her friend. *"No, I do not think so. This is very frustrating. It was a very good idea."*

"Well, it would have been a better idea with someone a bit... lighter than me."

Tikid blinked. *"What do you mean? You are lighter than me, are you not?"*

"Yes, but for a human my age, I'm too heavy. I like food in general, and sweetcakes in particular. Anyway, let's forget about it for now. If you're going to hurt yourself, I don't think it's worth it," said Meeryle with a pang. The idea of flying was so tempting. "When do you think you'll be big enough to carry me?"

"It will be at least another ten years before I come to maturity. Then I will continue to grow, but at a much slower pace."

Meeryle sighed. Flying would have to wait. "So what can we do? The only thing that comes to mind is to warn the village that dragons might be coming and try to explain the situation." She snorted. "But they didn't listen the first time. It's useless."

"Then I will go."

"Tikid, Navee and Tarkin were scared when they saw you and terrorized when they heard you. They both heard you, too. They just think they are crazy and hearing voices that don't exist. It's brave of you, but I don't think anyone is willing to listen just yet, regardless of who talks."

"I will fly over the village to see what your kin is doing, then report to my kin. This is all I can do

159

for the moment." Her tone was apologetic. "*I will have to leave you here. Do not worry, no harm will come to you.*"

"Be careful. When people are afraid, they do really stupid things."

Tikid nodded and launched herself into the air. As Meeryle watched her friend fly away until she was only a black spot in the sky, the angry words of the villagers she had overheard in the fire echoed in her mind. The image of hunters fully armed with bows, crossbows, and lances sprang into her mind. Her stomach was in knots. For some reason, she was sure she would never see the young dragon again.

CHAPTER TEN

Standing alone in the dragon clearing, Meeryle chewed her lip and pondered her few options. Waiting for the adult dragons could be a waste of time, as the creatures might not be quick decision-makers. She also didn't cherish the idea of sitting alone in the middle of the forest. The only thing she could do was to go back to the village. Her stomach growled, reminding her she hadn't eaten in over a day. While the berries had quenched her thirst in a remarkable way, they hadn't sated her appetite. Nor had she brought any with her. Home and food were sounding better and better.

With a chuckle, the plump girl got stiffly and slowly to her feet. She could always trust her stomach to steer her in a reasonable direction. If only her stomach also knew the direction to the village....

She was lost, hungry, thirsty, and tired. The effort of getting up took its toll: the trees suddenly became all blurry and the ground didn't feel stable anymore. Unable to keep her balance, Meeryle once again fell to the ground.

She blinked to clear her sight and realized that nothing was wrong with the forest. Exhaustion had finally caught up with her. Meeryle tallied up everything that had happened in less than a day: the "excitement" of facing the entire village, her escape and flight through the forest during the night, the crossing of the rift, and the Healing, as well as the sensory assault of so many dragons.

"Let's not forget using this stupid gift of mine." Speaking aloud cleared the last of the muddle. Meeryle knew she had to get rest and food. Rest was the only thing she could provide for herself now. She wasn't sure how long she had slept on her way in the forest, but it hadn't been enough.

A wet nose on her hand made her yelp in surprise. She met Suqi's black eyes with pleasure. "You're up! Too bad you didn't come a few minutes ago, you'd have met Tikid." Something occurred to her. "You know, now that I think of it, you're always gone when dragons arrive. Could it be that you don't like dragons?" The fox projected feelings of mockery. Meeryle could swear the little animal had lifted an eyebrow. "Let's say you're afraid of dragons, then." Suqi was now offended. "Well, what else am I supposed to think? That you're a dragon in disguise and that Tikid or the other Greens might recognize you?" The fox rolled her eyes. "Ah, forget it. Since you're here, you might help me find a place to sleep."

Under her pet's watchful eye, Meeryle once again got carefully to her feet. The dizziness was still threatening her balance. She surveyed the clearing, not wanting to sleep in the open. She was still in the forest, dragon clearing or not. The one place she deemed safe would be an actual dragon dwelling.

Where were the dragons' shelters? With nothing which looked like a house in sight, Meeryle didn't know where to start. Just as despair brought tears to her eyes, Suqi brushed lightly against her leg. The girl gulped and blinked away the unwanted tears. She still had a friend, albeit one even stranger than a

162

dragon. Reassured for the moment, she took in a deep breath and thought. The only possible things that could be dwellings in the vast clearing were the mounds. The closest one was not very big, barely taller than her and a few feet in length, and was covered with grass and small white flowers. She stopped and pulled her tangled hair, doubting her first instinct. This couldn't possibly be a dwelling. Suqi barked, looking over her shoulder, beckoning Meeryle to follow. She went around the mound and found what could only be an entrance. It reminded Meeryle of a giant rabbit hole, and not a very welcoming one at that. Meeryle hesitated. How could she possibly fit in there? She was big and the hole was small. Discouraged, the girl resigned herself to sleep in the open. Annoyed, Suqi barked again and ran into the mound. Meeryle wasn't sure if the fox was able to judge the difference in size. Exhaustion set in. At this point, she didn't care if she looked like an idiot crawling inside a burrow. She resolutely went down on all fours, shoulders stooping, and followed the fox.

The entrance was tunnel-like and narrow; she had to squeeze her arms and shoulders as tightly as she could against her body, thus blocking any light coming in through the tunnel. "I guess dragons don't need windows," Meeryle muttered. Her words didn't carry; the sound of her voice was absorbed by the walls. Meeryle peered in the darkness, trying to make out the contents of the dwelling. Then again, the mound she was exploring might not even be a house; it could be a storage room... if dragons had anything to store.

It didn't matter. The inside was dark, but warm and cozy. Kneeling on the ground, she moved to the side to allow a bit of daylight in, and felt her way to the end. Her hand almost immediately met the wall, which felt the same as the ground: beaten earth. Not the most comfortable place to sleep, but it was safe. Suqi had settled on the ground, rolled up in a ball. Following her example, Meeryle curled up, her back touching the wall, and fell asleep, lulled by the regular breathing of the animal.

***

A gentle yet insistent shake woke her. Meeryle blinked, slowly remembering where she was. She felt around for Suqi, but the fox had already pulled her disappearing act. Meeryle was now used to the dimness of the dwelling, but she still couldn't make anything out. Something was blocking the entrance.

"Are you awake?"

Meeryle jumped to a sitting position, startling the dragon who had woken her. She peered at it, but the only thing she could make out was its general shape. She was surprised to see that it was much smaller than Tikid.

"Yes, yes, I'm awake. But I can't see you, so if you don't mind, let's get out of here."

She sensed its agreement and it turned deftly, almost running out of the mound. Meeryle followed on all fours at a much slower pace. She blinked in the bright light and stretched. She had slept soundly, although probably not too long, at least according to the bit of sunlight she could make through the trees. She was sure the sun hadn't moved. Her stomach grumbled, but she still wasn't thirsty. Should she try to find more of the berries?

Something poked her leg, interrupting her musing. The little dragon was still there. Now that she could see it clearly, she was shocked by its small size; it barely came to her shoulder while sitting on its haunches.

"You are the human, are you not?" Meeryle smiled at the eager tone. The dragon was a very young one. *"They said to watch for you, just in case you needed something, but to be careful because you could not hear us unless we touched you. I am Lir. What is your name?"*

Meeryle laughed. "I'm Meeryle."

"You are Tikid's friend, are you not? She is gone."

"What?"

"Enough, Lir. I will speak with Meeryle now."

Lir made a face that looked so much like a pout Meeryle had to stifle a giggle. The little dragon turned and left with as much dignity as it could muster, but its diminutive size kept it from being taken seriously. Young ones were the same everywhere.

Shaking her head, Meeryle turned to the dragon who had sent Lir away. This one was bigger, a head higher than the human girl. It walked closer to Meeryle, sat in front of her and held out its three-digit paw. Meeryle examined the "hand." For its smallness, it still had extremely sharp talons. The digits were shorter and stubbier than Tikid's, but they already held the promise of becoming the long and large paws she had seen on Korad.

Meeryle took the extended "hand" in her own.

165

"I am sorry for Lir. It is the youngest one of us and it does not know when it is rude. I am Tar. We had to wake you and Lir was there before we could stop it. We need your help."

Fascinated, Meeryle looked around at a dozen young dragons staring intently at her. The smaller one was Lir, and Tar, the bigger one by far. In both instances, she had not been able to identify the sex of the dragon speaking to her. Like most youths, their voices were rather neutral. Yet she found it odd that Tar would refer to Lir as an "it." "Tar, why do you say "it" when you talk about Lir?"

Tar cocked its head to the side, puzzled. *"Because Lir is too young to choose. We all are."*

"Choose what?" The young one's answer was even more cryptic than Tikid's.

"If we are to be ids or ads."

Meeryle stood wide-eyed. "And what might that be?"

The dragon's red eyes stared back at her, confused. *"What is what?"*

"An id or an ad."

The creature burst out in laughter. Unlike the adults' laugh, it didn't resonate in her bones, but tingled in her ears. Soon, all the youngsters were laughing, filling the clearing with palpable amusement. Meeryle sighed. "Well, I can see this is something all dragons know for sure, but don't forget I'm not a dragon."

"Obviously," piped a new voice.

"Vir, she is right. I was wrong to laugh. I am sure humans have everyday things we would find strange," interrupted Tar. It was trying very hard to

be mature, but its mouth was deformed from trying to bite back laughter.

"Well, why don't you tell me, then? That way you can get rid of your giggles, hmm?"

Tar nodded eagerly. *"An ad is a male and an id is a female. How do you call yourself? An eele?"*

"No, I call myself a girl. And my opposite would be a boy. Once we get older, then we become men and women."

Her answer created a stir among the dragons. Meeryle's mind filled with the young ones' overlapping questions, objections, and comments. The noise became too loud for the girl and she broke contact with Tar. She sighed with relief at the sudden quiet. As with children, the young dragons thought that louder was better. "I pity anyone who can't block out dragon voices," she mumbled, scratching her head.

In doing so, she realized her hair was filled with earth from the mound. She shook her head and tried to brush the dirt out with her fingers, but the tight curls were tangled and would not relinquish their hold on the dirt.

Tar grabbed her ankle, startling her. *"You let go. I have been speaking, but you did not hear,"* it said, annoyed.

"I'm sorry, but everyone was speaking at once. Let's forget about ids and ads, all right? Now, let's get back to why you needed to wake me. Lir said Tikid was gone. But I knew that."

"Yes, she left and is now in trouble." The dragon was suddenly very solemn. *"We heard her call for help, but we cannot call to anyone yet. We*

are not strong enough. And we cannot fly yet. Can you help her?"

Panic twisted Meeryle's stomach. What could have happened to Tikid? She imagined only the direst situation could make the dragon call out for help. As the image of hunters carrying a severed dragon head crossed her mind, Meeryle swallowed bile. What could she do? She was lost and tired, alone, without any resources; she didn't know where Tikid was and what had happened to her. The hopeful look on Tar's face reminded Meeryle that these youngsters were relying on her. She just couldn't let them see her fear for Tikid, so she forced the panic away. "I will try to help in any way I can. But why can't you fly?"

"We are fledglings. We remain so until our wings are big enough, then we choose how we will come of age."

Meeryle had to admit the wings weren't as well-proportioned as Tikid's. Otherwise, the fledglings were miniature replicas of her friend, even if the smallest ones were a bit on the chubby side. She steered the discussion on the subject at hand. "Right. What happened to Tikid?"

"We are not sure. We heard her cry for help, but since we cannot ask questions back, we do not know exactly what happened to her. The only reason I think she would ask for help is because she is hurt." The young dragon's voice was heartrending. *"I am afraid she sounded so scared that her life might be in danger."*

"But how? What could possibly happen to her?" Meeryle started to feel dizzy again. The hunter image came back with more details. But if that were the case, her friend couldn't have called for help. Meeryle reminded herself that nothing could harm Tikid when she was in the sky and that she could blend in the forest and become invisible. Then she remembered the archers, and that Leena had bragged that her stepmother was the most skilled, hitting a flying bird at a hundred paces. A dragon was a much easier target than a bird. Could the villagers really have already started their hunt and made Tikid their first victim? The young dragon meant no harm, quite the opposite.

She took in a deep breath and calmed down. "Do you know from which direction her call came?"

"That way." Tar pointed its muzzle towards the west, from where Meeryle had come. *"We are sure she is that way, but we do not know how far. Can you help?"*

"Of course. Tikid is my friend. But you are not coming with me, right?"

Tar gave her an affronted look. *"We know better than to leave the clearing. Fledglings never leave the grounds until they come of age."*

Meeryle bit her lips to hide her smile. "I don't doubt you, I just wanted to make sure. Thank you for counting on me."

Tar let go of Meeryle's ankle. Meeryle left the clearing, feeling the youngsters' eyes on her back.

As soon as the trees hid her, Meeryle stopped. The panic she had successfully hidden from the young dragons suddenly overwhelmed her. She couldn't breathe anymore and her ears were filled with a rushing sound. Her hands were shaking.

"Tikid, how can I possibly help you?"

The wind blew her hair in her face. She heard briefly the rasp and groan signature of air. Meeryle noticed her headache was gone and no longer hindering her Mage-sense. The panic subsided as Meeryle clenched determined fists. She could do this. When she really thought about it, the reason why all of this happened in the first place was because of her. She hadn't wanted to share the dragon with anyone. Instead, she had wanted to live the adventure by herself, and now, not only had she cost Leena her apprenticeship, she might have even caused the death of her dragon friend. She had to fix it all, somehow.

Meeryle recalled bitterly how everyone, whether they were her age or adults, thought her spineless because she walked away from confrontations. She had never told anyone about the churning anger that would appear in the pit of her stomach when people would scoff at her and mock her weight. The comments had enraged her at times, and she had redirected the feelings into more and more cakes, eating them one after the other, her hunger seemingly endless. Meeryle was starting to wonder if the hunger and the tears hadn't been a safeguard she had unconsciously erected against her Mage-gift. Right now, she was past being hungry. The only thing she felt was anger: at herself, at the villagers, at everything in general. Everything had once again taken on an orange tinge. She was not spineless. She would accept her responsibilities.

Her determination smothered the anger. She would prove to everyone-and herself-that she knew what she was doing. The first step was to find Tikid and help her. Then apologize for putting her in peril in the first place.

Meeryle was somehow sure that the humans had harmed the dragon. If Tikid hadn't gone back toward the village, nothing would have happened to her. Everything was really her fault.

Meeryle closed her eyes. The anger was getting in the way of her trance. As if summoned by magic-Meeryle smiled at the thought-Suqi was suddenly there, projecting soothing feelings and ... strength? As strange as it sounded, Meeryle, though she was still hungry, no longer felt drained. Since she hadn't known she was drained (of what?) in the first place, it made the feeling stranger yet. She gave the fox a thoughtful look. Now that she was rested, her questions came back. The fox always seemed to appear when she needed her the most, yet she avoided the dragons. Suqi had made it clear the big creatures didn't scare her-and that was the crux of the problem. Meeryle could feel the fox's emotions. Suqi obviously wasn't an ordinary animal. Then what was she? The term "guardian" came to mind; Meeryle wasn't sure if she would have made it this far without Suqi's help. She even had Healing abilities, a fact that would interest Leena to no end-if she ever got to speak with her again.

The fox cut short Meeryle's thoughts by barking and running into the forest, leaving the girl on her own. Meeryle shook her head, promising herself she'd figure out the Suqi enigma later, and set to seeking Tikid with her gift.

A few minutes later, she heard the breathing sounds of air. She concentrated her efforts towards the west and was rewarded by the faint sound of a dragon wing flapping. Meeryle frowned; it did not sound like a dragon taking flight or landing.

She gulped as she looked at the way ahead of her. The trees formed an impregnable wall in front of her. She was sure they had moved closer together since she had arrived. She couldn't possibly have made her way through there! The branches were taunting her to brave their foliage.

"You're only trees. Now move out of my way."

The girl started boldly forward, daring the trees to hinder her. If she hadn't been afraid of tripping, Meeryle would have walked with her eyes closed. She did not relish having to cross the forest again. The sun still lit the treacherous trees, showing roots waiting to grab her ankles and trip her. She ignored them, ignored the laughter of the leaves moving with the breeze.

Eventually, Meeryle stopped hearing the mocking sounds of the forest. She came to admit to herself that she had probably imagined it. Still, she wasn't ready to completely give up her impression. Tikid spoke with the stupid trees, didn't she?

Meeryle had to concentrate on finding her friend. "Dumb trees. Can't they help instead of making fun of me?" The girl shook her head and focused on her task. Her progress was very slow, as she stopped often to listen for Tikid. She heard another strange wing flapping, grunts, and suddenly, a voice. The sound rooted her on the spot. She was sure it came from the same area as Tikid.

Panic gripped her. She was right: her friend had been hurt by someone and that person was with her. She did something she not only had never done, but didn't know she could do: Meeryle anchored her

172

Mage-sense in that voice. It was the oddest feeling: she felt tied to that particular spot. She now knew where she was going and set out running. Thanks to the magical tie to the voice, she knew exactly where the voice was, even if she didn't hear what it said. If she went in the wrong direction, the tie snapped at her until she was going the right way.

Meeryle felt as if she had wings on her feet. She avoided every rock, root, branch, and hole in her way. No twigs caught her hair or clothes, no bush slowed her down. Jumping stumps like never before, she was amazed until she heard the faint murmur of earth. Smiling, she sped up. Air was guiding her and earth was helping her. The Mage-gift was indeed useful.

When she arrived at the rift, she refused to let the fallen tree daunt her. Since air had guided her, she imagined earth could do the same. She took the time to examine the great trunk with the Earth sense. Some patches seemed to glow slightly with a brown light. She climbed on the trunk and stood, facing ahead, and asked: "Well, Suqi, what do you think? Can I do this?" She felt encouragement coming from the animal. "Well, here goes!" She closed her eyes and took in a deep breath, relaxing her muscles as much as she could, while listening to Earth. When she opened her eyes, a path was glowing for her to follow. With air and earth whispering to her, Meeryle ran across the rift.

The journey, so long and painful the first time, barely lasted minutes on the way back. Once on the other side, without thinking, she jumped down. Air wrapped around her and dropped her rather heavily on the ground. Meeryle didn't even pause to think about what she had just accomplished. The tie to the voice kept tugging at her urgently.

She broke into a run, zigzagging between trees and bushes. The sun was slowly setting in front of her and soon it would be dark. The tug of the tie to the voice was getting more and more insistent. She could only guess it meant she was getting closer.

Finally, just before the sun set completely, Meeryle burst into a clearing. She cried out and stopped her in her tracks, heart in her mouth. She had found Tikid. The dragon was lying on the ground, head on her front legs, her left wing spread wide. Blood was oozing down the wing. Someone was kneeling before the wing, back turned to Meeryle.

"Leave her be!" yelled Meeryle, her anger smoldering and quickly turning to rage. She was ready to rip this person to shreds. Seeing everything orange, Meeryle started to run, teeth bared, fists tight. She was even feeling the rumble of a growl in her throat.

Her enraged charge was cut short when the person who jumped and faced her turned out to be Leena. Meeryle stopped and gaped at the tall girl's mixed expression. She seemed taken aback by the aggressive attitude, then surprised and happy when she realized who had been running towards her. But most of all, Leena was extremely sad.

"Meeryle! Tikid was shot by an arrow. Her wing is ruined and...." She burst in tears. "Meeryle, I don't think she can be Healed."

CHAPTER ELEVEN

Meeryle was stunned. She wasn't sure what shocked her the most: Leena's presence or Tikid's wound. She remained motionless, eyes going from the dragon to the girl. They were both staring back at her, Leena drying her tears and Tikid's ruby eyes full of sorrow. Meeryle gulped down her own tears and clenched her fists. Leena had let her down and allowed her to go into the forest on her own. After all Meeryle had been through by herself, how could Leena be there?

Because she cared. She cared about her and she cared about Tikid. Friendship took over; Meeryle ran and embraced Leena in a tight hug. This time, Meeryle didn't hold her tears back.

Leena squeezed her and hiccupped. "I'm so glad you're here." She stepped back and turned towards Tikid. "I heard her calling me. And I came and... and...." She hid her face in her hands and turned away, sobbing.

Meeryle knelt by Tikid's head. The dragon closed her eyes and leaned her head on the girl's lap. "*I hurt. I have never felt anything like this before.*" Meeryle looked at the wing. Even in the failing light, it looked bad. "*But you came, with Leena. You both came when I called.*" She closed her eyes and sighed.

"Of course we came. I was sleeping in one of the mounds in that clearing when the youngsters woke me. They had heard your call."

Tikid's eyes snapped open. *"They did? They could hear me this far?"*

"Is that strange?"

"Well... I am not sure. Leena heard me, but I think she was close by. But the fledglings...." The dragon shifted her head so she looked in Meeryle's eyes. *"I did not know our voices could carry this far."*

"Unless... Tar said you sounded like your life was in danger. Maybe the need gave you more strength."

"Maybe. I am glad they told you to come to me. I will have to thank them." Tikid closed her eyes again. Through the touch, Meeryle could feel some of her pain, as well as panic. The dragon had never been in such a situation. Only the presence of her friends kept her from going mad with pain and fear.

"She's in a lot of pain." Leena sniffed and wiped her nose with the back of her hand.

Meeryle smiled. "I know. And I hope you'll wash that hand before you try to dress her wound." Leena stared at her, taken aback. "You just wiped your nose with it."

Leena looked at her hand, then at Meeryle, then at her hand again. Her mouth twisted with disgust and she rubbed her hand against her tunic. When Leena looked at Meeryle, both girls burst out in a nervous laugh.

"You're right. I'm not completely myself. Truth is, I don't know what to do. I've never seen a wound like this one and I just don't know enough about dragon wings." She shrugged helplessly and knelt beside Meeryle and Tikid.

The dragon opened her eyes to look at her friend and closed them again. "*I hurt, but I am sleepy. I feel so strange.*"

"You feel sleepy because I used a bit of my gift to calm you down. You need to stay still. If you want, I can try to make you sleep."

"*Yes.*" The voice in Meeryle's mind sounded just like Lir's for a second. The girl's throat tightened. Tikid was terrified. She was so helpless, lying on the ground like this.

"All right. Here I go." Leena put both hands on the dragon's shoulder and closed her eyes. Meeryle looked intently. This was the first time she ever saw Leena Heal. At first, nothing happened. Then Meeryle heard something that almost sounded like earth. It hummed, getting louder until all the sound moved into Leena's hands. The sound stopped abruptly and Tikid's head became much heavier on Meeryle's lap.

"She's asleep." Leena sighed with relief. "I wasn't sure if it would work. I've done this on people before, but never on something as big as a dragon. I wasn't sure if I would have enough strength."

"Well, I didn't see anything, but I heard you. It was like... a hum."

Leena nodded. "I guess you could say it's the sound that life makes. I also feel something like a vibration."

The girls gazed upon their sleeping friend in silence. Meeryle realized that now that she had found her gift, however unwanted it was, she couldn't imagine life without it. The rasp of air had become a reassuring background noise; her gift had also allowed her and Leena to become even closer,

177

and was now something they could share. She had heard the hum of... whatever that was through Leena; maybe Leena could hear one of the elements through Meeryle when the time came.

Pain in Meeryle's legs interrupted her thoughts. She broke the silence when she realized her legs had started to fall asleep. "Help me with her head so I can move. My legs hurt."

Leena grabbed Tikid's chin with one hand and wiggled her other hand closer to her throat. "Be quick. I'm afraid I might choke her like this, but I can't grab one of the spikes on her head: there's no grip there." Meeryle nodded. "On three. One, two, three." Leena lifted the dragon's head and Meeryle dragged herself to the right. Leena struggled to put down her friend's head as slowly as possible, but Meeryle knew how heavy it was. She went to the rescue and placed her hands beside Leena's. A few seconds later, they managed to rest Tikid's head softly on the ground.

The girls moved away from the sleeping dragon. Leena settled on a boulder and Meeryle stood, shaking her legs. When she could feel them again properly, she sat by Leena.

"You think she'll be all right?"

"For now." Leena bit her lip. "I'll think of something for her."

"Well, in the meantime, let's start at the beginning. What are you doing here? I thought you were going to wait for the council to throw you out of the village."

"You... You got me thinking."

"Wait. It's pretty dark and I'm getting cold. And I'm thirsty. Let's start a fire first, then you can tell me all about it."

Leena handed Meeryle her gourd. "Here, I have plenty."

Her thirst quenched-the berries had be effective, but water was so much better-Meeryle quickly gathered branches and leaves with her friend's help. For the first time in her life, she didn't care about feeling hungry, about being less than clean. Tikid was much more important. While she was relieved that the dragon's life wasn't in danger, she nevertheless couldn't stop worrying about her friend's safety. Would the villagers find them? A fire would be a beacon, wouldn't it?

Leena shrugged when Meeryle shared her concern. "Yes and no. The trees are thick around us and I had Tikid to guide me. They don't, so they have to search quite a bit. Either way, we need the heat and the light."

By the time they had picked up a respectable pile, full darkness was upon them. Meeryle closed her eyes and coaxed the wood to take fire. They soon had a small blaze reflecting on Tikid's scales, making her look unreal. They settled down as comfortably as possible close to the fire.

"So," started Meeryle. "How did you get here?"

"Well, about a candlemark after you left, I decided to go with you. But as soon as I stepped out the window, I heard voices, so I had to hide. It turned out to be the hunters, getting ready to chase dragons." She wrinkled her nose in scorn. "They acted brave and all, but I'm sure that deep down, they were afraid."

"What makes you say that?" interrupted Meeryle.

Leena took her time in replying. "The answer to that is a bit long."

"We're not going anywhere."

"True. Remember I told you I wanted the Mage-gift?" Meeryle nodded. "I wanted it because I thought I had it: I was hearing something only I could hear. So I researched it and found books on the Mage-gift. In it, they say that each element makes a specific sound and they give the exercises needed to hone the skill."

"So that's how you knew which exercise I was supposed to do. But I thought you said they were Healing-gift things."

"They partly were. Let me finish. The one thing in the books that bugged me was that it said that the Mage-gift was latent until puberty. So that means, no hearing the elements, no playing with them." She forestalled Meeryle's objection with a raised hand. "I told you that you're an exception. You are, trust me. In my case, I had been hearing the noise since I was six years old. I can even remember when it started: it was when my cat died. She was old and very sick and I was holding her, willing her to get better. I heard this hum and then it stopped. That's when the cat died. Since that day, I've been able to hear that hum when I concentrate.

"So here I was, showing what I thought was a Mage-gift, only it couldn't be that. I tried the exercises and I heard nothing at all. Eventually, the Healer found me trying to hear water and explained that I had the Healing-gift. It can manifest itself at any time. I learned to listen to what's called the hum

180

of life. As soon as I touch someone, I know if their hum is normal or not. That's how I know how bad a sickness or an injury is, and technically, how much power I need to use to fix it.

"Anyway. When I got you practicing, it got me thinking that I could maybe do the same as you and start listening to the hum, but while not touching anything, by listening at a distance. I'd never tried it, but since it worked for you, why not for me, right? So I tried it last night. Meeryle, it worked!"

"How? How did you know they were scared?"

"Well, when people are hurt, they're usually afraid. A Healer has to calm them down first and reassure them. It helps for the Healing. So I know how someone scared feels like; I've touched enough of them." Meeryle nodded encouragingly. "First, the heart beats a certain way and I guess the brain does something too. I'm sorry I can't explain it better; I'm not great with explaining theory. Fear somehow affects the hum in a very specific way. And let me tell you, the mighty hunters were extremely affected last night. I don't think I've ever heard the hum of fear so loudly before!" She giggled nervously. "I thought it was odd that they would be so scared, so I followed them. They were going house to house, collecting people and weapons for the hunt."

"They never saw you?"

"No, why would they look behind? Besides, they were making so much noise, they wouldn't have heard me if they tried. Eventually, they had gathered everyone who wanted to join, including Jetyaa." Meeryle winced at the mention of the name. Jetyaa was Leena's stepmother, the most skilled archer of the village, the one who could hit flying birds. She

181

was one of the village's most valuable hunters. "She was leading the group and my father was at the rear. Actually, I was at the rear." They chuckled. "It was dawn when they finally set out. I don't even know how they figured out which direction to go. Maybe they coaxed it out of Navee or Tarkin. They were very slow and trying to be quiet, so it took them a while to get anywhere, really. I guess quite a few candlemarks had gone by, because it was full daylight when Tikid came by." She paused and shook her head. "Meeryle, it was the worst thing I've ever seen. I mean, what they knew about the dragon, they had heard from Navee and your brother. When they actually saw her, I swear, they were terrified. I heard the fear so loudly, it was almost a scream. I'm sure a few wet themselves. Eventually, they all screamed and ran everywhere. Some even ran into trees and knocked themselves senseless!"

"What happened next, Leena?" asked Meeryle softly.

"I saw Jetyaa standing there, rooted to her spot, staring at Tikid. She was so white, I thought she was going to faint. Then she let fly an arrow. Tikid screamed so loudly, I think it drove Jetyaa over the edge. I know it felt like my heart had been wrenched out. She ran away, screaming like a madwoman that the demon from her dreams was finally dead. At that point, everyone was gone but me. So I listened for Tikid's hum and found her." The last was a whisper.

"Leena, this wasn't your fault. I can't even say it was anybody's fault. Tikid had come back to check on the village. I guess she just happened to be where she shouldn't have been."

The girls were silent. The popping of the fire startled them.

Leena snorted. "Look at us. We're jumping at shadows." She stared ahead, not really seeing anything. "Meeryle, what do you think is going to happen?"

"I don't know. I met with the dragons." Leena gave her a startled look. "Believe me, I like younger dragons better. They're huge! And a lot more scary looking than Tikid."

"But how did you find them?" interrupted Leena.

"With Suqi's help...."

"Where is she, anyway?"

"Well, I'm starting to think Suqi's not a normal fox."

Leena snorted. "You figured that out just now? The black and white fur is a sure indication she would be part of a coat if she hadn't been your pet, but the fact that she actually came into the village to follow you is downright extraordinary. Adult wild animals don't become pets overnight, you know."

"Leena, I can sense feelings from her. Just like with Tikid. Only when I touch her, I hear no words."

Leena frowned in concentration. "The only thing I can think for now is that Suqi is somehow linked to your gift."

"Speaking of gift, Suqi has one of her own: she can Heal." Leena's eyes opened wide. "I hurt myself badly crossing that rift Tikid told us about. She basically licked my wounds until they were Healed."

Leena frowned. "I've never heard of animal Healers."

183

"Well, you'll have to figure it out later. She also guided me and... I was able to find the dragons thanks to my gift." Leena's eyebrows went up. "It turns out I can listen for things with air just like I can with fire. It took me all night and I got nice scratches and a few bumps on my head, but I found them. Surprisingly enough, they took me seriously right away. They all flew off somewhere to meet with other Green dragons and decide what to do. We were afraid that they would get angry enough to be violent, so Tikid decided to see if our 'hunters' were on their way. You know the rest."

They looked bleakly at each other. Despair made its way into Meeryle's heart. Jetyaa had held her ground and done what any hunter would do; as a result, any hope of peace between the two races now seemed even more remote than ever. Once again, Meeryle wondered if things would be different if she had shared knowledge of the dragon much earlier with the villagers. Maybe the Healer would have been an ally instead and Leena would still be his apprentice. Then maybe Jetyaa wouldn't have seen Tikid as a demon to be destroyed at all cost.

Leena interrupted her descent into hopelessness. "All right. I think I've calmed down enough to be able to take a look at Tikid's wing. Come on." She got up and went to kneel beside the sleeping dragon.

Meeryle followed her. She wasn't sure where to place herself and hovered. "Do you want me to do anything?"

Leena frowned, thinking fast. "Well, I'm not sure. To be honest with you, I don't really know how to proceed. It's not like I ever went over the procedures for the treatment of a wounded wing with the Healer. Sit by me and listen in. Maybe you'll hear something differently than me." When she looked at Meeryle, Leena's eyes were wide with fear. "Help me in any way you can, Meeryle. I am so lost." Her statement shocked the plump girl. She had never heard her friend say anything of the sort. Leena never admitted helplessness. The young dragon must mean a lot more to her than she ever showed.

"You'll do fine," said Meeryle earnestly. "Remember when little Hamon hurt his ankle? You managed to fix him up even though the Healer was away and now he can run better than any other boy his age. I have no idea what you did then, but I remember the Healer saying he had never used that technique before. If anyone can do anything for Tikid, it's you."

Leena smiled, somewhat reassured. "All right. First, I need to wake her up. I don't know enough about dragon anatomy and I need her to tell me if I'm wrong or right."

Meeryle sat cross-legged beside Tikid, close to Leena. She put her left hand on the dragon's neck and her right on Leena's shoulder. The tall girl nodded and put both hands on Tikid's body. Meeryle watched her friend intently. Once again, she heard the hum build and disappear.

Tikid blinked. She turned her head back and stared at the two girls, as if she were unsure who they were. "*What?*"

"Tikid, it's us, Leena and Meeryle. You were hurt and we're going to help you."

The dragon blinked again and her eyes came into focus. "*Yes. My mind feels... foggy.*"

"That's because I forced you to sleep. You needed it, remember?"

Tikid carefully nodded. "*I was hurting. I still am.*" She twisted her neck even further to look at her injured wing. "*Something hit me out of the sky. I fell.*"

"Yes. You managed to land without breaking anything and you called for help. Now, I will see what I can do to Heal your wing, but I need your help because I don't know a thing about dragon wings."

The dragon chuckled. "*You mean to say none of your peers ever hurt one of their wings before?*"

Meeryle smiled. "Well, Healer Leena, it would seem your patient hasn't broken her sense of humor in her fall!" Leena smiled back. The dragon's comment had given her back her full confidence.

"Tikid, I am going to take a 'look' at your injury. You shouldn't feel anything, but if for some reason you do or you feel uncomfortable, tell me." The dragon nodded in assent and Leena closed her eyes. Meeryle did the same and went immediately into her listening trance. She heard the hum instantly. Since she was touching Leena, she also felt the vibration her friend had described. It still reminded Meeryle of earth, but she thought she heard a strange rustling. The groan of air made itself heard; however, it was so brief, she wasn't sure she heard it at all. She shook her head slightly and concentrated on the hum and her friend.

Leena was somehow moving the hum around. It started on the dragon's shoulder, where the wing began, and slowly made its way around the wing. The closer Leena got to the injury, the stranger the

186

hum became, until it was so discordant, Meeryle winced and opened her eyes.

Unconsciously, even with her eyes closed, she had moved her head to follow the hum. When Meeryle opened her eyes, her line of sight was directly on the wound. The girls were placed in such a way that they weren't blocking the fire at all, allowing the flames to glow brightly on Tikid's injury. Meeryle gulped. She had only seen a bloody mess when she had burst into the clearing. She was now getting a clear view and it was not pretty. The dragon's wing had four sections separated by fine bones that started on the upper part of the wing and fanned out to end with a small claw. The membrane of the wing stretched between the fingerlike appendages. The arrow had pierced the second section, leaving the leathery membrane in shreds. Meeryle could see the glint of bone on one side. She was thankful for the night and the blood, both of which partly hid the wound.

Leena was still probing the wing, frowning deeply. After what seemed like an eternity, she opened her eyes and clasped her hands in front of her. Meeryle removed her hand from the tall girl's shoulder, but left the other one on Tikid. She wanted to hear the dragon.

"Tikid, the damage is restricted to only a part of your wing. The bones aren't broken; however, the membrane is torn extensively in that part." She gulped. "How would you treat such an injury amongst yourselves?"

"*We would not*," answered Tikid, clearly puzzled. "*Our injuries are usually broken limbs or torn muscles, easily healed by infusing ourselves with the essence of the forest. I have already tried it, but I was only able to take care of the torn ligaments in my legs. My wing remained as it was. I have never heard of a dragon wounded as I am."*

Leena took in a deep breath. "Well, I can only guess, but I think you cannot heal your wing because pieces of it are missing. They were ripped out, Tikid. I can sew what's left together, but that's all I can do."

Meeryle could not believe her ears. "But you can use your gift! Come on, you've Healed things before."

"Never like this, Meeryle. Everything was always there; all I had to do was to meld the pieces together. Well, a little bit. I've never done a complete Healing. I've told you before, it could kill me. You Heal part of the wound and the body takes care of the remainder naturally with rest. In this case, it wouldn't work." Tears were forming in Leena's eyes.

Meeryle was so distraught that she couldn't find any meaning in Leena's words. All she could think was that the beautiful wing had to be fixed. Nothing else was possible. Tikid had to fly; she had to grow and carry Meeryle in the sky. Leena was going to fix it, no matter what. "Why can't you do this? Why can't you make Tikid's wing whole?" demanded Meeryle angrily.

"Because... because I would have to force the body to create the missing pieces."

"Do it then!"

"I can't, Meeryle, I can't! I'm not strong enough. I don't even know if the Healer would be."

"Leena, you cannot do anything besides... stitching the wing," stated Tikid softly. *"Are you sure?"*

"Yes," whispered Leena. The fire lit the tears on her cheeks. The dragon hiccupped in a familiar way. Meeryle blinked and tears ran down her cheeks when she realized Tikid was crying too.

"Then I will never be able to fly again."

CHAPTER TWELVE

Tikid's statement broke Meeryle's heart. She could not think of anything to console her friend. What can anyone say in such a situation? Leena stared at the ground, looking just as miserable.

Dragons could walk, but only for short distances. Even then, they relied on their wings for balance. Meeryle had two arms and two legs; losing the use of one of them would be devastating. She could well imagine the pain of losing the freedom to do the things she took for granted. However, it felt worse for Tikid. To Meeryle, flight was the symbol of freedom; flying creatures could go anywhere and protect themselves by taking to the air. Tikid was going to lose all that if she didn't do something.

"That's just wrong," blurted Meeryle. "We can't allow that!"

"You talk as if you had a say in it," replied Leena. "You don't, Meeryle. That's the way it is."

Leena's attitude bothered Meeryle. She couldn't understand her resignation in the situation. "You're talking nonsense. Of course I have a say in it, and so do you. You're a Healer, Leena. Stop feeling sorry for yourself and do something already."

Leena glared at her, fists tight, teeth clenched. She got up and loomed over Meeryle. "Feeling sorry for myself, am I? And who do you think you are to even talk to me like that? You're the reason why we're here in the first place, need I remind you?"

Meeryle cringed under the assault, but she did not relent. She stood to face Leena, anger slowly stirring. "So get over it! You didn't have to go along with it and you know it. Don't dump it all on me. You made decisions and you have to accept them! You always tell me that you have to see to your duties. Well, there's one right here. Someone needs care and it's your duty to provide that care. You're just giving excuses. What's your problem?" Meeryle was starting to see everything with an orange glow.

The glow intensified as Leena shouted back. "My problem? How about yours? Why can't you accept that things can't always go your way?"

A resonant roar interrupted them. Tikid was sitting on her haunches, left wing sagging miserably, and glaring at the both of them. Meeryle didn't have to touch her to know what the dragon was saying: she radiated disapproval. Leena confirmed it with her answer to Tikid. "I'm sorry. You're right. We'll stop."

The girls looked at each other with guilt. They had been so involved with their own problems that they had forgotten Tikid. Meeryle quickly ran to the dragon and embraced her awkwardly, mindful of her wounded wing. "I'm sorry too. And I think I should apologize to you too, Leena. I don't know what came over me."

"Apology not only accepted, but also offered on my side. I think we're all just too tired. Fatigue is the worst thing for tempers. Plus I think it's safe to say we've had a rough day."

Tikid snorted. Meeryle broke her embrace and sat beside her, grabbing the tip of the dragon's tail in her hands. "*That tickles*," said Tikid with a deep and vibrant giggle.

"Sorry, but it's the only thing I think I can touch without hurting you. Anywhere else and I'm afraid I'm going to make you move your wing in a bad way."

"All right," said Leena, sitting down. "Let's be calm about this. But first, can you do anything about the fire, Meeryle? It's getting awfully dark here."

"Not a problem." She closed her eyes and willed the fire to burn brighter. "We're going to have to add wood. I can't make it burn like this for a long time with so little fuel left."

Leena got up and added the few dead branches left from their earlier foray. Once settled back down, they stayed silent for a while, not knowing where to start. Leena broke the silence hesitantly. "Meeryle, remember when you got angry back in the barn?" Meeryle nodded, frowning. "Your eyes turned orange all of a sudden."

"Yes, so?"

"I'm not sure because it's dark, but just now, they were orange again."

Meeryle pursed her lips. Unease stirred in her stomach. "It's just you. It was dark."

"What about in the barn?" insisted Leena.

"It was dark there too. This is dumb, Leena. Leave it be." Meeryle glared at her friend. The unease had morphed into a churning that threatened to make her throw up. She didn't want to think about the orange glow things had taken on numerous occasions.

Leena gave her a sideway glance. "The mage thing again?"

"Ah.... Yes, I think so," answered Meeryle. As soon as she thought about it, the sick feeling in her stomach relented.

"It'll take a while to get rid of it, but you'll get there." Leena gave her an encouraging smile.

"I ... I get angry." Her stomach clenched.

"Really," replied Leena with a smirk.

Meeryle burst out in nervous laughter, dispelling all unease. "Yes, incredible, isn't it?"

"You want to tell me more?" asked Leena in a gentle tone.

Her throat tight, Meeryle shook her head.

"Later, then. As long as you accept it, it'll help, all right?"

Meeryle nodded and they fell silent once again. Tikid had settled herself by lying down and resting her chin on her foreclaws. She had extended her injured wing on the side and leaned its tip on the ground.

In an effort to make sure the sick feeling was completely gone, Meeryle concentrated on the dragon. A solution had to exist. After all, she could do magic, couldn't she? A thought popped into Meeryle's mind. Hope stirring, she cleared her throat. "Tikid, do you remember you said that Leena was a great Healer?" The dragon nodded. "You said something about a glow. What does that mean?"

"That we can tell how much power and the kind of power every living creature has. Animals have very little in general, but I discovered that the power in humans changes dramatically from one individual to the other. Like the ones who followed you, they have almost none. But both of you have that glow, just a very different one."

Leena's eyes opened wide in surprise. "A glow? I glow?"

"Hush for now. Tikid, what I want to know is how much of a glow do we give off?"

"*About the same, just a different... color is the best word, I guess. Yours is white, Meeryle, and Leena's glow is golden.*"

Meeryle turned to Leena with triumph. "You said I had a special Mage-gift, right?" Bewildered, Leena nodded. "I think that if your glow is as strong as mine, then your gift must also be exceptional."

"Meeryle, where are you going with this?"

"I'm trying to show you that you're as strong a Healer as I am a Mage. That you can do and Heal anything with your gift, including Tikid's wing. That's where I'm going. Am I not making sense?"

"I... This is kind of farfetched, you know," answered Leena hesitantly. "The Healer said I hadn't come into full power yet and...."

Meeryle interrupted. "Stop right there. Forget what the Healer said. Look inside yourself and tell me that I'm wrong."

Leena licked her lips. She looked at Meeryle and Tikid, searching their faces for an answer. Both human and dragon were staring at her earnestly. Her face fell and she shook her head. "My Healing gift is not a strong one. It never was."

"How can you be so sure?" asked Meeryle softly.

"Because... Because it's the wrong gift."

"*How can your gift be wrong? It is. It cannot be otherwise than right,*" commented Tikid, puzzled.

Meeryle clenched her fists. "I think it may be something you haven't fully understood, Tikid.

194

Leena thought she was a Mage, but it turned out she had the Healing gift instead. And it would seem that she's still yearning for the Mage-gift so much that she's ignoring her potential as a Healer." Meeryle was glaring at Leena. "How can you still doubt yourself?"

"It's easy for you to say! You're the one who's been making amazing progress with your gift. You're learning to do amazing things with it, things I can never do."

"Of course not, but you can do amazing things I could never even dream of. I've said it before; you can make the difference between life and death. If that isn't the ultimate thing, I don't know what is."

Leena didn't answer immediately. She bit her lips and looked from Meeryle to Tikid. "I... I never had the courage to tell you, but I've never actually completed a Healing before."

Meeryle's eyebrows went up. "How come?"

"Well, I would calm down patients or make them sleep, but every time I was supposed to Heal a wound, I'd start, but then, I'd... I'd get scared and I would tell the Healer I wasn't up to finishing it."

"Didn't he find it strange? And what were you scared about, anyway?"

"*The wielding of great power can be a frightening thing*," said Tikid.

"Actually, it's nothing like that at all. I thought... No, I was sure I was a Mage. When it turned out I wasn't and that I was kind of a failure, I guess it stayed with me. I'm just too afraid I will either fail or that something will go awfully wrong. That's why I didn't want to Heal you when you hurt your ankle. I just couldn't take the risk of making your injury permanent."

Meeryle couldn't believe her ears. All she had just heard was so at odds with the Leena she knew, she wasn't sure what to say. The person she had looked to for inspiration and stability had basically been lying to everyone. Yet she couldn't be angry with her friend. She could understand why Leena had wanted to maintain her image. She didn't necessarily agree with it, but she knew how hard it was to fit in with the villagers. They had accepted Leena as an apprentice-Healer, but they may have rejected her in another role.

Tikid, however, was at a complete loss. *"This is making no sense to me. You could not possibly use your gift the wrong way. It would go against your very nature to do harm unto another with your power."*

Meeryle and Leena exchanged a look. "Are all dragons always sure of themselves and do they always know what to do?" asked Leena.

"Ah... What do you mean?"

Meeryle intervened. "Let's pick an example. You have to learn how to fly, no?" The dragon blinked in assent. "When you first started to fly, did you immediately start acrobatics?"

"Of course not!"

"Why is that?"

"Because I did not know my limits. I could have twisted my wings or developed a dizzy spell. Ah! I see what you mean, now. Only for Leena, it is not about hurting herself by accident, but another." Tikid frowned. *"I still think you have no reason to doubt yourself, though."*

"Thank you, Tikid; your confidence is very much appreciated."

The dragon nodded and suddenly winced.

"What is it?" asked Leena.

"*I still hurt.*"

Meeryle ground her teeth. If this mess was indeed her fault, even indirectly, she was going to fix it. Another idea formed in her mind. "Leena, would you know what to do?"

"To do what?"

"To Heal the wing."

"I told you...."

"I know what you said. Let's just pretend for a minute, all right?" Leena reluctantly nodded. "Do you technically know what needs to be done to repair Tikid's wing?"

"Technically, yes. But I've never felt the life force of a dragon before and even if the same principles as those of humans apply, people don't have wings. I kind of know, but it's an educated guess."

"So you know what to do. You just lack the power, right?"

"Ah... Well, it's simplistic, but yes. Meeryle, you're making me nervous. Come out with it."

"I can give you the power."

Leena blinked twice, clearly confused by what she had heard her friend say. "Give me power. Just like that." Meeryle nodded vigorously. "Oh, well, then, let's do it!"

"No need to be sarcastic. It's a good idea." Meeryle frowned. "It does make sense, doesn't it?"

"It's not so simple, Meeryle. You can't just give me some of your power."

"Why not?"

"Well, because it's not something that's done."

"Has anyone ever tried it?"

"I don't know!"

"Then how can you know it can't be done?" Anger was slowly stirring and formed an uncomfortable warmth in Meeryle's stomach. "It almost sounds like because it's a good idea and you didn't come up with it, you don't like it."

"Don't be ridiculous. It has nothing to do with you...."

"Really?" cut in Meeryle. "As soon as I mentioned it, you rejected it. What's wrong? All the great ideas have to come from you?"

Leena glared at her friend. "Well, so far, your ideas aren't turning out so nicely, are they? First, secrecy about the dragons made me lose my apprenticeship, then the hasty fix-up cost Tikid her wing. Sorry, but from now on, I'm going to be cautious."

"You are not being fair, Leena. You talk as if I was merely a leaf carried by the wind. It is not so. I am the one who decided to fly over to your village, not Meeryle. And it was not she who shot the arrow that injured me."

Meeryle was extremely thankful for Tikid's intervention. Leena's words had made her so angry, things had once again started to take on an orange tinge. She took in a deep breath and forced the anger away. "Look, we're not getting anywhere. All we're doing is getting angry at each other. I want us to try something in order to Heal Tikid. I don't care if it's never been done before. I'm sure a lot of things we do now weren't done before and someone had the guts to try."

Leena slowly nodded. "Actually, the very first Healing was done completely by accident. That's what I learned, anyway."

"Let's try it, then."

"It's not that simple, Meeryle. What if...."

"Never mind, what if! We're doing it, no doubts, no hesitation, all right?"

Leena gulped under Meeryle's gaze. Not trusting her voice, she nodded. Meeryle smiled briefly, then frowned in concentration.

"*Is there anything I need to do?*" asked Tikid.

Meeryle looked to Leena, who shrugged. "I can't say," said the tall girl. "This is going to be completely new. Just watch and tell us if you think something is wrong or right."

"Leena," said Meeryle, "you get comfortable first. You're the one doing the Healing, I'm just going to be your helper." The tall girl nodded. She sat cross-legged on the ground in front of the injured wing. Once her friend was settled, Meeryle hesitated. "Do you think I need to touch you?"

"I guess it would be best. Keep on touching Tikid too, just in case."

Meeryle got up and sat back down beside Leena. She put her left hand on Leena's shoulder and held the tip of Tikid's tail in the other. "I was able to hear the hum when you were looking at the wound the first time. Start and I will follow."

"How?"

"I'll improvise. Let's be honest, I've always been improvising with my gift. We'll be fine. Start when you're ready." Meeryle made sure she sounded confident. For the first time, she was the one leading. She didn't want Leena to know the fear of failing was twisting her stomach in knots, that she really didn't know what to do and that she was hoping her instincts would guide her. So far, it had seemed to work.

Leena gave her a penetrating look. Meeryle stared back confidently. Leena nodded and closed her eyes. Almost immediately, Meeryle heard the hum of life. She listened closely and heard faintly the murmur of earth. She closed her eyes to concentrate. The murmur was not always present and another sound was interfering. For some reason, the murmur of earth came and went, and Meeryle couldn't find a pattern, but the other unidentified sound was getting louder and louder. Frustrated, she frowned and decided to ask Leena about it, when the noise that had interfered in her trance became something she could not only hear with her gift, but with her ears. Branches breaking, people walking, people yelling, people crashing through the forest into the clearing.... The hunters had caught up with them. Meeryle had completely forgotten about them, and apparently, so had Leena. The fire! It was much, much brighter than normal, thanks to her gift, and must have been a beacon for them. Otherwise, how could they have known to come in this direction?

Yells of anger and relief jarred the quiet that had settled over the girls and the dragon. Meeryle and Leena stared around, bewildered.

However, as soon as Tikid raised her head, the humans stopped at a respectful distance. Not a word was uttered. The hunters' arrival had scared away any animal or insect, making the night eerily silent.

A man came forward. Leena swore softly when she saw it was her father. He stopped a few feet from the young dragon and glared at the three friends. "What are you girls doing here? How did you get out of the barn? And when? And that creature...."

A flurry of wings interrupted him and screams of fear broke the silence. People started running back into the forest, some stumbling, other falling. Meeryle looked up: the dark dragon shadows landing in the clearing suddenly hid the stars.

Meeryle, Leena, and Tikid exchanged a desperate look and braced themselves against the upcoming confrontation.

CHAPTER THIRTEEN

Humans and dragons stared at each other across the clearing without uttering a word or a grunt. Meeryle was used to feeling emotions projected by Tikid on her own, but she was not prepared to feel the joint emotions of a crowd of dragons. The anger and scorn of the huge creatures washed over her, making her shudder. Fear controlled her heartbeat and she had to make a conscious effort not to bolt. She closed her eyes and forced her instincts away. These were friends. Angry friends, but friends, nonetheless. She knew the dragons wouldn't harm them, but the sea of negative emotions made it hard to believe.

A quick look towards the human crowd confirmed that Meeryle wasn't the only one sensitive to the dragons' mood. The hunters were suddenly very hesitant. Since she was touching Tikid, she knew the dragons hadn't spoken yet. The humans had come closer together behind Parin, a mass of heads exchanging uncertain looks. It was one thing to hear the description of frightened youths and to see a single young dragon flying in the sky, and quite another to face a crowd of adult dragons.

Leena's father had stayed where he was, looking from the three friends to the adult dragons, assessing the situation with a practiced hunter's eye. Meeryle tensed, inadvertently pinching Tikid's tail. The young dragon yelped, breaking the silence and the stillness.

All eyes turned on them. Meeryle bit her lips, her stomach turning cold and hard. All the encouraging words she had said earlier to both Leena and Tikid, all her resolutions to make the situation better vanished under the accusatory looks. She wanted the ground to swallow her. Not trusting herself to say anything, Meeryle gave Leena a pleading look.

The tall girl shrugged and got up. "Hello, Father."

Father and daughter glared at each other, unmoving, for what felt like an eternity. The humans were exchanging looks and the dragons were shifting warily. None dared to make an abrupt move that could be deemed threatening. Feeling Tikid's tail quivering with fearful anticipation in her hands, Meeryle reminded herself to breathe.

In the end, one of the dragons moved towards the three friends. All the humans gasped; a knife even zinged out of its sheath, but no one came forward. Meeryle sighed with relief. She turned and found herself face to snout with Larid, Tikid's mother.

"*Well, children, what a fine mess.*" Her words were answered by the panicked whispers of the humans. Meeryle couldn't make out the exact words, but she could easily guess their uneasiness. Once again, all they had were Tarkin and Navee's word. It was very hard to really believe in hearing words inside one's head. The big dragon turned to Leena's father. "*Yes, as you can hear, I am speaking to you.*"

His eyes went wide, but he stood his ground. "What are you and what do you want?" At first, his voice quivered, but he regained his confidence

203

quickly as he spoke. His shoulders were squared and his head high.

"*Strange that you would ask such a question when you are the interlopers here.*"

This time, all the hunters truly heard Larid. Some gasped, a few screamed, and two ran into the forest. With a nod, Leena's father sent two others after them. Meeryle was relieved. Even with dawn nearing, the forest was still very dark, making it very easy to get lost. Most of the villagers were farmers; only a few were foresters like Leena's parents.

The incident had given Parin the chance to completely compose himself. He stared boldly at Larid and moved forward. The dragons hissed and he faltered. Nevertheless, he stood where he was, as his pride didn't allow him to back up.

"My name is Parin. I repeat my question. Who are you and what are you doing here?"

"*We are the Greens. We are the guardians of the plants and this forest is our home. You are trespassing and destroying the plants. But worse, you are... aggressive,*" answered Larid. While she was talking, she had straightened up to sit on her haunches. Tikid's mother was a big dragon and she used her size to her advantage. She looked down on Parin menacingly. The man gulped and took an involuntary step back.

"You... You were the ones who were hostile in the first place," he stammered.

"*Oh? Really? Where are your wounded?*"

"At the village! A girl and a boy both lost their minds when this dragon threatened them." He pointed an accusatory finger at Tikid.

204

"I never threatened them. All I did was to ask them to leave us alone." Tikid was outraged at the accusation. Astonished by the answer, Parin gaped at the younger dragon, who misinterpreted his expression. *"You doubt my word?"* She stood on all fours, ready to charge at the insult, wound forgotten. When she flared her wings, she cried out in pain and fell to the ground, dragging Meeryle, who was still holding her tail.

Leena knelt quickly by her side, shaking her head. "He wasn't questioning your word, you silly thing. He just wasn't expecting your answer." She threw her father a resentful look. "He didn't even let me say as much as you did. Now calm down and don't move."

Larid roared, startling everyone. *"Was such a request worth maiming my daughter for life?"*

"Your... daughter?" said a woman's voice. The crowd parted to make way for Jetyaa. "This beast is your daughter?"

"Tikid is not a beast. Who are you?" asked Larid.

"I am Jetyaa. I was the one who shot the arrow that wounded your... daughter."

Larid's anguished howl pierced through Meeryle's body, making her very bones shudder. Leena closed her eyes and bit her upper lip. No matter how peaceful Tikid claimed the dragons to be, Larid's roar made it hard to believe. Jetyaa was trembling.

Leena got up and took her hand. The woman blinked, surprised to see her stepdaughter. "I was there, Larid, when Jetyaa shot her arrow. It was an accident. Dragons are a scary sight. She panicked."

205

The dragon shifted her gaze on the tall girl. *"You defend her. Why?"*

"Because it's the right thing to do. I don't want you to think she would hurt Tikid on purpose." Leena squeezed Jetyaa's hand reassuringly and it gave the older woman courage to speak.

"What she is not saying is that I am her mother," said Jetyaa with a quivering voice.

"Ah! It is ironic that such a skilled Healer would share the family bonds with a killer."

"I am not dead!" interrupted Tikid. *"This is getting tiresome. I hurt. Meeryle and Leena were trying to help when you all arrived."*

Larid looked from Meeryle to Leena and shook her head. *"It is very kind of you both to try to do something for Tikid, but I am afraid it is not possible."*

"Stop it right there, all of you," interrupted Parin. "Jetyaa, what is the matter with you? You're apologizing to animals!"

Listening to the meaningless squabble had erased the guilt that had surfaced under the humans' gaze. Instead, anger flared and melted the cold rock in Meeryle's stomach. "Dragons are not animals!" she shouted. Her outburst surprised everyone, including Larid, who took a step back. She stood, squeezing Tikid's tail in her left hand. "You spoke to Larid and heard Tikid. Since when do animals speak to you?"

"Meeryle, girl, you're blinded by your fantasies," replied Parin.

"Fantasies? What fantasies? Do you not see? What's wrong with you?" Meeryle could feel her cheeks getting warm and her stomach was starting to churn. Parin's denial was infuriating her. "Are you so stubborn you refuse to believe your own eyes?"

"Meeryle, that will be quite enough." The Healer's voice rang clearly and dampened the fire in Meeryle's stomach. When had he arrived? How had he known where to find them? His appearance had subdued her anger enough for her to notice that Corvin was sweating and out of breath. She assumed that he could use his gift to guide him the same way she had. She thought wryly that the Healer would think his presence essential, whatever the situation. He had probably made his way through the forest as soon as he had fulfilled his duties.

Now that Corvin was here, the hunters respectfully let him through, some even looking relieved by his presence. He stopped by Leena and Jetyaa, shaking his head. "Parin speaks for many of us. Look at your dragons. How can we not see an animal?"

"Well, talk to them, then. You'll see that you're the ones who are fantasizing, not me." Meeryle had to put her temper in check. His words were, as usual, condescending. He was looking at her with so much scorn, Meeryle had started to see things take on a slight orange tinge. The phenomenon was reoccurring at an alarming rate and was really starting to concern her. Special gift or not, it just wasn't normal.

The Healer simply nodded and addressed Tikid. "How did you get wounded?"

"*An arrow hit me while I was in flight.*"

The Healer's knees buckled and he had to sit down.

"What's wrong?" asked Leena with a frown.

"I... Hearing a voice in my head is... Well, let's just say that I wasn't expecting this at all." He sat in silence for a while, staring at the young dragon. He then got up and moved closer to examine the injured wing. He circled Tikid, pulling his lip. Neither humans nor dragons dared interrupt him. Meeryle reminded herself to breathe and hoped Tikid's answer had been enough to convince the Healer. Suddenly, he said: "This is very bad. But is there anything I can do?"

Larid and Tikid exchanged a look. They might even have exchanged words, but Meeryle didn't hear them. Larid lowered her head and rested it on her forepaws, staring intently at the Healer. Even when she was not towering over the man, the dragon emanated threat. The Healer gulped loudly, making Meeryle smirk. For once, Meeryle felt warmth fill her without seeing everything in orange; she was glad to finally see the Healer humbled. His constantly haughty attitude grated, and the way he dismissed Leena and the dragons rankled deeply.

Larid's voice interrupted her thoughts. "*I thank you, but I do not think you know anything about dragons, let alone how to Heal such a wound. I believe Leena and Meeryle were interrupted in their attempt to fix the wrong that was done.*"

Larid's comment warmed Meeryle's heart. The dragon now thought they could do something for Tikid. One adult had decided to trust her and Leena, unlike the Healer, who gasped in outrage. "But Leena is a mere apprentice-or, rather, she was-and Meeryle doesn't know the first thing about Healing."

"*You were certain dragons were only animals, were you not?*" replied Larid scathingly. The Healer winced, but Larid continued. *"You seem to dismiss readily your younglings. Have they never anything interesting to say?"*

"Well, Leena has proven herself unworthy," answered the Healer, regaining his composure. Leena looked down at her feet and clenched her free hand in a fist.

Another dragon stepped forward. Meeryle thought at first it was Korad, but this dragon was bigger. As all the other dragons moved to let it pass, Meeryle surmised this dragon held special standing. When it stopped and sat, the girl gaped at its size. The creature was much bigger than Korad, almost twice his height, and she was sure the darkness concealed part of him. Meeryle realized also that this dragon was male. While he hadn't spoken, he somehow projected maleness. Her impression was confirmed when the big dragon voice resonated in her head.

"You are weak, human, and you know it."

Startled, the Healer blinked. "If by that you mean that my gift is not strong, you are right. I cannot possibly Heal something so extensively damaged. Unfortunately, since part of the tissue is missing, I don't think anyone can Heal this."

The dragon chuckled loudly, making Meeryle's entire body vibrate, almost like a deep tickle. *"I mean a lot more than that."* He stooped his head down until his pointy snout almost touched the Healer's face. *"Now, will you let your blindness and vanity rule you and interfere, or will you learn?"* The Healer trembled, rooted in place. Meeryle started to feel sorry for the man. She could commiserate; she was getting used to the great

209

creatures, but this dragon was making her feel uncomfortable. The glee in his eyes seemed out of place and his sheer size was intimidating.

Leena broke the standstill. She squeezed Jetyaa's hand briefly and let go. "Well, if you want us to do something, get out of the way, then." She faced the dragon with her hands on her hips.

The creature chuckled again. *"Ah, Korad was right. Human younglings do have spirit. Tikid trusts you. So will I."* He bowed and turned, flicking his tail playfully. He quickly took flight in a whirlwind of unseen dust, much to the dismay of the humans, who coughed and sputtered.

Leena looked questioningly at Tikid.

"This is Rutad. He is my sire and he enjoys... teasing others."

"I'm not sure 'teasing' is the word I would use. One thing is sure, your dad is just like mine: he enjoys making others feel uncomfortable," replied Leena. She gave the Healer a glance. He was visibly troubled by the dragon's words and seemed oblivious to his surroundings. For once, Meeryle thought he looked older than his age. She glanced at the other villagers and found they had settled mostly by sitting down on their side of the clearing. They weren't as nervous anymore, but they watched the dragons, probably still unsure the creatures didn't pose any immediate threat.

The dragons had also made themselves comfortable. Most of them had lain down and curled up, looking surprisingly like great cats. In the first light of dawn, they were mounds of gleaming scales of all shades of green, punctuated by the bright red of their eyes. She caught two staring at Leena. The

210

tall girl stared back, lifting an eyebrow. The deep rumbles of their laughter shook everyone.

Leena and Meeryle exchanged a puzzled glance. Meeryle felt her cheeks heat up. "What's so funny?" she asked angrily.

The two dragons lifted their heads and fixed their red gaze on her. Tikid's tail flickered in her hand and answered for her. *"They find it funny that Leena can look at them in the eyes."*

"How can that make them laugh?" asked Meeryle, confused.

"Usually, the young ones are the ones who show meekness, not adults." She paused, trying to grasp the right words, then gave up. *"I do not think dragons and humans find the same things funny."*

"Well, I certainly don't get it."

"Neither do I," added Leena. "So, since Tikid's dad seems to trust us, do you want to try again?" she asked quietly.

"It would at least give us something to do. They're all giving me the creeps, staring at each other like that," replied Meeryle.

Their conversation had been quiet, so no one had heard her comment. She was glad, because she felt guilty about it. Dragons were still fearsome in her eyes; her fellow villagers had every right to be wary of them. As for the dragons, humans had suddenly become predators, wounding one of their young. The situation was still volatile and she wanted to avoid another mishap that could end in bloodshed.

"All right, let's get back the way we were," said Meeryle, springing into action. She was suddenly eager to see if her idea would work. The mere sight of her friend's sagging wing choked her with unshed tears. She let go of the dragon's tail and knelt by her neck. Her sudden movement startled Larid and the three closest dragons. Unheard questions came her way but she couldn't hear them as she was no longer touching Tikid. Shrugging, she ignored them.

Leena joined her and Meeryle cut everyone out but her friends. She closed her eyes to go immediately into her trance. She heard the beat of the fire loudly. It's reassuring sound steadied her and made her smile. As she put her left hand on Tikid's neck, Meeryle groped for Leena's shoulder with her right hand. The sound of life drowned out the beat of the fire and made her gasp. She opened her eyes and met Leena's gaze. "Why is it so loud?" she whispered.

Leena shook her head. "The only thing I can think of is the presence of all the dragons."

"Not the people?"

"No. I've listened to crowds and it's never as loud as that."

Meeryle shrugged. "Do you think they should leave?"

Leena snorted. "I don't think they would want to. We'll just get used to it, that's all." She closed her eyes and Meeryle followed her example.

Once again, she was rushed by the sound of life. However, after a while, she was able to make out a difference between the sound of the dragons and the one emitted by the humans. The dragons' sound was deeper and more vibrant than the humans'. Meeryle concentrated and was surprised to hear the murmur of earth intertwined with the dragons' song of life. The more she listened, the more evident it became.

"Leena, can you hear the earth?" she whispered, keeping her eyes closed.

"Is that what that sound is? I've never heard it before. Is it the dragons?"

Meeryle frowned and concentrated on the humans. At once, the sound became a slightly discordant lighter music. "I think so. The humans don't seem to have it. They don't sound as good either."

"That's the sound of fear," answered Leena. "I told you it affects people. The dragons don't seem to be afraid. Then again, I don't have much experience with scared dragons."

Meeryle shifted her attention back to the dragons. "Tikid, I can hear the earth when I listen to your... life sound. Is that normal?"

The young dragon was silent. Meeryle felt her give a dragon shrug. It was Larid who answered. *"Greens are closely linked to the earth, as are the Browns. That our life song should reflect it is indeed normal, Meeryle."*

"Ah. Thank you." The dragon's statement aroused her curiosity. She opened her eyes and started to ask if other types of dragons were linked to the other elements, but she curbed her enthusiasm. Tikid's wing was more important. Her questions could wait.

She pondered the meaning of the link between the dragons and earth, and was struck by a thought. "All right, Leena, I know what to do. I'm going to funnel earth energy to you."

"You are?" Leena looked dubious.

Meeryle answered with an exasperated sigh. "I'll try, all right? We're both improvising,

213

remember?" She fought down the too-familiar warmth in her stomach. Tikid's steady heartbeat under her hand helped her put a check on her temper. Now was not the time to let Leena's doubts enrage her and make her see everything in orange.

She gave her friend an encouraging nod and closed her eyes. This time, she ignored the beat of the fire and the song of life to concentrate on the murmur of earth. At first, the same problem came up; the murmur came and went. She ground her teeth in frustration. The beat of the fire became stronger and calmed her down. She suddenly realized that every time she lost the murmur, she heard the beat of fire. The element, so familiar and reassuring, was hampering her for some reason.

"Anytime, Meeryle," interrupted Leena.

"Hush. I'm having a hard time. Fire's getting in the way."

"Then I will extinguish it. We no longer need it; the sun is up," replied Larid.

Meeryle couldn't believe she had been awake all night. While she expected to be tired, she found she was very awake and in tune with everything around her. Larid didn't give her much time to think. Within minutes, the fire was silent. Meeryle concentrated, pushing aside any thought of fatigue. She found the murmur of earth and was able to hear it constantly. Meeryle then realized she had never used that element as she had used fire. She knew how to find it, but she wasn't sure how to affect earth. She briefly analyzed how she lit twigs and found it was quite simple: she willed them to burn.

Yelps and shouts from the human crowd made her jump. She opened her eyes and found herself surrounded by tiny flames. Each grass blade around her was burning.

"Meeryle, this is not earth!" Leena's eyes were wide, echoing the villagers' fear.

"I'm sorry, I'm sorry." With a thought, she willed the flames out. "Give me a second." She could will things to burn and flames to extinguish, but what could she do with earth? She closed her eyes and listened intently to earth. The murmur seemed equal everywhere, except around rocks.

"I know!" she exclaimed, opening her eyes. "Earth makes things grow."

Leena gave her a look. "You just figured this out?"

"Yes. No! I mean, this is how the earth power works. I can will things to burn, because that's what fire does. So I have to will something to grow, but give you the power instead." She faltered. "Leena, how am I supposed to do that?"

"*Will Leena to grow*," said Tikid. "*She is not a plant, she has no roots, so the power will be within her. She will decide how to use it.*"

"This is probably the strangest thing I've ever heard," replied Leena.

"Yes, but it makes sense to me," said Meeryle. "Let's try."

"Sure! The worst that will happen is that I will grow even taller," commented Leena wryly.

Meeryle ignored the comment. "Ready?" Leena nodded and they both closed their eyes to concentrate on their task. Meeryle immersed herself in the murmur until her skin was covered with goosebumps. She smiled at the feeling. Where fire had heated every fiber in her, earth was caressing

215

her, warming her slowly from the outside in. When she felt saturated with the strange energy, Meeryle willed it to shift to Leena. Nothing happened. She bit her lip and fought down panic. It had to work. She was doing something wrong. After taking a deep breath, she remembered she had to will the power to do something, not to go somewhere.

She changed her thought from going to doing and felt the difference immediately. All the earth power slowly moved towards her right arm. Her left arm lost its goosebumps, then her shoulder. The shift was taking too long. *Faster,* thought Meeryle, *you have to move faster*. Once again, the change was immediate. The power moved quickly throughout her body and gathered in her right arm. *Go,* she thought, *go and make Leena grow*. Her hand pulsated and the power was gone. Meeryle felt cold and shivered from the shock of losing the energy so suddenly.

Leena gasped. "This is amazing," she whispered. "Here I go."

Meeryle kept her hand on Leena's shoulder and her eyes closed. She listened intently to Tikid's life sound through Leena. The screeching sound emitted by the injured wing made her wince. This time, since she was expecting it, she didn't break the contact with her friends. She felt Leena gather the power in a way she didn't understand. The murmur intensified. Leena was mumbling under breath. Meeryle caught the words "grow" and "heal".

The sound went slowly from screeching to harmonious. The murmur of earth diminished and the vibrant sound of dragon life filled her body. Meeryle opened her eyes and looked at Leena. Her

216

friend was exhausted, but she smiled. She looked at the dragon's wing. Meeryle did the same and whooped.

Tikid's wing was completely healed and as good as new.

CHAPTER FOURTEEN

At the sound of Meeryle's shout, dragons and humans alike arose to peer at the three friends, moving in to see the results of the Healing. Some of the dragons, especially the ones further back, stood on their hind legs, dominating the clearing. At the sight of the standing dragons, the humans stopped.

Only the Healer came closer, shaking his head in awe. "I don't believe it. You reconstructed the wing." Oblivious to his surroundings, the Healer pushed Meeryle and Leena aside to grab Tikid's wing. He pulled it out and peered closely at the leathery membrane, which was once again flawless. "This is impossible. You can only mend with what's there. How? How, how, how?" He started to poke the wing with his finger, until Tikid had enough.

Meeryle wasn't touching her, but she could guess at Tikid's words when the Healer jumped, startled, and backed up, apologizing. The young dragon sniffed loudly and moved to settle down beside Meeryle, wrapping the human girl with her tail.

"... *not to touch me unless you ask*." Her tone was icy. Even if she was young, Tikid was much bigger than a horse. She drew herself up and glared down at the Healer.

The man's eyes went wide. "Once again, I'm sorry. I got carried away. I mean, this is not possible!"

"*You keep on repeating it, yet you have the proof in front of you. It almost seems as if you wish it had not been accomplished,*" replied Larid.

"You don't understand me. In all my studies, I have never encountered such a thing. A Healer can only Heal what's there. Parts of the wing were missing, yet they are back. Where did the missing parts come from?"

"Probably from me," interrupted Meeryle.

He looked at her with surprise, as if he hadn't noticed her presence before. "How so? You were just sitting by Leena."

Meeryle ground her teeth. Hadn't he heard anything that had been said? And when she had worked her magic, where had he been? Still in his own little world? Everyone had seen the flames she had unwittingly called. Was that not reason enough to at least wonder about her and her gift? The dismissing tone of the Healer woke an anger she had thought gone. "Tikid's father is right. You're so weak, it's not funny."

"Meeryle!" cried Leena.

"Let me talk. I've had it with his attitude, anyway. He's been looking down at you for too long as far as I'm concerned." Meeryle turned to the Healer. "You knew there was something about me, didn't you? I saw how you looked at me. Yet you didn't do anything about it." Meeryle was surprised by the pride in her own voice. She realized that the gift she hadn't wanted was truly part of her, just like her cooking skills, and could be useful indeed.

The Healer interrupted her. "You simply were not worth it," he said condescendingly.

Leena gasped. "How can you say something like that? How can anyone not be worth it? Meeryle is very much worth it."

"Leena, that will be quite enough," interrupted Leena's father. "Mind your elders, girl."

"Ha! Respect is earned, not due. Meeryle's just done something exceptional and none of you want to recognize it. I wouldn't have been able to Heal Tikid if it weren't for Meeryle. She believed in me more than I believed in myself and obviously more than you both do." Leena was glaring at her father and the Healer. However, they weren't quelled by her look and her speech. Parin crossed his arms and looked down on his daughter.

The Healer snorted and asked: "What did Meeryle do, then?"

"She fed me power from the earth, which allowed me to force Tikid's wing to grow and heal."

Parin blinked, taken aback. The Healer turned to Meeryle and stared. He opened his mouth to speak, but he was cut off by movement among the dragons, who had been following the conversation eagerly.

The big creatures were moving to the edge of the clearing and looking up expectantly. Meeryle did the same and had to shade her eyes with her hands from the early morning sun. Rutad was coming back. She was now able to fully appreciate his size. He was bigger than she had estimated earlier and for some reason, he looked different, as if he were brighter.

She felt Tikid's tail tug at her. "*Come, we must make way for Rutad. I think....*" Bewildered and awed, Meeryle disengaged herself from the young dragon's tail and missed what she said. She looked for Leena, who was gaping as well, and grabbed her hand. The three friends made their way to the very edge of the clearing. Tikid sat on her haunches and the girls leaned against her chest, watching.

The great dragon swooped twice before landing in a flurry of leaves and twigs flying in the whirlwind created by the dragon's huge wings. Once the leaves and the dust had settled back down, Meeryle had a clear view of the dragon. He stood on his hind legs, tail curled around him. His front legs hung by his side while he towered majestically over the entire clearing.

"Why does he seem different from last night? He was almost mocking and now, he looks so serious and... grand," whispered Meeryle to Tikid.

"*Because he represents the Great One of the Greens. In that sense, Rutad is our leader,*" answered Tikid in a neutral tone.

Meeryle and Leena exchanged a puzzled glance. Leena shrugged. "And the Great One is...."

"*He is the very essence of the Greens, the source of the Green dragons' power. Without the Great One, the dragons would fare poorly, if not die altogether. As he cannot be everywhere at once, he has a representative amongst all the Green enclaves across the Kin. The dragon who represents him can become him in a certain way. He has all his powers and he can communicate directly with the Great One. I have to admit this is the first time I see Rutad fully assume the Great One's function.*" With her eyes riveted on the big creature, Tikid didn't see the confused faces of her human friends.

"Tikid, you completely lost us," said Meeryle. "Why would this Great One be here?"

"*Well, I am guessing the result of Leena's Healing, as well as the meeting with humans, was communicated to him and he wants to see it for himself.*"

Leena sighed. "Would you mind explaining this last bit? How do dragons communicate, anyhow?"

"*By thought, of course. How do you communicate with other humans?*"

"We speak to each other, Tikid. Out loud. Like right now. If someone is far away, we write and have to wait for the letter to get to them. Depending on the distance, it can take months for the person to get the message."

The dragon was taken aback. "*Months? Being out of touch for so long is... frightening to me. Adult dragons link and can send their thoughts very far.*"

Meeryle looked at Leena. "Link?"

Any other question was forestalled as the huge dragon turned his eyes on the three friends. Meeryle looked into the big ruby eyes and everything around her disappeared.

She was in a pool of power where colors pulsed. She was surrounded by every possible shade of green, from the palest pastel to the most vibrant emerald. Tones of gold appeared and disappeared at random, giving off an eerie light. The only sound was the murmur of earth, but it resonated in a strange way.

"*Hear the earth imbued with the power of the Greens, young Mage. You have truly joined both within my young kin.*" The voice echoed in the green space. Meeryle looked to see where it came from, and found that red eyes were suddenly there, staring intently at her. "*It has been a very long time indeed*

222

since your kind has attempted such a thing. Be proud, but wary of your gift, human. It may prove lethal if you do not harness it." The voice was so deep, it made Meeryle's bones vibrate. She closed her eyes and shuddered.

A hand was shaking her roughly. She opened her eyes to find Leena's concerned face hovering over her. Meeryle blinked and looked around. She was lying on the ground. Her view of the clearing was blocked by dragons' backs.

"What happened?"

"You went limp and crumpled to the ground. My turn to ask what happened," replied Leena.

"I... Rutad looked at me and took me... somewhere. I was surrounded by green energy and I could hear the earth very, very clearly. It was really strange."

Leena bit her lip. "Meeryle, you were glowing with a greenish tinge for a while. Tikid said you'd be all right, that the Great One was talking to you through Rutad."

"He was. He said...."

Jetyaa came running, a concerned look on her face. "Meeryle! What are you doing on the ground? Are you feeling well, girl?"

"Yes, I'll be fine. What's going on?"

The woman wrinkled her nose. "I'm not too sure. When that huge dragon landed, we were all frightened, but none of us could move to run away. It looked around and focused on something, but I couldn't see what. You won't believe this, but it... changed colors for a few minutes. It was a bright, shining green, almost like emeralds. Then it went back to normal and we could all move. I looked where it had been staring and saw you on the ground."

Jetyaa backed up to make room for Tikid, who immediately put her paw on Meeryle's shoulder. Leena's stepmother closed her eyes and gulped.

"I want to apologize, dragon. I don't know what came over me, but when I saw you...."

"It was a mistake. I frightened you to the point where your mind took you elsewhere. I also need to apologize," replied Tikid.

Jetyaa jumped slightly at the voice in her mind. "This is very awkward."

"Don't worry, Mother," said Leena. "You'll get used to it."

"The good thing that came out of my injury is that both your gifts are now truly in full bloom," said the young dragon.

"Tikid, I don't think you can say that about gifts," said Meeryle with a raspy voice. "Only flowers bloom. Help me up, will you? And your paw's getting heavy."

"Sorry." The dragon slipped her front paws underneath the big girl's shoulders and lifted her into a sitting position. Meeryle blinked, disoriented. Tikid sat on her haunches and pulled her friend back until she leaned on her. *"Use me for support."*

"Thanks."

"I don't believe what I just saw," said Jetyaa.

As Leena sat down beside Meeryle, the two girls looked at each other, puzzled. "What do you mean?" asked Leena.

"Meeryle is leaning against a dragon."

"She needs support and she has to touch me in order to hear me. I thought my solution was ideal."

224

"It is, Tikid," said Leena with a smile. "What my mother means is that she's amazed that anyone could trust a dragon the way Meeryle does."

"*Dragons are trustworthy creatures,*" replied Tikid, hurt.

"I know, Tikid. So does Meeryle. But it would seem we are the only humans who can appreciate that." Leena turned to her stepmother. "Do you think Father would believe me now?"

A shadow loomed over the small group. Meeryle looked up into Parin's face. He kept his expression strangely neutral. Beside him, the Healer was rubbing his brow, as if trying to chase away a headache. Larid was following them, and Tikid's sire was hovering over the two men, the mischievous twinkle back in his eye. He was still as large, but no longer held the strange awe-inspiring energy of the Green dragons' leader.

The Healer cleared his throat. "Well, it would seem the dragons are agreeable to letting us go without harm. Leena, your Healing seems to be a token of our goodwill."

"Man, you're rambling," interrupted Parin. "The big fellow dragon was quite clear about it. The only reason they haven't killed us outright is because of the two of you."

"*We would never kill you,*" said Tikid, offended. "*Dragons do not kill.*"

Parin gave the young dragon an unkind look. "You could have fooled me."

"*You are not to address my young one in such a manner. It irks me.*" Parin turned and found himself nose to snout with the male dragon. The man blanched. "*Remember, to maim is not to kill. My name is Rutad. Do not forget it."* The dragon exchanged a look with Larid and left.

Parin closed his eyes and took in a deep breath. They all remained silent for a while. A gentle breeze rustled the leaves and birds were flying overhead, chasing insects. Meeryle could hear the mumble of human voices and the occasional rumble of a laughing dragon.

She startled the others when she spoke. "Well, everyone seems to be getting along now."

"You could say that," said the Healer. "That big dragon...."

"*Rutad,*" interrupted Tikid and Larid at the same time.

"All right, Rutad spoke to us and said that if we were to take care of you, everything would be fine."

"Ha! You mince your words, Healer," said Parin. "The dragon's exact words were: *I would be extremely displeased if anything were to happen to the young Healer and the young Mage.* His words are still echoing in my head and it's not a pleasant sensation, let me tell you." He rubbed his temple. "Now, the young Healer is Leena, of course, so I guess the Mage would be you, Meeryle. This is the first I hear of it. Why is that?" He moved forward and loomed right over the girl, making her squirm.

Larid flicked her tail and hit Parin's buttocks. The big man yelped in pain and outrage. "*Be glad it is I who remind you of this warning, not Rutad.*"

"But I wasn't doing anything wrong," sputtered Parin.

"*You were menacing. The girl is exhausted, both from the Healing and the contact with the*

226

Great One through Rutad, and you stand over her as if you were to punish her."

The big man was at a complete loss for words. Meeryle looked down to hide her smile. It was refreshing to see his flustered expression. Everyone was intimidated by Parin. He knew it and took advantage of it. Meeryle was glad to see that someone could stand up to him that way. She had heard that Leena's mother had been the only one who could look and yell him down. Since her death, none had dared, not even headstrong Leena. Maybe to a dragon, Parin was a small creature. He certainly didn't inspire any respect in them. Meeryle tucked the image of the man's flushed face in her mind, promising herself to recall it the next time he loomed over her.

The Healer cleared his throat. "Well, lady Larid, we're puzzled, you see. Meeryle's gift is a surprise. Her parents have never mentioned it. I had thought she had the Healing-gift, but after studying her, whatever I felt from her was gone. To find a Mage among us is an event, but a Mage of Meeryle's potential, if we are to trust Rutad's word, that's even more important. We just don't understand why she never said anything to anyone about it." He looked at her questioningly.

Larid smirked. *"Humans do not see the life essence. It is obvious to me that Leena and Meeryle are powerful.*"

The human adults looked at each other, bewildered. Leena chuckled. "I know how you feel. Dragons always talk like that. Eventually, you'll understand them, but it takes a while."

227

The Healer shook his head. "But I do understand what she means and it makes no sense. You can feel and hear the life force or essence, as you call it. But you can't see it!"

"Well, dragons can," interjected Meeryle. "Dragons are very different from humans."

"Now, that was an understatement," mumbled Parin. "Look, girl. Seriously, since when have you been a Mage?"

"All my life."

"You're sixteen and you're just saying something now?" asked Jetyaa, incredulous.

"Actually," interjected Leena, "she didn't say anything. I found out by accident."

All eyes turned to Meeryle, who blanched. "I... It just seemed normal to me, nothing special," she managed to mumble.

"Your parents never noticed anything?" asked the Healer, bewildered.

Fear choked Meeryle. She couldn't say anything, she wasn't allowed... Cold sweat broke out, dripping down her back.

Leena intervened before anyone could berate Meeryle for not answering. "Someone put a block on her, forcing her to never mention her gift."

"How is this possible?"

"Another mage."

The Healer shook his head. "I don't know anything about Magecraft. However, I'm thinking it makes sense." He frowned, as if trying to recall something. "This reminds me of someone. When I examined you, Meeryle, I had felt something similar, but...."

"Teerane's mother," said Leena.

"Oh, she died a long time again," offered Parin. "What can she possibly have anything to do with this?"

Corvin's face lit up. "Ah, but you weren't with us at the time. Yes, now I remember. A fire of some sort?"

Terror gripped Meeryle and she choked.

"Enough!" yelled Leena. "Come, I'll explain over there. Meeryle, calm down. Nothing will happen, all right? Remember what I told you; just breathe and concentrate."

While Leena spoke with her father, the Healer and a few others, Meeryle stayed put, thinking only of Tikid's warm presence. Larid didn't ask anything; she simply sent some sort of soothing thoughts her way, something very strange, yet calming. It took her a while, but finally Meeryle realized Larid was feeding her energy from the forest.

Soon, her heart had found a somewhat regular rhythm and the cold sweat had stopped. By the time Leena had finished explaining the situation, Meeryle felt like herself again and realized that she was making people nervous. They all returned to her side, and remained quiet for a while. Jetyaa was giving Meeryle sideways looks and Parin was openly glaring at her. While it irked her that he should be angry with her for something that wasn't her fault, Meeryle couldn't help smiling when she noticed that he made sure his back was turned to Larid, ensuring the dragon wouldn't see his face.

"Well, what is done is done," said the Healer. "Right now, we can't do much about this, but we'll discuss it later."

Meeryle wanted to tell him it wasn't his place to say any of this, but the mumbles from the other villagers became louder as the dragons started to move, preventing her from voicing her opinion. They all turned to see the reason of the commotion: Rutad was making his way toward the small group. Leena moved closer to Meeryle and Tikid wrapped her tail around both her friends. The adults moved back, awed. Jetyaa stepped on a rock and stumbled. Larid caught her before she could fall. Eyes wide, Jetyaa looked at the huge paw and thanked the dragon with a shaking voice.

"You see, you have nothing to fear from me," said the dragon, chuckling.

"None of you have anything to fear unless you contravene my wishes," said Rutad. He lowered himself until his head was level with Meeryle's. The plump girl took in a surprised breath and smiled. He smelled like pines and flowers, like leaves and moss. His head was as long as she was tall, yet she wasn't frightened. He was projecting feelings of well-being and kindness. His voice-or was it the Great One's?- resonated once again in her mind. *"Remember, harness your power."*

With that comment, he backed up and unfurled his great wings. Tikid shifted to protect her friends from the whirlwind of dust and leaves. The adults, who had no such shelter, turned, covering their eyes and mouths as best they could with their hands.

Eventually, the flurry settled and Meeryle watched the great dragon fly away.

"Well, we will also take our leave," said Larid. *"I believe we've all had a wearying night. I hope to*

230

see you later, Meeryle, Leena." Tikid's mother nodded and left, following her kind into the sky.

The Healer cleared his throat. "Well, the lady dragon was right. We're all exhausted. We should go back to the village and rest. Any other matter can wait."

Meeryle sighed with relief. She wanted her bed very badly. Not only could she feel every little scratch intensely, she felt wary to the bones. A nice hot bath would also be welcome.

"Hum... What about you, youngster?" asked Parin warily.

To his dismay, Tikid got up and flicked her tail eagerly. *"I will come with Meeryle and Leena. My dam did not recommend that I try my wing and fly quite yet, so I cannot cross the rift. Besides, it is too far on foot to my home."*

Meeryle and Leena exchanged an elated glance. The tall girl had a twinkle in her eyes. "Now that's going to be very interesting."

CHAPTER FIFTEEN

Tikid followed Meeryle and Leena on foot. She kept her wings as close to her body as possible, but she was the first creature her size to tread the tiny forest trails. Room was scarce and her wings managed to snag every branch on the way. Nevertheless, the young dragon was excited to finally see her friends' home. Meeryle didn't have room to touch the dragon, but Leena was giving her a summary of the running commentary of the gleeful creature.

They were delayed by Suqi. The little fox suddenly appeared in their path and stopped in front of Tikid. The dragon projected intense surprise and delight. The two creatures touched noses and seemed in deep conversation.

"Leena, What are they saying?"

"Well, I don't know. Tikid shut me out; I can't hear her at all anymore."

"Yes, she's done that before. And here I thought Suqi was afraid of dragons."

The conversation was short. Soon, Suqi shook herself and sauntered off. Meeryle managed to grab hold of Tikid's tail. "What was that all about?"

"*An interesting companion you have, Meeryle. I like her. She said she would be around the village. I look forward to meeting her again,*" answered the dragon smugly.

"That's it? That's all you have to say?"

"*Yes, why?*"

Meeryle gave her friend a dubious look. "Well, you felt rather... elated when you first saw her. And you shut out Leena, which you almost never do."

"You're also very full of yourself right now," added Leena teasingly.

Tikid raised her head haughtily and snorted. *"What was said is between Suqi and myself. Now, shall we go?"*

Meeryle sighed. "I guess the big Suqi mystery won't be solved any time soon."

Leena laughed and motioned them on. They carried on merrily, clearing the way for Tikid by holding branches back. When the three friends finally made their way out of the forest, they found Rokin hovering behind a tree, waiting anxiously for them. As soon as he spotted the trio, he jumped and came to meet them. "Leena! There you are. The wildest rumors have been going around and I see they're right." He eyed Tikid with open curiosity, but didn't ask any questions. He quickly turned his attention back to Leena. "I'm sorry I wasn't able to come and help you."

"Why did you think I needed help?" asked Leena with a perplexed frown.

Rokin turned an interesting shade of red. "Ah... I kind of stayed around the barn the other night and saw Meeryle get out. When you came out, I followed you, but I had been forbidden to join the hunt, so I had to stay behind. Will you forgive me?"

"Rokin, there's nothing to forgive. I wasn't counting on you in the first place."

Meeryle smirked at the offense on the handsome boy's face. "And it was a good thing she wasn't depending on you, either, right? 'Cause you

233

had been forbidden to go in the forest. You always do what you're told, don't you, Rokin?"

Meeryle took a sudden dislike to the youth. Why had she never noticed that everything he did seemed carefully thought out to make sure he looked good? He was rather full of himself, really. He never did anything wrong and was always very conscious of what others thought of him. Meeryle had thought it nice that Rokin liked Leena so much, but she now wondered if his interest was genuine or if Leena just seemed the type of girl everyone expected him to court. His words made Meeryle think the latter was more likely; otherwise, he would have come. He was a fake and it hurt to think she had liked him, both as a friend for herself and a suitor for Leena. Meeryle made a face.

Leena seemed to have reached the same conclusion, but did not show her disgust the way Meeryle did. "That's the problem with you, Rokin. You just do what you're told. You don't take any initiative. That's why you'll never be more than a friend, and not a very close friend, either."

Rokin's face went from red to white. Meeryle's dislike abated somewhat. If he didn't have any feelings for Leena, the boy wouldn't have shown such raw emotion. Nevertheless, she now knew that Leena had been right: Rokin was wrong for her.

The tall girl gave the handsome boy a sad smile. "I'm sorry, Rokin, but I'd rather be honest with you. Now, we have to go. We need to introduce Tikid to everyone." She gave him a pat on the shoulder and pressed on.

Rokin was so distraught, he didn't even see the dragon looking at him with interest. Meeryle shook her head and motioned Tikid on. The dragon was projecting intense curiosity, but Meeryle didn't think the time was right to explain the situation.

When they cleared the forest and arrived at the village proper, a silent crowd welcomed them dubiously. Every villager who hadn't joined in the hunt was standing quietly, watching for the coming dragon. The people who had seen the creatures in the forest were milling around, trying to reassure the others with a word or two, some of them still unsure of the dragon.

Meeryle was reminded of the other day, with its sea of unfriendly faces. Tikid snaked her tail in front of the plump girl and Meeryle grabbed it with gratitude, reminding herself that the situation was not the same. However, when she saw the woman elbowing her way in front, Meeryle's doubts came back.

"Meeryle!" The girl winced. Her mother looked frankly annoyed. "I don't know what to do with you. First, you get your brother raving mad, then you run away, and I'm told you're a Mage and that I have to treat you with consequence. What have you got to say for yourself?"

"*She only meant to help me,*" said Tikid.

Meeryle's mother made an ugly squawk. She had been so intent on her daughter, she had missed the looming figure of the dragon.

"Mother," said Meeryle hesitantly, "this is Tikid. She's a very good friend of mine, and Leena's too. Her wing was hurt. Leena and I Healed it, and now she needs to wait a bit before she can fly again. She'll be staying with us for a while."

235

The woman's mouth opened and closed a few times without making a sound. She looked at the dragon with wide eyes. "I heard something."

"Yes, you did. It was Tikid. You can tell Tarkin he's not mad. He really heard a voice in his head. That's how dragons talk."

The woman looked at her daughter as if she were a stranger. "This... thing better get away from me." She turned and bolted away, leaving her daughter stunned. Meeryle had never seen her mother so disturbed.

"It would seem that my dam is more trusting than yours."

"I'm not even sure if this has anything to do with trust. I think she really saw me for the first time and she doesn't know how to deal with me." Meeryle paused. She wasn't sure herself how to deal with this new side of her mother. She shrugged and pushed the thought out of her mind for the time being. "Come, let's introduce you to the others and hope we won't scare everyone to death."

"I still do not see what is so scary about me. I have often been told I am a bit of a runt."

Leena chuckled. "I'm tall for my age. You've seen my father, he's a big man. Yet you're a lot bigger than he is. You're no runt among us, Tikid. Some might see you as a monster out of their worst nightmares."

"But... but I am a Green, not a Red! And I am young and not fierce. You are not making sense."

A chuckle stopped Tikid's offended speech. "You have to understand that the color of a dragon means nothing to us, Tikid." Jetyaa had made her way silently towards the group. "I heard your

236

mother, Meeryle, and she reacted better than I did the first time I saw a dragon."

"*Does your dam know how to shoot an arrow, Meeryle?*" asked the young dragon, worried.

The three humans laughed. "No, she doesn't. I think she knows how to hold a sword, but not what to do with it," answered Meeryle. "My mother is well known for her aversion to weapons of any kind. It's a good thing I'm the cook at home, otherwise, we would eat very big pieces of food. The only knife she'll hold is the table knife."

"*Good. I feel safer already.*"

"Come on," motioned Leena. "You have other humans to meet."

By the time they had joined the waiting crowd, Parin and the Healer had reassured everyone. The faces were no longer as scared and some were even curious. Yet, as they moved closer, the crowd took a single step back. The only exception was a small boy, who was looking around frantically, but not at the dragon. Meeryle couldn't place him for a minute, then remembered his name. Nirvin was very shy, except with animals. He and his little white dog were inseparable. He would hardly speak to people, but opened up to his pet. The dog always listened diligently to his little master's endless flow of words.

The little dog was nowhere to be seen. Nirvin moved forward, panic distorting his face. "Dowie! Dowie, come here!"

Meeryle caught a white flash from the corner of her eye. She turned her head and smiled. The shaggy dog was sitting on its haunches, matching Tikid's position, its little nose up, neck muscles strained to their maximum. Tikid was stooped down, her snout touching the dog's.

"No! Nirvin, come back!"

Meeryle jumped at the shout. She didn't have time to find out who had made it as Nirvin ran past her and grabbed his dog in an embrace so tight, the animal squawked.

"Be careful, little one. You will hurt him."

Nirvin blinked and looked around, slightly loosening his grip on the dog. Finally, his gaze met Tikid's, who tilted her head to the side and chuckled. "You speak?" he asked.

"Of course. So does your dog and he was greeting me. He is very happy to meet a dragon. He has never seen one before."

"Me neither. What else did he say? And how come he doesn't speak to me, anyway? I always talk to him."

Tikid lay down to meet the boy eye to eye. Meeryle stopped listening by letting go of the dragon's tail. The boy's mother was approaching cautiously. Tikid chuckled again. The sound was reassuring and gave the mother the courage to sit beside her son and take part in the ongoing conversation.

Leena took Meeryle's hand and squeezed it. "I think everything will be fine." She jerked her chin toward the other villagers. All the children wanted to sit by the dragon and they swarmed Nirvin and his mother. The parents could only follow. Soon, Tikid was surrounded by a sitting crowd.

"You're right, Leena," said Meeryle. "We'll be fine."

The biggest problem was hospitality. Meeryle and Leena were told by a shocked Tikid that dragons slept in their mounds, not under the stars. "*Animals sleep outside, not dragons.*" They couldn't get an explanation that made sense out of the young dragon, so they started to hunt for a dwelling. However, a creature this big couldn't fit in any house and very few doors were opening in welcome. Meeryle also refused to leave her friend on her own. Leena proposed an elegant solution: the barn in which they had been jailed had plenty of room for both human and dragon.

A village-wide effort cleaned and refurbished the barn for Meeryle and her guest. As the summer and its harvest were upon them, little space was taken by the remaining winter grain stores. The few barrels left were easily reshuffled into a much neater stack. The unused plowing equipment was removed and placed outside. Two farmers pounced on it, finding a hundred uses for the previously forgotten apparatus.

Soon the barn was clean and organized, ready to welcome its unusual guest, lacking only sleeping accommodations and any furnishings Meeryle would need.

"That big critter of yours, Meeryle, what does it want to sleep on?" asked old Makin.

"It's a she, Makin, not it. And I don't know. I slept in one of their mounds, but it was only bare earth."

They consulted Tikid, who snuffed and scratched at the ground inside the barn, much to the dismay of the old man. "Now, slow down, girl. I don't mind you using my barn and all, but if you dig a hole, it's just not going to work out."

"Your earth is not pure enough. I need to dig to get to the right layer."

The old man scratched his head. "What do you mean, not pure? It's the same ground that was there when my grandfather built the darn thing!"

"Precisely. You have never cleaned it."

"Say what?"

"The earth that covers the ground of the entire barn is dead. I need live earth to sleep in and infuse."

"Meeryle, you take care of this, but I want my barn back the way it was when Missy here leaves. Understand?"

Meeryle nodded solemnly, trying very hard not to laugh. The barn was basically the only barn worthy of the name and Makin's family had always owned it. In return, the villagers paid him a fee to house winter fare. That barn was his life and his obsession. Seeing it invaded by a mystical creature wasn't the issue; only what the creature did to the building mattered to him.

"That man seems very strange."

"I think you'll find everyone here strange," said Leena with a smile. "Makin is special, though. According to him, doing anything to his barn is a high crime."

Tikid settled into the slight hole she had dug, and Meeryle sat against her friend. Leena carried in blankets and lanterns, stacking them neatly on the ground and placing the lanterns by the walls.

"Back up," said Meeryle. With a thought, she made the lanterns flare.

"Showoff," said Leena. Meeryle smiled smugly. "Anyway, here's bedding for you. You may want to lay out some straw. You stirred up quite a bit of dust, Tikid. Oh yes, what do you want to eat? Everyone is willing to give a bit, like a chicken or a rabbit. My dad even offered a pig."

The dragon's head came up abruptly. *"I certainly will not eat any of this."* She was outraged.

"Well, then, what?" asked Meeryle, puzzled. "You have to eat something. Every living being does, right?" Leena nodded in support.

"I sustain myself with the essence of the plants and the earth," replied the dragon.

The girls exchanged a bewildered look. "And just how do you do that?" asked Leena.

"It is easiest when I sleep. I dug out the dead earth and I will lie in the ground and soak in its essence. Normally, I would have earth and plants around me, but this should be enough."

"You're saying that earth can be dead?" asked Leena, curious.

"Yes. When all the minerals and fertilizants are gone, the earth is dead. It cannot feed me. I could make it live again, but it takes time and practice. Besides, I am the one who needs to replenish, not the earth here. And it has been dead too long, anyway."

"Do all dragons feed this way?" asked Meeryle.

"Yes. Different Colors need different essences, though."

"Tikid, for every answer you give, ten more questions come up," said Leena with a sigh. "So, what does the color have to do with anything?"

"The Greens need plants, the Browns need earth, the Whites need air, the Purples need water, and the Reds need fire."

The girls looked at each other, eyes wide. "Leena's right. Your answers are very confusing," said Meeryle. "Let's try to understand this because it sounds very important. You said Greens need plants, right?" The dragon nodded. "Then how come you're digging a hole instead of rolling yourself in leaves?"

"In order to roll in leaves, they would have to be on the ground, and therefore dead. I need live plants. In the forest, the trees can be enough, but it is better if we can also imbue ourselves with earth. Plants need earth to grow, and in a sense, we are just like plants. So our dwellings are a perfect mix of earth and plants."

"Do you need to be watered too?" asked Meeryle with a giggle.

Tikid blinked before her laughter shook the barn walls. *"We are not plants! Greens like water; we sometimes drink it. Most of the time, we get water from the plants themselves. Purples need water much more than Greens."*

"So you can 'borrow' from another color?" interrupted Leena.

"In a way. Since Greens are the essence of plants, we can also use water and air to sustain ourselves."

"By using water, do you mean submerge?"

"Yes, or drink it. Greens are very versatile, you know. But some Colors can only survive in their own environment, like the Reds, though they can use air too."

"And just what is this environment for the Reds?"

"*Fire, of course.*"

"Is there a Red dragon in all fires?" asked Meeryle, hopeful.

Tikid chuckled. "*Only in very big fires. The Reds live in the center of the world and in the volcanoes. I do not think they have ever had contact with humans. They have very little contact with the rest of the Kin.*"

"The Kin?" Leena looked like her head was about to burst.

"*The name of the dragons. We are the Kin.*"

"Meeryle, wipe that grin off your face. We're not going after Red dragons."

"But fire is my element!"

Tikid's laugh resonated once again in the barn. "*If you really want, when I can carry you, we will fly together and find a Red for you.*"

"See, she understands."

Leena rolled her eyes. "You two are impossible. Now let's go. I'm hungry and no amount of earth bathing is going to fix that. Do you want to come, Tikid?"

"*No, thank you. You will be eating dead live things and it will be wrong to my senses. Go ahead. I will sleep in the meantime. This day has been very taxing for me and my wing.*"

The girls left, laughing at the understatement. A few people were waiting anxiously outside the barn to find out what to prepare for their guest's meal.

"Nothing. It turns out dragons don't eat the same type of food we do," explained Leena.

"So what, then? Grass? Hay?" asked the Healer.

243

At the mention of hay, Makin raised his voice. "Now, she better not start eating the hay left in the barn. It's meant for the cows, not for some strange dragon-thing."

"Don't worry. Your hay is safe," answered Meeryle.

"I'm just saying, that's all." Satisfied, the old man left to hover by the open door of the barn and peer inside to make sure the dragon wasn't doing any more damage.

"Well, then, no feast?" asked the Healer.

"No."

"Home it is, then."

"Well, I'm sure we can organize something with Tikid and everyone, just not around 'dead live things,'" said Leena.

"Dead live things? Now, there's a rather peculiar description of food," said the Healer with a wry face. "I will see you later, then. We need to talk about this Healing of yours."

The rest dispersed. "Do you want to come home with me for your meal?" asked Leena.

Meeryle hesitated. "I really should go home, you know. I have to face my mother eventually."

"All right."

As Meeryle watched her friend walk away, she prepared herself for the upcoming confrontation. She was pretty sure her mother would act oddly, but she didn't know how her father and brothers would react to her actions. She shrugged. It didn't matter, really. Her life was finally set; the dragons were at the center of it. She would make sure everyone everywhere would know about dragons and how to respect them.

The thought lifted her heart and she stepped lightly to her house. She was stopped by a bark. Suqi was looking up at her, head cocked to the right. "Ah, well, now you show up! Tikid didn't want to say anything about what the two of you discussed. I don't suppose you'd like to elaborate?" Meeryle put her hands on her hips and stared at the fox. Suqi made a noise that sounded suspiciously like laughter. The little animal was definitely projecting feelings of mockery. "Well, I guess you're entitled to yet another secret. I wonder if I should tell the Healer about your abilities. He'd probably throw a fit!" The fox flicked her tail disdainfully and led the way home. It seemed Suqi felt just as Meeryle did about Corvin. The girl smiled and followed her strange pet.

As the windows were open to let in the breeze, Meeryle heard the voices of her parents and brothers, which stopped abruptly as soon as she opened the door. All the faces turned to look at her. Meeryle gulped.

Tarkin, who had been pacing, almost ran up to his sister and grabbed her shoulder. "It really speaks?" he asked. Meeryle, bewildered, nodded. She had never seen such a look on her brother's face. He was always the joker and usually displayed a small smirk. Tonight, however, he was serious, almost frighteningly so. "It speaks in my head?"

"In everybody's. The only sounds dragons make with their mouths are... I guess roars." Tarkin blanched. Meeryle quickly added: "They laugh, too."

The young man stood still. "I didn't imagine it."

"No, you didn't. Mother heard her too, you know."

"I'm not sure anymore," she protested. "It could have been Leena or someone else. Or maybe a trick, Meeryle. Aren't Mages supposed to be able to do things like that?" Her eyes were wide and her face white. Meeryle closed her eyes, took in a deep breath and summoned as much patience as she could.

Before she could say anything, however, Alvyl, her father, stepped in. "That will be enough, Meera. Everyone who went into the forest agreed they heard the dragons inside their heads rather than with their ears. If you refuse to believe it, it's your decision, but don't use it as an excuse to badger Meeryle. And as for that Mage thing...." Meeryle's father came to his daughter. Tarkin moved away, making room. Alvyl put his hand on Meeryle's shoulder and smiled. "I'm proud to have a Mage in the family. It was time you found yourself, girl."

Meeryle-and her mother-were wide-eyed with astonishment. The girl had never expected to hear such words from her father. Happiness filled her with a rush. She blinked and held back tears. Even Leena hadn't been so happy about her gift. For the first time in years, Meeryle threw herself into her father's arms and hugged him.

"I'm glad too. And I found dragons."

Alvyl smiled. "It's been a long time since you've mentioned them."

"Turns out they aren't just stories, though," said Meeryle with a smile.

"No, they're real. Almost too real for some. But come, let's eat. It won't be like one of your meals, but we'll survive. You can tell us all about this dragon friend of yours."

***

At first, Meeryle had a hard time speaking. She was intimidated by her father and brothers, as well as the sour looks her mother was throwing at her. She concentrated on her food (definitely not her cooking-not enough spices), playing with it on her plate. Eventually, the memories overcame her shyness and she came alive in the telling of her adventure. Even her mother became captivated and the meal cooled on the table, forgotten.

Her younger brother, Marvyl, then asked to meet Tikid. Infected by his enthusiasm and Meeryle's, the rest of the family voiced their own curiosity. They trouped out and were making their way to the barn when they were intercepted by Parin.

"Come, I was going to meet you at your house. Since we couldn't have a banquet for the dragon, we decided to have a general meeting. We wanted to do this before nightfall. The Healer also has a word to say."

"Is Tikid already there?" asked Meeryle.

"Yes. It gave old Makin a chance to inspect the barn. I don't think he wants to go in there if the dragon is already in it," chuckled Parin.

When they arrived, the village's square was already crowded, with Tikid taking almost a third of the space on her own. She was surrounded by chairs occupied by adults, and children sitting on the ground. Some, braver than others, were touching her. Nirvin and his dog were cradled by the dragon's long tail. Leena, who was petting Dowie's shaggy head, smiled and waved at Meeryle. The plump girl spotted Rokin hovering at the back of the crowd. Leena's rebuke seemed to have made him hesitant. Normally, he would have been sitting right beside Leena, beaming with pride. Tikid's presence had everyone's attention, so his aloofness remained unnoticed by the bevy of girls who usually tried to convince him that their company was more interesting than Leena's.

After their encounter in the woods with the boy, while the barn was being cleared, Tikid had questioned Meeryle mercilessly on the meaning of the relationship between the tall girl and the handsome boy. She'd explained that like humans, dragons did court one another, but much later. For Tikid, the thought of a mate was far from important, as, in her opinion, she was much too young. *"I only came of age last spring. I still need to fully understand what it means to be an id."* The young dragon hadn't been able to clarify her statement, so Meeryle had continued in explaining why she now thought that Rokin would be a bad choice for Leena. Tikid agreed. *"He just does not seem worthy, neither of Leena nor of you."* When asked why, Tikid had given a dragon shrug. *"He does not have sufficient power to match either of you."*

"So we would need a powerful man?"

"Well, certainly. Do you not wish to be with your own kind? A Mage with a Mage and a Healer with a Healer."

Meeryle was amused by Tikid's simple view of love. She tried to explain why she found Rokin

248

attractive, whether he was a Mage or not, but in vain. *"I fail to see what is so attractive about him. His appearance just seems wrong."*

"How so? I mean, Rokin is quite the looker. Even in the big cities, I'm sure he'd stand out."

"Well, the muscular balance in his upper body is really off. His shoulders are bulging, and he has strange bumps in the muscles of both his upper and lower arms. The legs are no better. I think he looks ugly, especially compared to the both of you. Your beauty differs, as you are soft and curvy, and Leena is nice and long, but you are both much nicer to look at than this male of yours." The dragon had punctuated her statement with a nod. Meeryle had given up with a laugh, promising herself to relay the dragon's unique view of human beauty to Leena.

The tall girl was attractive in her own way. Her almond-shaped eyes were always kind, especially with children. While the villagers were gathering, Leena was talking with Nirvin and two other children, encouraging them to touch Tikid and speak with her. Meeryle smiled and agreed silently with the dragon; Leena did have her own inner beauty. Whether Rokin had seen it or not was irrelevant. Meeryle was sure someone else, the right man, would see it also one day.

The Healer had erected a makeshift platform in the middle of the square and was standing on it, looking for someone. As soon as he spotted Meeryle, he smiled. "Please, everyone, we are ready to start."

As Meeryle made her way to Tikid's side, the crowd slowly quieted. When silence was complete, Corvin spoke.

"As you know, we have a rather unexpected guest." A few dared to chuckle. "If you haven't met her already, this is Tikid. This youngster will be among us for a few days while her wing fully heals."

Meeryle sat on the ground in front of Tikid, who put her right paw on her shoulder. *"He is very eager about something. He kept asking about you."*

Meeryle shrugged. "I'm sure he'll tell me."

She was hushed by the ones surrounding her. Meeryle looked up and back at Tikid and rolled her eyes. The young dragon chuckled, the rumbling cutting off the Healer's speech. All eyes were on them.

"We are sorry. Please do go on," said Tikid calmly, while Meeryle felt her face heat up.

Corvin harrumphed. "As I was saying, Tikid's wing still needs to heal. However, what you are all seeing is the end result. The dragon's wing had been damaged almost beyond repair. Thanks to Meeryle's inventiveness and Leena's skill, Tikid will fly again." Meeryle was speechless. She never thought she would be recognized in public. She looked for Leena and when she met her friend's eye, they both smiled.

"Now," continued the Healer, "I cannot attest to Meeryle's skill, but I can certainly do so for Leena. If you could come up here, Leena."

Bewildered, the tall girl obeyed. The platform was narrow, so she stood very close to the edge. "Even if I retracted your apprenticeship, Leena, I don't think you need it any longer." He took out a green and gold scarf and tied it around Leena's neck. She stared at it and shifted her gaze to the Healer, mouth gaping. The old man smiled. "Now, normally, you would give me your green scarf, as a symbol. But since I took it from you the other day, I already have it. I did keep it, have no fear. Now I can cherish it." Leena closed her mouth and nodded. The Healer smiled and turned toward the audience. "Leena is no longer an apprentice. The Healing she performed on Tikid was her first Healing as a full Healer."

Stunned, Leena looked around the applauding crowd. Meeryle got up and tried to run to her friend, but Tikid was already ahead, making everyone scramble out of the way. Meeryle caught the tip of the big creature's tail and followed her. Leena grabbed the dragon's neck in a tight embrace.

"Thanks to you, Tikid, I'm a Healer."

"*You always were. Now you just know it*," said Tikid, smugly.

Meeryle smiled. "For once, Tikid, I understand you perfectly. Come, let's celebrate."

CHAPTER SIXTEEN

Meeryle crumpled into a chair and took the cloth the Healer gave her to wipe her mouth.

"Here, drink this, it'll help with the taste," he said in a gentle tone.

The drink was bitter, with only a touch of sweetness, but it did block the lingering taste of vomit. She was sweating profusely, shaking from head to toe and had finally thrown up, but she had managed to relate the memories leading up to the death of Teerane's mother.

Both the Healer and Parin were looking at her pensively. Leena squeezed her hand in support; the tall girl had warned her that this could happen, but Meeryle had wanted to get rid of the memories' hold on her. The person for whom she had forced herself to face the gut-wrenching fear of these memories stood motionless, tears running down her cheeks.

"You killed her," whispered Teerane.

"Now, Teerane," started Corvin.

"You made me forget, you made everyone forget what you did!" she screamed, fists tight.

Meeryle cringed. Bile filled her mouth and she gagged, trying very hard not to throw up once again.

"Enough, Teerane!" bellowed Parin. "You can't just choose what you hear. You listened, didn't you?" The older girl ground her teeth. "Didn't you?" insisted Parin, his voice almost growling.

"Yes," she answered reluctantly.

"Now, child," said the Healer, "I'm also angry, but not at Meeryle."

"You should be!"

"I said quiet, girl!"

Teerane cringed a bit under Parin's menacing gaze, but her eyes were still full of hatred.

"As I was saying," resumed Corvin, "I'm angry at your mother, Teerane." He lifted his hand to forestall her from saying anything. "Think about it, will you? She was ready to kill a child in order to hide the fact that she had the Mage-gift. Why? A Mage is very useful and their services usually bring them, if not fortune, at least respect. To me, this can only mean that she was planning to use the people in this village. How, I'm not sure. Of course, it no longer matters, since she's gone."

"But... but...."

"And now I also wonder about your father's death all those years ago. He drowned, didn't he?"

Teerane blanched. "You mean...."

The Healer nodded. "But of course, we'll never know for sure. This is speculation."

"But it makes sense," whispered the girl.

"So, you understand that Meeryle was not at fault?" asked Parin.

The words lifted a weight Meeryle hadn't known she was carrying. If neither Parin nor the Healer thought her responsible, then maybe she really wasn't. She knew that all she had done was defend herself, yet somehow, it didn't make it right.

Teerane shook her head and wiped away new tears. "This is really messed up. Did my aunt know? Why didn't she tell me?"

"She was your father's sister, so she probably didn't know. I think, from what Meeryle remembers, that she used her gift to get what she wanted and affected the memory of those she used so they wouldn't recall what she did. Once again, I'm guessing. What's important now is that you do know and that you accept it."

"Corvin's right, Teerane. What was done is done. I will change the village records to indicate the approximate time of her death and I'll let everyone know what happened."

"But...."

"They deserve to know," insisted Parin. "It won't change how people see you, Teerane. At least if you make an effort to be kinder to Meeryle than you have been." He chuckled at the surprise on both girls' faces. "What, you didn't think I hadn't noticed?"

"No," said Meeryle. She was glad that he had, though. Her head was spinning a bit with everything that was happening: she wasn't considered guilty; at least a few people had known about Teerane's bullying, yet hadn't done anything about it; and now, she had just found out Teerane's father might have been murdered.

"I had, and others too," said the Healer. "When Leena became your friend, however, things got better, so I didn't do anything about it."

Teerane didn't say anything; she only looked down.

"Well, your actions are a bit more understandable, but they will no longer be tolerated," said Corvin. "Am I clear?"

The older girl was still quiet. Meeryle suddenly felt sorry for Teerane - nothing about what she knew about her parents was true. "Teerane." When she finally looked up, the older girl's face was blank.

"Teerane, I'm really sorry." Meeryle was surprised how true it was. Tears welled up and ran down her cheeks. She had killed someone! It was so wrong....

"So am I, Meeryle, so am I." Teerane left the Healer's cottage, sobbing.

Corvin, Leena, Parin, and Meeryle looked at each other, all taken aback by Teerane's abrupt departure.

"Well," said Leena, "I guess that's that."

"I'll keep a watch on her," said Parin. "In the meantime, I'll inform the rest of the village."

***

The village settled down over the next few days. People slowly accepted the fact that they now had two Healers, one of whom was of an unusual kind. They also acknowledged Meeryle's new status as a Mage and her participation in the demise of Teerane's mother by taking the time to stop and talk to her or simply by giving her a nod usually reserved for adults when meeting her on the street. This reaction left Meeryle uncomfortable. She hadn't come to terms with the fact that she had killed someone, and while she was obviously not found responsible, everyone's solicitude in that matter left her with an awkward feeling. All she wanted was for things to go back to the way they had been. So for the most part, she ignored this new attitude toward her. When someone spoke to her, she answered politely and escaped as soon as she could without being rude.

Her escape was Tikid. She spent every available moment with the dragon, showing her friend every corner of the village, explaining the rationale behind every building and every tool.

Objects were of great interest to Tikid. Dragons never used them, so any object became subject to a lengthy explanation. The concept of tables to eat from baffled her, and tools fascinated her. Dragons didn't use tools, as they possessed the strength and dexterity to do without them. The human solutions filled her with wonder. The tools used to plow the earth and to harvest were the most captivating.

Meeryle couldn't answer all the dragon's questions, so she sought the villagers who did have the knowledge. At first, they were hesitant, intimidated by Tikid's size and appearance. Her endless curiosity and her ebullience soon broke the barrier of physical differences and all answered her questions eagerly.

Tikid had decided to stay at the village even when her wing was fully healed, much to the dismay of Makin. The dragon agreed to use only a small part of the barn in order to make space for the harvest. The old man erected a small picket fence inside the barn, delimiting Tikid's area. Meeryle thought it rude, but Tikid shrugged. All she wanted was a roof of some kind.

With the dragon's presence, Meeryle's gift and the circumstances that brought forth the death of Teerane's mother were, if not forgotten, put aside. Teerane remained quite aloof, isolating herself in her aunt's house. Meeryle didn't really mind not seeing the older girl around-and spending so much time with Tikid, she barely thought about that dreadful day anymore.

At her father's request, Meeryle didn't share the barn every night with the dragon and spent one night out of two at home. She understood it looked strange to the rest of the villagers for a girl to sleep in the barn. Meeryle didn't particularly care what others thought on that score, but she wanted to please her father. Father and daughter were seeing each other in an entirely new light, and Meeryle didn't want to ruin the newfound relationship.

Tikid quickly became part of everybody's life. People would wish her good morning as they did to anyone else, as they stopped fearing her and seeing her as a novelty. The dragon had become such a part of the village, people forgot to warn visitors from other villages. After their first encounter sent a visiting couple screaming, everyone made a point to introduce any visitor to Tikid, with ample previous explanations. None of the villagers wanted the reputation of harboring a monster, and no one wanted to hurt Tikid's feelings further. Once visitors got over the shock, they were quickly conquered by the young dragon's positive attitude and answered- and asked-questions eagerly. When guests left, most were pleased with the encounter, but a few remained dubious. Meeryle was puzzled by their attitude, but Leena pointed out that not everyone would like dragons, just as not everyone liked other people.

Life would settle back into its routine and Tikid would once again become a taken-for-granted part of the village. The children were an exception: they couldn't get enough of the young dragon. Wherever Tikid went, at least one child was lurking. Even the older ones found a reason to be outside to see the dragon.

Tikid also found children strange. She questioned their appearance and their clothes. Her questions on that subject reminded Meeryle of the fledglings and how funny they had found her when she hadn't known the different names of the dragons' sexes. She now understood their mirth when Tikid questioned her about things that were self-evident- for a human.

"What do you mean, how is their sex determined?"

"Well, who determines it for them? Nirvin is obviously male, but he has not come of age yet. Who made the decision for him?"

"No one did. He was born this way," answered Meeryle with a smile. "Just like all the animals."

Tikid blinked a few times. *"But animals are different, they just are. They do not have the capacity to choose. I did not get the feeling humans were like animals. They think and decide, do they not?"*

"Well, yes, but..."

"So what happens if Nirvin no longer wants to be male when he comes of age?"

"He won't. You can't just change your sex. You're a boy or a girl for rest of your life."

"So you did not just choose to be female?" asked the dragon, puzzled.

"No! I've been a girl since I was born. It's not the same for dragons, is it? The fledglings mentioned it to me and laughed at me when I asked questions."

"Well, they are young and do not know that humans may be different in that manner. Deciding your gender is a very important decision. Only once

258

a fledgling comes of age can it decide if it would be more suitable to be an id or an ad. Then, it immerses itself in the essence of the Greens and comes out male or female."

"And you went through this process?" asked Meeryle, eyes wide.

"Of course. Last spring."

"So what were you before?"

"I was Tik. I then decided I was best suited for an id, so I became Tikid."

"And if you had decided to become a boy?"

"I would have been Tikad."

Meeryle had related the conversation to Leena, who was fascinated. "But how do they know to balance the males and the females? Do they ever have too many of one kind?"

"I don't know, Leena. The whole thing was really strange to me. You should ask her for details, not me."

The new Healer listened to her advice and sought the dragon. Meeryle listened briefly to Tikid's explanations, but they were a repetition of her earlier conversation with the dragon. Leena's questions remained unanswered as the young dragon didn't have the information she wanted.

Instead, the young Healer began to systematically question her friend on dragon anatomy. The sheer amount of questions made Meeryle dizzy. Some were interesting and some were boring, but Meeryle stayed and listened, trying to understand the answers.

The purely physical side of dragons was fascinating. They moved around on all fours like animals, and for a brief moment, Meeryle couldn't help but compare her friend to a horse. The explanations on movements and problems were indeed similar to that of horses, in particular the description of injuries like sprains, scratches, and fractures. However, dragons lacked the techniques to care for these injuries and unlike horses, they had no one to tend to them. Leena was outraged to learn dragons had to sometimes suffer for months before a wound healed on its own.

Tikid found Leena's reaction funny. *"We have no Healers like you, Leena. Dragons imbue themselves in the essence of their environment and redistribute it as needed. We cannot use it the way you do. That is why the Healing of my wing is a miracle. Mind you, it would be virtually impossible for a dragon to hurt itself in such a manner in normal circumstances. We are not usually clumsy."*

"So let's say Meeryle and I hadn't been around and you managed to tear your wing. What would've happened?"

"It would have eventually healed, tear and all. I might have been able to hover slightly, but no more."

"So you would've had to develop your leg muscles," said Leena thoughtfully. She circled the sitting dragon. "Can you go down on all fours, Tikid?" The dragon complied. "Well, you certainly weren't meant to walk, at least for long periods of time."

"What do you mean?" asked Meeryle, suddenly interested. She had been sitting with the tip of Tikid's tail in her hand.

"Look at her. Her front legs are shorter than her hind ones, by a lot. Think of your brother's dog. He's meant to race, so the hind legs are a bit longer and stronger, but not like Tikid's."

Meeryle examined her friend. Her rear end was much higher than her front, but her long neck allowed her head to be level with her back end.

Tikid turned and looked at herself, amused. "*I have never thought about it. But you are right, Leena, we do not walk very long. It is straining and it can be awkward among the trees.*"

"But then, why are your hind legs so muscular?" asked Meeryle.

"*Apparently, they are not muscular enough to lift off with you,*" teased Tikid.

"What! You can't mean...."

Meeryle blushed at the humiliating memory. "Yes, that's what she means and leave it alone, Leena."

"Yes, well, anyway," snorted Leena. She turned to Tikid. "You use your hind legs to lift off, right?" The dragon nodded. "You use both your wings and your legs when you lift off."

"*I tuck my front legs in when I fly.*"

"All right, now spread your wings out and let me have a good look at them," said Leena.

Meeryle sighed and left her two friends. The examination was becoming much too tedious to her taste. Her stomach grumbled. It suddenly seemed like an eternity since she had taken the time to prepare a fine meal. Meeryle headed home, her head full of meatloaf and pastries. Maybe Tikid might like sweetcakes. They contained no meat, after all. Stunned, Meeryle stopped and thought it through. She could make sure the sweetcakes contained no "dead live things." Elated at the possibility of getting Tikid to enjoy the most wonderful thing in life-eating-she started running in anticipation.

***

Over the following months, a routine settled in. Every other morning, Meeryle would walk from the barn home to have breakfast. She would then tour the village with Tikid, answering the dragon's questions or finding someone who could. They would part at lunch, then meet with Leena, who was taking copious notes on whatever Tikid could tell her about dragon physiology and habits. Meeryle usually left them, finding the conversations difficult to follow, since most of the time she couldn't touch Tikid, as Leena was making the dragon move around too much.

She also left Tikid to fend for herself when the dragon went into the fields. Tikid had wanted to try the tools used for harvesting and discovered that she was not only much better with her paws than with tools, but that she enjoyed the work tremendously. "*I am a Green. I have helped plants grow and heal, but I have never sown one. Moving the earth this way feels very good.*" However, fieldwork was not for Meeryle; after making sure dragon and farmers got along without too many mishaps, she decided that her friend was in better company with them when it came to sowing, and later, to harvesting.

Meeryle would go back home and launch herself into the creation of sweetcakes and pastries, bathing the area surrounding the house in the most appetizing smells. Tikid could not eat anything she prepared, though. All of it came into the "dead live thing" category, even if the products were transformed, like flour or butter. However, the dragon immensely enjoyed the smell of food prepared with such products. The scent of pastries was a new sensation for her. Meeryle was beside herself with joy. Now, every time she ate something, she took the time to analyze the smell, trying to guess if the dragon would like the scent of the food she was sampling. She guessed right most of the time. As long as the food contained no meat, the dragon was fine. Seeing Tikid's eyes close with bliss as she inhaled over pastries brought the warmest feeling to Meeryle's stomach. Delighted by her friend's reaction, the human girl was becoming a very creative cook indeed.

Leena was shocked to discover that Tikid-or any dragon-didn't have any teeth, and questioned her mercilessly.

Tikid cocked her head and blinked in surprise. *"Why would we need teeth? We do not eat. We infuse ourselves with essence."*

"Yes, I know. But you still need teeth."

"To what end?"

"Well... to help you hold something, like when you're building something."

"We do not build."

"What about your mounds?"

"They are created when fledglings come into being, then we dig them as needed."

"What about to defend yourself?"

"Against what? And I would use my paws and claws; they are much less awkward than my mouth."

Leena threw her hands up. "I give up. I forgot that you don't kill to eat. Never mind. It's a good thing sweetcakes don't agree with you." She gave Meeryle a wry look. "If they're not good in large quantities for humans, they wouldn't be great for dragons either."

Tikid snorted. "*She tried, but flour is still a live thing. They smell good, though, not dead.*" The dragon added eagerly: "*She always has different new ones, too!*"

These new creations, along with her new status as a Mage and as a survivor of a Mage's attack, unexpectedly opened doors for Meeryle. Everyone wanted to taste her food or know her opinion on special dishes. Although she had already had a good status as a cook, her opinion suddenly became more important. At first, people expected Mage tricks. When none came, Meeryle became less interesting, but no one wanted to pass the chance to see magic at work. So they listened, politely at first, then with great interest. Meeryle's comments and ideas on cooking eventually wiped their memories of anything having to do with magic. Her work in the kitchen was supplanting her Mage status-to the point where she would forget all about her gift. Meeryle was truly fitting in for the first time amongst her peers and her elders.

Once evening came, Meeryle would hurry back home for dinner-which she usually prepared-and would regale her mother with the village's gossip. Her daughter's point of view was new to Meera and she enjoyed Meeryle's comments on the villagers and their cooking disasters or successes.

The relationship between mother and daughter had mended and bloomed to the point where Meera would sometimes accompany Meeryle after dinner to speak with Tikid. Some of the children would already be crowding the barn, asking Tikid either to tell them stories or to find out what their pets were saying. After a few candlemarks, parents would seek their offspring to put them to bed, much to their disappointment. Meera-when she was there-would help with the children-gathering. When she was not, Tikid would chase the children-and sometimes the parents-out of the barn with terrifying roars. The shrieks of fear and delight pleased her immensely and she would roll on the ground with laughter, shaking the barn's walls.

On these occasions, Makin would sometimes barge in and shake his fist at the dragon. "Now, listen, missy. You can't go around and destroy this barn. It's much too valuable. Settle down and behave, now, will you?" Tikid would blow air in his face-a very rude thing for dragons to do, apparently-and rumble. The old man would snort and leave, saying: "I've got my eye on you, critter. You watch yourself," making Meeryle and Tikid go off into peals of laughter.

Once night had fallen, Tikid would settle in her hole and fall asleep. One evening out of two, Meeryle would curl up against her friend and fall asleep to the rhythm of the dragon's heartbeat. On other nights, she would walk slowly home, thinking of pastries and red eyes full of delight.

Suqi had also become Meeryle's shadow. Everywhere the big girl went, the black fox followed. Only Meeryle and Leena noted it, though; Tikid had drawn everyone's attention, and the villagers had already grown used to the little animal's presence.

The dragon kept stubbornly silent when it came to Suqi. When questioned, she would answer: *"She will tell you when she is ready."*

"Tell me what? Am I supposed to hear her?"

Tikid would shrug and cock her head. *"If you cannot hear her, then neither she nor you are ready."*

As enraging as they were, Meeryle had to content herself with these cryptic answers. She even tried to question Suqi, but how did one carry on a conversation when the other couldn't answer? Eventually, Meeryle had simply hugged the fox and told herself she would wait until later, when "she was ready," as Tikid had put it, to delve more deeply into the meaning of Suqi's presence.

Putting any thoughts of the fox's strangeness aside, Meeryle lived what she felt were the best months of her life. Between the cooking and the dragon's presence, the girl was in heaven. She did notice that Suqi stopped following her some places. For example, when Meeryle was meeting with the women to discuss new dishes, the fox didn't accompany her to the house designated for the meeting. As soon as the destination became clear, the little animal would run in another direction. As Meeryle became more and more involved with the village women, she saw less and less of Suqi. She would only meet her at night, when she slept in the barn. By that time, Meeryle was usually too tired to ask any questions and simply fell asleep rolled against Tikid, cuddling Suqi.

The days Meeryle noticed that Suqi wasn't following her, she missed the fox and her cocky attitude. She also realized that Suqi was the only one who had managed to get her to use her gift appropriately. Since Tikid had arrived at the village, Meeryle had barely touched fire except in the usual way to cook. It was almost as if Suqi's presence and sarcastic feelings were necessary to encourage Meeryle. Between Suqi's absence and Tikid's presence, the young Mage had lost all desire to pursue her gift.

Once in a while, though, Leena would remind Meeryle of the exercises she needed to do in order to train her gift. "You've mastered fire, but you've only barely touched the other elements. You need to focus on them too, you know."

"I used air and earth to find the dragons. I'm fine," answered Meeryle.

"What about water?"

"It's the opposite of fire, right?" Leena nodded. "Well, then, I don't want to have anything to do with it. My element is fire."

"Meeryle, a Mage has to master all four elements."

"Says who?" asked Meeryle, annoyed.

"Say all the books. There's even a hint of a fifth element, the one that Healers use. But that would need some looking into. I'm not too sure about it, but the Healer maintains that's why we were able to Heal Tikid. We used all elements conjointly."

"I'm busy. It's almost the end of summer and there are preserves that need to be done. I'm needed."

"Meeryle, the Healer and I need you too. We can't redo that Healing without you. We've tried, but we can't even touch the other elements. We need a Mage for that."

"Later, all right?" Meeryle would compromise with a smile. She was so happy with her life, her temper seemed extinguished. She didn't get angry with Leena or anyone anymore.

But later never came, as Meeryle always found excuses. The harvest was coming; she had promised all the village women to teach them how to make that wonderful new pastry; Tikid had found a new way to plow and sow; Tikid needed a new home, because the barn was getting full and the space was needed. Eventually, Leena gave up, much to Meeryle's relief. The problem was that, as always, she didn't want anything to do with the Healer. He was giving her strange looks, both condescending and respectful, and maybe even fearful. The last troubled Meeryle deeply and stirred memories of Teerane's mother. Were they wondering if she would she use her gift in a similarly harmful way? No one should be afraid of her; it just didn't feel right. Developing her gift was therefore not a good idea.

Meeryle also felt extremely comfortable with her relationship with fire and didn't see the necessity to touch the other elements. The rasp of air and the murmur of earth were not as enticing as the powerful beat of fire. When she spent the night at home, before going to sleep, she would go into a trance to seek the hot presence deep in the ground and bask in it. She would let the heat engulf her and rock her to sleep. Her dreams were filled with churning oranges and reds moving to the beat of fire. Sometimes, she imagined she dreamed a Red dragon was lurking about and beckoning her to join it in the dancing colors. In the morning, she was full of energy and acutely aware of the fire burning in the hearth. Life was very good for Meeryle.

***

One day, as Meeryle was finishing preparing lunch, one of the boys came running to the kitchen widow.

"Meeryle, Meeryle! They're done!"

"Done what?"

"The house for Tikid!"

She closed her eyes and took in a deep breath, a huge smile spreading across her face. "I'll be right there." The boy left as quickly as he had come. Meeryle was beside herself with excitement. She had helped with the plans, trying to recreate a dragon mound like the ones she had seen in the forest. It hadn't been easy; the mounds weren't simply piles of earth, but shell-like protections created by dragon couples to allow their young to grow safely. The attempt to make mounds of earth had failed: the earth had collapsed since the mysterious dragon energy wasn't holding it together. When someone had asked Tikid to put in her energy, the dragon had been shocked: "*I am not only too young for this, but it cannot be done without an ad!*" After calming her friend down, Mccryle had suggested that they build a modified house. The roof was to be flat and covered with soil so grass could grow on it and the floor inside was to be bare earth.

Meeryle cleaned herself up and ran to the new house. People were already milling, all as curious as she was. She laughed with delight when she saw the low structure. As promised, the roof was covered

269

with newly planted grass uprooted from one of the fields. Tikid walked out and projected her happiness. Once Meeryle reached her and grabbed her tail, the dragon's excitement was clear. "*And they even left some loose earth so I can move it around when I wish!*"

"Well, that was the least we could do. You've been a tremendous help to plow the fields, Tikid," said Parin with a smile. "We've seen how quickly and well you move any type of soil. We thought you might want to do the same for your bed. After all, we change the sheets once in a while on our beds."

The gathering crowd laughed. They all took turns inside the house, Tikid guiding them with pride. Meeryle stayed outside, barely holding the tip of the tail. She smiled at the dragon's comments.

"*I will sleep here at first, then move this earth and sleep on this side after.*"

"But why, Tikid?" asked the current guest.

"*I do not want to kill the earth in order to replenish myself, so I need to shift it.*"

"Ah!" was the answer.

Meeryle giggled. Very few people understood this peculiar side of the dragon. They did see the difference her presence had made on the crops, though. The harvest had been the most plentiful anyone could remember. All the vegetables had flourished and the flowerbeds were threatening to overrun the houses.

Leena and the Healer arrived, the tall girl rushing inside the house to congratulate Tikid. Corvin stopped at the door and waited for the two friends to come out. They were a while, as Leena, the only person who could really understand Tikid's physiology at this point, was asking question after question. The dragon answered them all and in her excitement forgot to block the others out of the conversation. The entire crowd was privy to the details. Most were lost at once and eventually, the Healer interrupted.

"Tikid, Leena, come now."

"Sorry. I was explaining to Leena that...."

"Yes, we all heard," interrupted the Healer with a smile. "Are you satisfied?"

"Yes! Very much so. It is as promised."

"Will it be big enough, though?" asked Parin.

"Of course. The very old ones would not fit, because they are much bigger, but I doubt they would want to come."

Meeryle was startled by the comment. "What are you talking about?"

"Well, Meeryle, we made Tikid a proposition. We offered to house a dragon every spring and summer. Tikid went home and presented our offer. They agreed to take turns every year," answered Parin.

"But you never told me about this, Tikid!"

The dragon hesitated. *"No? I was sure I told you I was going home."*

"And you did for a few days. But I thought it was because you wanted to see your parents." Meeryle was at a loss. "Besides, two dragons can't fit in here. Where will you go?"

"Home, Meeryle. I cannot stay here all the time. I need the forest. You knew that. I was to remain here to heal, then to learn."

"I thought you wanted all humans to know about dragons."

"*I do. They will.*"

Worry suddenly gnawed Meeryle. A cold feeling appeared in the pit of her stomach. "How, if you leave?"

"Meeryle, calm down," said Leena with a frown. "I've been trying to get you involved, but you always told me you were too busy. Tikid will go back to the forest for the winter, then in the spring, she will return to travel to other villages and cities."

Meeryle felt relief swell her chest. "So you'll need someone to accompany her, right? I mean, we all know how scared people get the first time they see a dragon. Though with our visitors, word of mouth should have spread. Maybe people will be eager to meet dragons!" She smiled.

The Healer shook his head. "It's hard to say, Meeryle. I'm sure some will want to see the creatures for themselves, but you know as well as I do that hearing about dragons and seeing them is... difficult for the mind. Others also won't believe dragons even exist, so their very sight could trigger a reaction similar to Jetyaa's. Between that and the traveling involved, it will be a very difficult road ahead, believe me."

"Well, this is a hardship I'm ready to take on. I mean, I'm the dragon expert, right? Just tell me when and I will get ready to leave with Tikid."

Corvin and Leena exchanged a hesitant look. "You will not be going, Meeryle. At least not with Tikid. You will be going to Sharitown to train your gift. I am not qualified to train you and neither is Leena."

Meeryle couldn't believe her ears. When had this been decided? Had anyone told her about this?

Maybe. She suddenly remembered Leena interrupting a baking experiment, where she had waved her away with annoyance. Leena had turned red and left slamming the door. Maybe that's what she had been trying to explain and Meeryle hadn't listened. If only Leena had picked a better time! But how come Tikid hadn't said anything? She turned to the young dragon. "Did you know about this?"

"Yes, but I have no say in this. I requested your presence, but it was refused for a valid reason. I agree, actually. Your gift is making you flare in the strangest colors. I am not sure I like it. It looks a bit threatening. You need to take care of yourself."

Meeryle's ears were filled with a rushing sound. She felt like a huge rock had hit her in the chest and she could hardly breathe. "Then who will be going with you?" she asked in a weak voice.

"I will," said Leena eagerly.

CHAPTER SEVENTEEN

Meeryle's ears were roaring. For a long moment, she could not see or feel anything. She wasn't even sure she was still standing. She took a step forward - she was standing - and bumped into someone. She blinked and saw the Healer. His lips moved without any sound coming out. She tried to move forward, but something was holding her back. She turned and saw Leena, also moving her lips. Something wiggled in Meeryle's hand. She was still holding Tikid's tail. She let go and ran, shoving everyone in her way.

Meeryle lost track of where she was. She kept on hearing Leena saying: "I will," over and over again. Tikid's concerned look at the mention of her colors being off became malevolent. Red eyes couldn't possibly be friendly. The only beneficial red thing was fire.

At the thought of her element, Meeryle sought the nearest source of fire and listened to it. The newly lit communal fire at the side of the barn was very low, but enough to still beat. The calming effect of the sound allowed Meeryle to regain her senses, but when she heard voices far behind her calling her name, she shut them out resolutely.

A sharp bark caught her attention. She looked down into Suqi's concerned black eyes. Meeryle gave the fox a disdainful pout. "Oh, so now you find me worthy of your presence. You know something? You're just like all the rest. You don't care about what I want, you only care about what you think I should want. I am old enough to make my own decisions. So get out of my sight!" She started to pass the animal when Suqi bit her ankle, projecting offence and concern. Meeryle yelped in pain and tried to kick the fox, who evaded her. "Just leave, will you? Leave me alone!" Afraid that Suqi might bite her again, Meeryle ran into the barn and pushed the doors closed.

The darkness was welcoming. She wanted to be alone and wallow in her sorrow. The barn was perfect for that, particularly since she could lock herself inside. She had always wondered why one would want a lock inside as well as outside a barn, but today, she was glad for this quirk. Meeryle dragged the locking bar and put it into the door brackets. Unless the villagers were willing to ram the doors down, they would not be able to come in. She smirked, thinking they probably didn't know where she was. She waited a few moments by the door, listening for Suqi. The black fox sniffed under the door and made a very unfox-like snort before leaving. The little paws made soft thumps on the dry ground and grew fainter, until Meeryle was sure Suqi was gone.

Meeryle gulped and shook her head. Suqi's bite had hurt in more than one way. She had never thought the fox would turn against her, just like everyone else. She had been betrayed by everyone, but mostly by Leena and Tikid. The thought of the dragon tore something inside her. Her friend was going to leave without her. Tears burst out, accompanied by a rasping sound. She realized it was her voice. She put both hands on her mouth and crumpled to the ground.

Her body was racked with sobs. With Tikid leaving, her life was over. The young dragon had been at the center of it and was her inspiration for everything she did: the pastries, the house, the activities with the children. Everything to make Tikid happy, to ensure she understood what it meant to be human. Everything to right any wrong she had done to the dragon. Healing her wing, showing everyone dragons weren't monsters. Braving the forest to find the dragons and warn them of the danger humans might represent. All the events of the past months came tumbling back in her mind.

Through it all, Leena's comments intruded. Leena, who didn't even believe in dragons. Leena, who always knew what to do. Leena, who wanted to be a Mage. Meeryle's sobs stopped. Leena was to blame for all this. She knew what dragons in general and Tikid in particular meant to Meeryle. Yet she had accepted the task to roam the world with Tikid without even consulting Meeryle, knowing all along it had been her lifelong dream. Sure, she had said she'd tried to involve Meeryle, but had she really? The enraged girl didn't remember anything of the kind ever being mentioned.

Leena was getting back at her for being a Mage. She couldn't steal her gift, so she was stealing her friend. Tikid had asked for Meeryle, but Leena had managed to convince her it would be wrong. Tikid was naive; she didn't understand deception and lies. The dragon was as much a victim as Meeryle.

The young Mage's tears had dried and her cheeks were stiff from their salt. She rubbed her eyes and looked around. The barn had been stocked with the grain from the harvest and bales of hay for the cattle and the horses. They hadn't refilled Tikid's hole, but rather taken advantage of it and filled it with dried clover, the biggest pile ever, thanks to the young dragon.

Everywhere she looked, Meeryle saw the touch of her friend. The barrels of buckwheat were a new addition. Tikid had concentrated on the tiny patch and it had truly grown for the first time. If it hadn't been for Tikid, these barrels wouldn't even be there. If it hadn't been for Meeryle, the dragon would have never come to the village and made this possible. Anything linked to the dragon had been caused by her directly. Instead of thanking her, they were casting her aside.

For the first time in months, anger stirred. Teeth grinding, recalling every single thing she had done for the villagers to accept Tikid and to make them understand what she could do for them, Meeryle remembered the nightmare of her escape into the night and the forest. She counted the scars on her arms from all the scratches she got when she thought she'd been running for her life and from the dreadful crossing of the rift when she sought the dragons.

She was seeing everything with a tinge of orange.

Anger transformed into rage. Its heat glowed in her stomach and spread out slowly, like lava. They dared use her, reap the fruits of her labor, and cast her aside. Without her, they would never have known how to go about building a house for dragons. Without her, they wouldn't even be planning on a harvest as fruitful for the following year. Without her, they would still be scraping the last skinny grain out of the soil.

The heat had reached her face. Meeryle was now seeing everything in red. Leena had mentioned her eyes were orange once. Were they red now? If they were, what would Leena think? That she was a monster? That she didn't know what she was doing?

Rage gave way to fury. Leena didn't know a thing about Magery. All she wanted was the gift for herself. Leena had everything she wanted, did anything she wanted. Everyone looked to Leena as an example. This time, though, Leena hadn't been the one who did something right. Meeryle had. And now, out of spite and jealousy, Leena was trying to take that away from her. She wanted revenge for not being a Mage. She blamed Meeryle for taking the gift from her. Well, the Mage-gift was Meeryle's. She was the one who heard fire.

At the thought, Meeryle closed her eyes and reached for the fiery heat in the ground. It engulfed her. Her heat and the heat of the center of the world joined. When she opened her eyes, Meeryle still saw everything red, but with a pulsing aura. She stared, fascinated. The barrel of buckwheat pulsed with a peculiar mix of red and orange. The beat of fire was strong, making her body vibrate. When she turned to look at the haystack, its pulse was pure red and the beat of fire became quicker.

Entranced, Meeryle swayed to the beat of fire. The power of fire that filled her to capacity made her feel mighty. When she held her hand up, it was red. Was her skin actually red, or was it the effect of fire on her vision? She laughed. What would Leena think now? Would she dare smirk at her? Would she cower before such potential?

It occurred to Meeryle that while she couldn't know what Leena thought about her, she could find out what she was saying about her. All she had to do was to reach for air, throw some of her power into it and set it to seek Leena and her treacherous words.

Immersed in heat, Meeryle closed her eyes. She allowed herself to bask in the heat and to savor it. She smiled, giddy with power.

Giving herself a mental shake, she sought air and heard its particular rasp immediately. She giggled. The rasp wrapped itself around her, tickling her. It swirled playfully in her hair. Meeryle reached for it and the air groaned. She willed it to mix with the fire suffusing her. The groan hiccupped. Startled, Meeryle opened her eyes.

The red was mixed with strands of blue, twirling around her, creating tentacles that were reaching out. Meeryle frowned. She concentrated on the red, willing it to stay in place. The blue strands muted. She took in a deep breath and reached once again for air, carefully willing it to mix little by little with fire. The groan changed. As the two elements mixed in front of her, the beat of fire started to match the beat of her heart. *Tha-thump. Tha-thump.* She smiled and willed in more air.

Suddenly, the groan became louder. The strands of blue became much more numerous and were beginning to incorporate the red into themselves. Meeryle willed them to slow down and let go.

Nothing happened.

The blue was still swirling faster and faster. Meeryle dug down into the earth and sought the mighty power of fire. She gathered as much as she could and fed it into the blue strands, willing it to overcome the power of air.

The groan became a shriek. The blue strands and the red melded to become a sickly green. Meeryle panicked. Power she didn't control was gathering inside her. Not only did she not know what to do with it, she quickly realized she couldn't really do anything even if she wanted to, as the power had taken on a life of its own. She did try to stop the flow of fire, but air had full control. Since she had never learned to master it the same way she did fire, she didn't know how to stop it.

The shriek of air became shrill. Green tentacles reached out and touched the hay, which burst into flames in front of Meeryle's horrified eyes. The shriek redoubled and the tentacles touched the barrels of buckwheat. The wood of the barrels boomed and caught fire.

Meanwhile, the fire in the haystack had spread to the bales. Soon, Meeryle was surrounded by greenish flames over which she had absolutely no control. Terror gripped her. The heat filling her was gone, replaced by the heat of the burning barn. Fire, which had felt so right minutes ago, was now completely wrong. Sweat dripped into her eyes. As she blinked it away, she realized she no longer had the red sight and was seeing everything painfully clearly.

Smoke brought tears to her eyes. She coughed. "What have I done?" she whispered hoarsely. The winter provisions were literally going up in smoke before her eyes. She was destroying their means of survival. Horrified, Meeryle tried to stand up, but her legs gave out and she fell. She was able to breathe a little bit easier, but not for long. Soon all she could see was smoke. She suddenly remembered she could call for help. But as soon as she opened her mouth, smoke choked her words.

The thought that she was going to die barely had time to cross her mind just before she lost consciousness.

CHAPTER EIGHTEEN

The noise was loud, disturbing and just downright annoying. Why couldn't her mother let her sleep in peace? She really could wait until later to move all that furniture around. One of the chairs was dragging on the floor, making a gruesome screeching noise that sent a sharp spike of pain into her head. Meeryle hated waking up with a headache.

And for some strange reason, Leena was helping her mother in her task.

"Stop it, Tikid. I see her. I know, I know, she looks bad. I don't know, I have to touch her. Because you're making too much noise!"

Leena was having a conversation with herself. How strange. She was usually much too down-to-earth for that.

"Can you move this beam?"

Suddenly, Meeryle found it much easier to breathe. She smiled and took in a deep breath.

"Did you see? She's alive, Tikid, she's alive! She breathed. Yes, I saw the smile too. I don't know. I guess she's happy to see us."

Was she dreaming or was Leena crying? Why would Leena cry when she was moving chairs around? This was not making any sense. She needed to find out what was going on.

Meeryle opened her eyes and blinked in surprise. Something was wrong with the ceiling of her room: it was gone. She blinked a few more times to make sure she was awake. The ceiling was still absent. She frowned, only to find her headache was also affecting her forehead, sending yet another stabbing pain, making her cry out. She wanted to rub it with her hand, but she found she couldn't move her arm for some reason. She tried the other arm and whimpered. It did move, but with difficulty and much pain.

"Don't move, Meeryle. You'll hurt yourself."

Meeryle turned her head and winced. Leena's face was hovering over her own, concern filling her eyes. Strangely, Leena was a mess. Her face was black with soot, with tracks where her tears had cleaned the dirt. Suddenly, a huge green head with red eyes moved in, almost touching Leena.

"Leena," croaked Meeryle, "what's going on? I feel strange. Am I seeing... a dragon?"

Leena burst into tears. "It's Tikid, Meeryle. She saved you. You can't hear her because she's not touching you. She can't because she's afraid to hurt you."

Meeryle looked into the big ruby eyes and memory came crashing back. Her fury, the fire, the smoke. She closed her eyes and felt hot tears trickling down the side of her face. "I thought I was going to die. I'm sorry, Leena."

"Hush. Save your throat. You've inhaled a lot of smoke. The whole barn crashed down on you. I think your left arm is broken and you have a lot of burns," said Leena. She smiled and looked at the dragon. "Tikid said we look even scruffier than the first time we met."

"Ha! Just wait for the next time she steps on her tail," answered Meeryle weakly.

Tikid chuckled and hiccupped at the same time, laughing and crying the dragon way.

"It's all right, Tikid. Leena'll fix me up," said Meeryle. The dragon moved her head closer and gently blew on the girl's face. She carefully smiled. "That felt good."

Crunching sounds interrupted. "Meeryle, thank Life you're alive!" said the Healer, bending down as far as his old limbs would allow. "You gave us quite a scare. Come now, we have to move you out of here, girl."

"I will put you to sleep," explained Leena. "That way, you won't feel anything."

"But what would I feel?" asked Meeryle, puzzled.

"Your legs...." Leena choked her sobs down. "It'll be better. Trust me."

Meeryle nodded wearily. The simple movement made her head pulse painfully. Leena crouched beside her as the rubble didn't allow her to kneel or sit, and put her hand on Meeryle's forehead. The girl felt a tingle and everything went dark.

***

Meeryle came to at the sound of earth's murmur. In the darkness, its warmth and fuzziness comforted her and made her smile. Earth was slowly spreading throughout her body, a bit like fire had, but it wasn't overwhelming. It touched her, but didn't fill her. She knew she couldn't will it to do anything as it was moving around with a mind of its own.

The thought triggered fear. What if it started to spread and destroy like fire and air had? She was reassured when she noticed the murmur didn't intensify but remained stable. She also noticed that it was doing something.

To her.

As she concentrated, she heard another sound, which matched the soft brush of earth. Meeryle winced at its discordance. In some instances, it was a screech. Eventually, the sound changed and became a most pleasant song. Mixed with the murmur of earth, it was the most beautiful music Meeryle had ever heard.

The music left abruptly. Meeryle tried to find it, but it was beyond her reach. Instead, she heard voices.

"*I am done. I cannot do anymore.*"

"That was a lot, Tikid. More than I had ever imagined. That's twice today!"

"*Yes. It was supposed to be beyond me, you know. It does not matter. Meeryle will be fine.*"

Leena and Tikid were talking about her. "Why would I not be fine?" Meeryle asked. Or tried to ask. The only sound that came out was a mumble.

"She's awake! Meeryle, can you hear me?"

Meeryle nodded.

"Can you open your eyes?"

Her eyes were closed? That explained the darkness, then. She opened her eyes. It was still dark. She blinked and was finally able to make out the shape of Leena and Tikid.

"Why is it so dark?" she whispered.

"We're in Tikid's house. No windows, remember?"

"Ah!" She frowned. "Why are we in Tikid's house?"

"It was the best place to Heal you with Tikid's help."

"Heal me? Oh! The fire...." Her mind was clearing. She had lost control of her gift and burned down the barn. It seemed she had managed to hurt herself in the process. "I'm thirsty."

"First, you will have to sit up."

"She can lean against me. I will move behind her." Meeryle heard a large shuffle. *"There. Help her to move her shoulder up, Leena. I need a bit of space for my paws."*

Leena gently put her hand under Meeryle's neck and lifted it. Meeryle helped as much as she could, but she was weak. She felt big hands slide down her back and move her into a sitting position. A dizzy spell forced her to close her eyes, but it soon disappeared.

Leena handed her a cup filled with water. "There. Can you hold the cup?" Meeryle nodded and took it with trembling hands. She managed to take two long gulps of the fresh water. Its coolness felt so good, she felt tears welling up. Leena gently took the cup back and put it down. "So, how are you feeling?"

"I... Weak. Stiff. But otherwise, no worse than when we came out of the forest after meeting Tikid for the first time."

"Good."

"What happened? I remember the barn burning down and the smoke, but that's all."

"We had to save you, otherwise, we would have lost you," answered Tikid.

Meeryle realized something was amiss. "Wait a minute. I heard you talking before you helped me

286

up. What's going on?" Meeryle looked up and met the dragon's gaze.

"*I helped Leena Heal you, just like you helped her Heal me. Only this time, it was a much more complex and long process. I am now able to pass the barrier of your power. Either that, or your ordeal helped you gain some control on the power.*"

Meeryle smiled. "It really is you. I don't understand your answer."

Leena chuckled. "Some things will never change. Do you want the rest of the story?" Meeryle nodded. "Well, after you left, we couldn't find you. Tikid was really worried because she said you were glowing red or something. I didn't understand her and delayed, asking questions." She smiled ruefully. "You know me, always wanting more details." The smile vanished and tears trickled down her cheeks. "It almost cost you your life." She took in a tremulous breath. "Fortunately, Suqi showed up."

Meeryle gasped. "She did? But she bit me and I tried to kick her away. I was sure she hated me for some reason."

"Oh, Meeryle, she doesn't hate you at all! Thanks to her, we were able to find you."

"And how did she get her point across? Did she bite you too?"

"No, she spoke to Tikid." Leena grew thoughtful. "The strange thing was Tikid's reaction. I never noticed before, but she treats Suqi with the same kind of respect she had when the Great One of the Greens came to talk to you.

"Anyway. Suqi told Tikid that something was very wrong with you, specifically with your gift, and we followed her to the barn. We saw the smoke coming out, but by the time we got there with pails of water, the whole thing exploded in flames. Tikid was along and said she would try to smother the fire with earth. I thought she was going to dig." Leena paused and smiled. "Meeryle, it was the most beautiful thing I ever saw. She was glowing emerald and gold. It was amazing. Then she... threw whatever it was at the fire and it stopped."

"Stopped? How can a fire just stop?" asked Meeryle.

"With the essence of the forest and the earth smothering it, the fire had no choice but to disappear. I did not know it would disappear so completely and quickly, though. It was the first time I ever attempted such a thing."

"Ah! That explains it all," said Leena, shaking her head and rolling her eyes.

Meeryle smiled. "I remember now. I heard you freeing me of the rubble. I thought I was hearing my mother moving furniture around! Then you put me to sleep, Leena."

"Yes, I had to. One of your arms was broken and so were your legs." The young Healer paused and gulped. "The skin on your entire body was burnt, Meeryle. We were afraid to touch you."

"But you Healed me. From the looks of it, you did a fine job, Healer."

"Yes, we did. Tikid fed me earth power and forced the skin to grow back."

"Actually, it would be more exact to say I fed you the essence of the Greens mixed with a lot of earth."

Leena shook her head with a smile. "Well, yes. Anyway, I Healed your bones and there you are. The

288

only thing I couldn't fix was your hair. It will have to grow back on its own."

"What!" Meeryle passed her hands over her head. Sure enough, it was smooth, except on the right side, where she felt a rough stubble.

"I guess you were lying on your right side when the fire caught you. Most of the skin on that side wasn't as badly burnt," said Leena apologetically.

The two girls looked at each other and burst into tears. Leena embraced Meeryle as tightly as she could and Meeryle returned the hug, though with less strength. Tikid's tail snaked around them and completed the embrace.

Finally, the tears dried up. Leena drew back and wiped her eyes. Meeryle did the same and squeezed Leena's arm with one hand and Tikid's tail with the other.

"I am so sorry. This is all my fault. You were right, both of you. I don't control my gift. I can only control fire, but as soon as I touched air, it was out of my hands. I have to get training."

"I feel just as bad, Meeryle. I set you off. I should have insisted and explained to you I meant to go with Tikid, not just give up on you like I did."

"*And I should also have communicated my intentions more accurately. I believe we are all to blame.*"

"What about the crops? I burned everything down."

"*I am sure a solution will present itself.*"

Meeryle jumped at the unfamiliar voice in her head. She looked for a new dragon, only to find Suqi, sitting on her haunches, looking smug. Eyes wide, Meeryle pointed at her. "She... she spoke!"

"Who? Suqi?" Leena frowned. "I didn't hear anything."

"*Of course not. You are the only one who should hear me. Aside from the dragons, of course,*" said the fox with a head bow toward Tikid.

"Ah... What?"

"*Familiars tend to want to keep private, you know. I did not want Tikid to tell you what I was before you were ready.*"

"Familiars?" Meeryle was confused.

"What's going on? What's this about familiars? Meeryle, talk to me!"

Meeryle smiled at Leena's frustrated tone. "Now you know how I felt when we first met with Tikid." Leena rolled her eyes, motioning her to continue. "Suqi said that she's a familiar." The fox snorted. "Um... My familiar?" Pink tongue lolling out, Suqi went to Meeryle and butted her head gently against her thigh.

"*Yes. I had chosen you and had you had proper guidance, you would have been able to hear me much sooner and avoid all this.*"

Leena sighed. "So, we know why Suqi's been following you around." She frowned. "But I thought an apprentice-Mage had to find and tame his or her familiar?"

"But I didn't try to tame her. She just came along."

"*Because you really needed me. Your power called to me, so I came. Usually, Mages have to work very hard for a goupil to hear them.*"

"She's talking, I can tell. What's she saying?"

"That apparently, she's not a fox, but a goupil and that my power attracted her...."

290

She was interrupted by a commotion outside the low house. They heard screams and yelling. Parin's booming voice drowned the screams and brought a sense of order. They couldn't make out his words, though.

"What's going on?" asked Meeryle.

"I don't know, I can't see anything. Hang on, I'll find out," answered Leena.

Tikid squawked. Surprised, both girls turned and looked at her.

"What is it, Tikid?" asked Leena.

"*Oh... It's the Great One again,*" she whispered in awe.

A great shadow filled the wide door of the house. Meeryle and Leena turned and found themselves staring at the huge snout of Rutad. Tikid was right, though. The dragon looking at her projected wisdom and tolerance, but none of the mischievous-if not malicious-airs Tikid's sire had sported.

"*Well, it would seem you did not heed my advice, little Mage. However, your lack of foresight has allowed my young kin to use her own gifts in a way dragons had forgotten. For that alone, I am most grateful.*" The voice filled Meeryle's mind. The red eyes suddenly filled with laughter. "*It is not often one sees a human female without hair. I find it most becoming.*"

"You're making fun of me!" said Meeryle, outraged.

The dragon's chuckle shook the walls of the house. "*Of course. I believe it was needed. Now, if I understand correctly, your misadventure has a downside for the rest of your kin.*"

"Misadventure? How can you call it that? It was a disaster!" Meeryle was annoyed. The big dragon was laughing at her again.

"*I did not think you would want to dwell on it so much.*" He cocked his head questioningly. Meeryle, offended, shrugged. The dragon chuckled again. "*Very well. I will get to the point. The Kin and I will foray for you to make sure you do not starve during this coming winter. It will not be much, as we cannot upset the balance of the forest, but it will be enough for this coming winter. Then, next spring, this wonderful house will accommodate Rutad, the first volunteer.*" At the name of her father, Tikid groaned. "*Yes, young one, your sire is most curious. Even now, I am having a hard time keeping the link between the two of us open. He is extremely eager and wants to know more about the humans who have allowed a lost skill to resurface.*"

"*The humans might not appreciate his sense of humor, Great One.*"

"*He will behave,*" answered the big dragon. The twinkle in his eyes was purely Rutad's and therefore contradicted his words, but Tikid remained quiet.

Leena was astonished. "Are you saying you will give us food?" The dragon nodded. "But... That's a lot of food!"

"*Like I said, it may not be as much as you think. But no quantity of food is too big compared to the skill Tikid has displayed. It may be a hard thing for a human to grasp, Healer or not. Do not dwell on it and simply accept the gift. I believe your sire and his companions already have. Only one remained chagrined and I do not understand why. One male called Makin?*"

Meeryle burst out laughing. "Oh, he's going to hate me! You see, the barn was his."

Leena was biting her lips, her face distorted by the effort of trying not to laugh. "It's not funny, Meeryle."

"Sure, it is! And it feels so good to laugh."

"Well, now, young ones, if you do not mind, this link is definitely becoming uncomfortable. I believe Rutad wants to speak, so I will leave and see you later, Tikid. I will travel to meet with you, as we have a lot to discuss." The dragon bid them goodbye and left. Meeryle was astonished by the change of expression in his eyes. She was now looking at Rutad, who immediately rumbled out in laughter.

"Get out, you mean dragon! You shouldn't laugh at me like this!" Meeryle pointed her finger to the door in outrage.

The big dragon turned, chuckling, and left to speak with the other villagers.

"Your dad is really something, Tikid. Next year's going to be a difficult one, I wager. I hope I didn't insult him too much by yelling at him."

"No, actually, this was the response he expected. He likes it when others stand up to him. He says it builds character."

"What about your dad, Leena? And the Healer? I mean, we'll have food, but they must be angry with me."

Leena sighed. "Well, actually, pretty much the entire village was ready to finish you off when they first heard the news. But as soon as they saw what you looked like when we pulled you out of the ruins, they kind of forgot about it. They just wanted to help you in any way they could. They're proud to have a

Mage and a great cook among them, you know. I think everyone understands. They're not happy, but the dragons' help will be enough for them to forgive you. A lot of them came to see you before you came to. Even Teerane."

"Really? What did she say?"

"Nothing. She's still dealing with her mother being a murderer, so I didn't press. I think she just needs to find herself."

The three friends were silent for a while. Meeryle petted Suqi, feeling much better. Things were going to work out, after all. She was alive! And she had a familiar.... She rubbed her bald head and smiled. "So, what do you think people in Sharitown will say when they see a bald Mage?"

Leena smiled smugly. "Well, I don't think they'll notice."

"Why not?"

"*Because I will distract them,*" said Tikid.

"What?"

"Tikid decided we would travel with you to Sharitown and make it our first stop to educate humans about dragons. I mean, we have to start somewhere, right?"

"Oh, Leena, thank you. This means so much to me." She closed her eyes, biting her lips in order to keep tears at bay.

She cleared her throat and changed the subject. "So no one else is coming along?"

"Well, Jetyaa offered, but she's needed here, so I thanked her and told her to let me grow up."

"You're sure you're okay with this?"

"Yes. I'm a Healer, so I need to offer my services. Corvin is enough for this village, so I have to find my place somewhere else. I just know it."

"So it's you, me, Tikid, and I guess Suqi. It'll be perfect. It's a great idea."

"*Of course, it is. Dragons always have good ideas*," said Tikid smugly.

"They certainly do," said Meeryle. "Let's make sure the whole world knows about it!"

ACKNOWLEDGMENTS

I would like to thank everyone who read the drafts and made the story better with their comments: Kevin McColley, who got me to the end of that very first draft, my beta-readers, Fabrice (my bro), Sarah Tuttle and Joelle Duran, and my editor, Marlene Setter.

I'm also really happy to say that this was the first fantasy story my mom ever read and that she's been hooked since!

But most of all, I would like to thank Melody Pena for creating her wonderful sculptures. A Dragon Medley was directly inspired by her beautiful dragons, who have invaded my home and are constantly staring at me in the hopes that I will tell more of their adventures and ways of life...